About the Author

Jeremy Dale has had a career as a scientist and University teacher, during which he has written several textbooks as well as many research papers. He has now combined his writing experience with his long-standing interest in folk music to produce this collection of short stories inspired by some of the traditional songs of Britain.

He lives in Glossop and is a regular participant at Glossop Folk Club and folk music sessions. As well as singing, he plays English concertina, whistle, and harp.

To Angela, who bought me my first concertina

Jeremy Dale

COME LISTEN TO MY SONG

AUSTIN MACAULEY
PUBLISHERS LTD.

Copyright © Jeremy Dale (2016)

The right of Jeremy Dale to be identified as author of this work has been asserted by him in accordance with section 77 and 78 of the Copyright, Designs and Patents Act 1988.

All rights reserved. No part of this publication may be reproduced, stored in a retrieval system, or transmitted in any form or by any means, electronic, mechanical, photocopying, recording, or otherwise, without the prior permission of the publishers.

Any person who commits any unauthorized act in relation to this publication may be liable to criminal prosecution and civil claims for damages.

A CIP catalogue record for this title is available from the British Library.

ISBN 9781785544088 (Paperback)
ISBN 9781785544095 (Hardback)
ISBN 9781785544101 (E-Book)

www.austinmacauley.com

First Published (2016)
Austin Macauley Publishers Ltd.
25 Canada Square
Canary Wharf
London
E14 5LQ

Acknowledgments

I would like to acknowledge a debt to many traditional singers, and especially to the members of the University College London Folk Club (particularly Pete Nalder and Mavis Pilbeam) who introduced me to the folk songs of Britain many years ago.

Cold blows the wind

There were 365 pebbles on the grave. Jessica didn't have to count them. She knew that it was exactly a year, to the very day, since Ian had died. Every day, whatever the weather, she had made the long climb up from the valley to the graveyard on the hilltop, with its view over the trees on the slope below, over the chimneys of the houses and the long dead mills, to the hills opposite. Some days, in the winter, if she got there before the snowplough, she had had to wade through knee-deep snow – in places higher than that, where the snow had drifted against the dry stone walls lining the lane. But today was a bright May morning. Some of the trees were in full leaf, while others were just showing buds. There was a cloud of bluebells in the wood below, and cowslips in the fields. The sun was shining, and birds were singing. She had placed the 365th stone on the grave. She sat down on a nearby bench and looked at the colourful pattern. She had started, originally, with pebbles collected from the little stream that tumbled down to join the main river in the valley bottom. She remembered the journey she had made to a shingle beach and the time she had spent carefully selecting a range of stones of different colours, even some pieces of coloured glass, worn smooth by the waves. Every evening, she looked through this collection, selecting the pebble that she would take up to Ian's grave the following day. Now she had a full year of them. But there were still many more at home that she could use before she would need to make another trip to the beach. Beautiful stones too – some of them pure black, jet maybe, or possibly coal; some emerald green speckled with white; some purple, pink, red. All sorts of shapes, flat and perfectly round, egg-shaped or round like a small ball, – even the irregular ones had a beauty of their own. She loved the feel of them, so smooth. All of them, in their own way, reminding her of Ian, and the many facets of his character. The happy days they had had together. She closed her eyes and remembered, as she did every day, how they had first met, and all that had happened since.

*****

It was her fifteenth birthday, and she was having a party. A momentous occasion, as it was the first time she had had a mixed birthday party, boys as well as girls. Patrick, who lived next door, would be fifteen next week, so they were having a joint party. She was inviting the girls and he was inviting the boys. She was somewhat apprehensive about this – it was her parents' idea, but she wasn't at all sure how it would work out. Nevertheless, it was sure to be exciting. She was starting to think about getting ready for it – what should she wear? – when Emily rang up. Emily was her best friend.

"Hi, Jess. I'm really looking forward to your party tonight. The reason I'm ringing is to ask if it would be OK if my cousin Ian came as well?"

"I suppose so, if he really wants to."

Jessica had often heard Emily talk about her cousin, but she had never met him, and she wondered why he would want to come.

"Yes, he really does. I'll let you in on a secret, but don't tell him I told you. Promise you won't tell?"

"I promise. What is it?"

"I think he's got a crush on you, that's why he wants to come."

Jessica started to laugh. "Don't be ridiculous. I've heard you talk about him, of course, but I've never actually met him."

"But he's seen you around, and that seems to be enough. He appears to know an awful lot about you as well. So it's OK if he comes?"

"OK. But I won't know what to say to him."

"Don't worry about that. You'll think of something. Or just let him do the talking. See you tonight." And she rang off.

Jessica stood by the phone, bemused by this development. How should she behave with this stranger who fancied her? Then her mother called out, "Are you going to get ready? They'll be here before you know it."

Once the guests started to arrive, Jessica was too busy to think about Ian. Then suddenly he was there, with Emily.

"Hi, Jess. I want you to meet my cousin Ian."

"Hello, Ian," said Jessica. "Emily has told me a lot about you. Only good things of course."

Ian mumbled something and stared down at his feet.

Emily grinned. "He's a bit shy. I think he said 'Thank you for inviting me'. I'll leave you two together while I go to find some food. I'm starving."

Ian raised a hand as though to try to stop her, but she had gone.

Jessica desperately tried to think of things to talk to Ian about, but she only got monosyllabic replies, almost inaudible. Eventually she had to give up as her mother needed some help.

Next day, Emily rang again. "Hi, Jess, Great party last night. You were a real hit with Ian. He can't stop talking about you."

Jessica protested. "But I hardly saw him. After you abandoned us, I couldn't get a word out of him. He just mumbled and stared at his feet. After that, I didn't see him again the whole evening."

"I think it was just being in your presence that was enough for him! I think you'll make a great pair – but you might need to encourage him a bit. Bye!"

But it didn't happen. Jessica often wondered if he was going to ask her for a date or something, but no, he made no attempt to contact her. It was almost a year later when they next met, at another party. Jessica didn't know he was there, and then she bumped into him. Literally. Some of his drink spilt over her dress.

"Oh how clumsy of me!" he exclaimed. "Let me try to mop it up." And he produced a handkerchief, not very clean.

"Don't worry about it, it'll wash out. It was my fault anyway, I should have looked where I was going." Then she looked up at him. "Oh, it's you. Ian, isn't it? I haven't seen you since my party last year."

He blushed and said. "I'm sorry, that was rather rude of me. I should have thanked you for inviting me. I had a great time."

Hello, she thought. This is progress of a sort. At least he's audible now. Seems that spilling his drink has loosened his tongue.

And indeed it had. They spent most of the rest of the time at that party talking to each other. The thing that intrigued her most was his interest in poetry. Jessica had never liked poetry. The stuff they did at school seemed so boring and incomprehensible. Why couldn't they just say what they meant, instead of dressing it all up in flowery language? And all that technical stuff – assonance and alliteration, metres and feet – what was it all for? But once he started reciting some of his favourite poems, it all seemed to come to life. She could *see* Westminster Bridge in the quiet of the early morning. He seemed to come to life as well. He was so animated and enthusiastic about it.

"It sounds so beautiful like that, just listening to the words. Why does it all seem so boring when we read it in class?"

"That's the point, really. It's like music, or at least the sort of poetry I like is. Start off by just listening to the sounds. Don't worry about what they mean – or not at first anyway. Set your mind free to paint the images for you. Opera is the same."

"Oh, opera! That's even worse. I can never hear the words, and it's usually in some foreign language anyway."

"Well, pop songs then. Can you always hear and understand the words there?"

"No, but they have a tune, and a beat. You can dance to them without understanding them."

"Exactly!" he said, triumphantly. "So does poetry. Listen to it, tap your feet to it if you want. Just let the words carry you away. Don't start off looking for meaning – it will emerge gradually, if you hear it over again."

"But how do I know that I'm getting the right meaning? How can I be sure that I'm getting what the poet actually means?"

"That's not important. It's what it means to you that is important. Even the poet probably can't tell you what he, or she, meant at the time it was written. It can mean something different every time."

She laughed. "That's not much good in an exam!"

"No," he admitted glumly. "That's the problem. The system demands a standard interpretation that students have to learn and regurgitate. It destroys the poem."

They talked about poetry for most of the evening, until Jessica looked at her watch. "Oh, God, I said I'd be back by eleven and it's gone that already. I have to fly."

Ian pulled a book from his pocket. "Here, borrow this, and read a few poems. Start with Westminster Bridge, that's nice and simple. On one level anyway. Like most poems, you can find deeper meanings if you want to. Browse through it, but I suggest sticking to the shorter ones. When you find one you like, read it over and over, preferably aloud, rather than just skimming through them all."

Ian's enthusiasm must have been infectious. To her surprise, and that of her parents, she found herself spending an hour or two each evening with her nose in the book of poetry, apparently talking to herself. Mr Griffiths was rather concerned about this, and he said to his wife "Mary, is Jessica all right? Is this poetry she's reading all this time? She's never been interested in poetry before. Why this sudden obsession with it?"

Mrs Griffiths smiled, knowingly. "At her age, that sort of behaviour usually means there's a boy around somewhere. And that's probably the case here. I was talking to Eleanor Foster the other day. Her Ian's a bit of a poetry geek, and she said that he had spent a lot of time at that party last month talking with Jessica. I think he's lent her that book. So perhaps she's got herself a boyfriend at last."

"Well, that would be nice. I like the Fosters, and he seems a good lad, although where all that poetry will get him, I don't know. But I hope it doesn't interfere with her school work, with her exams coming up and all."

"I think she's got her head screwed on properly. Let's just see what happens."

But nothing did happen. Months went past and she heard nothing from Ian. Her exams came and went, and she felt that she had done well enough. But she didn't understand why Ian hadn't contacted her. "He must want that book back, at least," she thought. "Even if he doesn't want to ask for a date or anything."

Then Emily rang. "Hi, Jess. What's up with you and Ian? You seemed inseparable at that party, months ago now, and everyone thought you would be an item by now. But no-one's seen you out together. Is it a secret romance? Do your parents object or something and you have to keep it quiet?"

"No," replied Jessica. "It's nothing like that at all. No romance, or even the start of one." She explained about the poetry, and how Ian had lent her a book. "I really thought that must be a good sign, because he would have to get in touch again even if it was just to ask for his book back. But I've heard nothing from him. Not a squeak. So I've still got his book, and wondering what to do with it. Perhaps I should give it to you to return it."

"No, don't do that, whatever you do. That would kill it stone dead. That's as good as saying you never want to speak to him again. Leave it to me. I'll find out what's going on."

Two days later, Emily rang again. "Hi, Jess. I've spoken to Ian, and you really are a couple of twerps. You need your heads banging together, probably literally. You're sitting there wondering why he hasn't asked for his book back and, you know what? He's sitting at home all this time wondering why you haven't given him the book back!"

"Oh. How daft is that?" Jessica groaned. "I thought it would look as though I was being, well, a bit forward, if I contacted him first. After all, it's usually the boy who makes the first move."

"I told you before, Ian's not like other boys. He's shy. He needs some encouragement. Don't worry, I've done the job for you. I've told him what's happened, and how you really are desperately keen to see him again."

"You didn't really say that, did you?" Jessica was horrified. "I mean, we had a nice time talking at the party, but I don't want to look as though I'm throwing myself at him."

Emily laughed. "No, I didn't lay it on quite that thick. But I did make sure that he understood that, let's say, further contact would not be unacceptable to you. So you should be hearing from him soon."

And it was soon. Immediately, as she put the phone down, it rang again. "Hello, Jessica? Ian here."

He did sound very nervous, she thought. She remembered what Emily had said about encouraging him. "Hello, Ian. Nice to hear from you. I've been reading lots from that poetry book, and it would be great to talk to you about it. There are a lot of questions I would like to ask." As soon as she had said this, she felt worried; was that too forward? It was virtually asking him for a date.

"I was hoping you would say that. Can we meet on Saturday morning, in the coffee bar, say eleven o'clock?"

"Great. I'll see you there then."

As she put the phone down, she thought "Saturday morning coffee. That doesn't sound like an exciting date! But I suppose it's a start, or it might be."

When they met on Saturday, Ian got down to business straight away. "How did you get on?"

"After Westminster Bridge, I turned the page and found Ozymandias. I loved that. Such a short poem yet tells such a complete story. The powerful king who builds a monument to himself. Now the kingdom has disappeared, and the monument is just a ruin. Making a mockery of the inscription 'Look on my works ye mighty and despair.' Now it has a meaning quite opposite to that intended. A beautiful poem, but you can also quite clearly see a message in it. I was a bit puzzled by 'The hand that mock'd them and the heart that fed.' If I think about it, I can't explain what it means, yet inside me I somehow know. Odd."

Ian nodded. "That's poetry for you."

"And the last line is beautiful. 'The lone and level sands stretch far away.' My head objects that the desert isn't level, and what does 'lone' mean? Lonely? Empty? But if he had written 'The empty sands', it wouldn't have sounded nearly so good. I guess that's what you mean by the 'music' of poetry. That line seems to sing its meaning to you."

Ian smiled. "You're getting hooked, I can see. Did you try 'Ode to a Nightingale'?"

"Yes," Jessica hesitated. "I didn't like that so much. Seemed to be too many words in it. They kept getting in the way. I couldn't stop trying to understand what it all meant, rather than just listening to it. Some beautiful bits, but ..."

"I know what you mean. I don't want to try to explain it to you. That's not the point. Except that the poem does get extra meaning in relation to Keats' life, and death. He will have seen a lot of suffering and death in his training as a doctor. And you know that he died young?"

"Did he?"

"Yes, about 25, of TB. So the line 'Where youth grows pale, and spectre-thin, and dies;' is rather prophetic. But he was probably just referring to other people's deaths from TB."

They went on to discuss many other poems, some that Jessica liked and some that she didn't. Before they parted, Ian pulled out another book from his pocket, and said "Now that you've got the idea of poetry as music, try some Dylan Thomas. I really like his stuff. Some of it anyway. Try 'And death shall have no dominion'. And 'Poem on his birthday.' Same time, same place, next week?"

Jessica laughed. "You make it sound like a tutorial!"

"Oh dear. I'm sorry, I guess that wasn't a good way to put it, but I get so carried away by all this. It's really nice talking to you."

****

Jessica opened her eyes and looked at the grave. It was still hard to believe that he was dead, and the birds were still singing. 'Fled is that music: – Do I wake or sleep?' Had the nightingale really gone? 'Was it a vision, or a waking dream?' All those 'tutorials' on Saturday mornings; he had opened her eyes in so many ways. But did we really talk like that? Seems a bit precocious for sixteen year olds. Maybe my memories have been enhanced by the ten years since then. Only ten years, such a short time. Yet so much time now, without him.

Yes, he really is dead. 'Where blew a flower may a flower no more Lift its head to the blows of the rain.' She still wondered if Dylan Thomas had originally written 'bloomed', and how inspired it was to make it 'blew' instead. "But Death does have dominion. He is dead, and will write no more. And all I have left is memories." She started to weep again, as those memories flooded back.

****

The weekly poetry tutorials went on for several months. They explored poetry of all sorts, old and new, poems written in English, and those from other languages. But only in translation. Neither of them had enough knowledge of any other language to be able to appreciate the originals. Jessica enjoyed these sessions immensely. Ian said that he was enjoying them too; the exercise was making him look again at familiar poems, and widening his horizons to poets that he hadn't looked at before. But Jessica did start to wonder if their relationship would ever go beyond just friends who liked talking about poetry.

One day, Ian surprised her. They had just finished their session, but instead of saying "Same time, same place, next week?" he said." Jessica?"

"Jess, please. All my friends call me Jess."

"But Jessica is such a nice name."

"I don't mind it, but it does sound rather formal."

"OK. Well, Jess, there's something I've been meaning to ask you. I've been summoning up the courage for weeks."

"Gosh," she thought. "It sounds like he's going to propose. That would be a bit sudden!"

"Um, I don't know how to say this. I'm not much good at this sort of thing."

"Go on," she encouraged, smiling at him.

"Er," he hesitated again, and then blurted out "Would you like to come to see a film with me?"

"Of course I would. I'd love to. When?"

"There's a good film on at the moment, but the programme changes today, so it would have to be this evening. But do say if you don't want to. I would hate to spoil our friendship."

"Don't be silly. I said I would love to. And this evening is fine."

He picked her up from her house and they walked down to the cinema together. She wondered if they should be holding hands, so she made sure that her hand was free in case he wanted to, but he didn't. Even when they were in their seats, he sat upright, avoiding contact as much as possible. "He still needs some encouragement," she thought. "This is strange. Everything I've heard and read suggests that girls need to fend off, or at least slow down, the advances from boys, and here am I, having to do just the opposite. I know what I'll do."

Under the pretext of attracting his attention, she touched his hand lightly, leant across, and whispered something in his ear. Then she left her hand there. To her relief, he got the message, and grasped her hand, albeit rather clumsily. She gave his hand a squeeze, as if to say "That's the thing to do."

After the film, they walked back to her house, hand in hand. When they got there, she said to herself "Now for a bit more encouragement." She reached up and kissed him. That certainly encouraged him. He put his arms around her and kissed her, tenderly. "I've been wanting to do that for so long," he whispered in her ear.

Inside the house, Jessica's parents had heard their footsteps approaching, then stopping. Then instead of the door opening and Jessica coming in, there was a very long pause. Mrs Griffiths looked at her husband. "I think they're getting somewhere at last," she said. When Jessica came in, eventually, she could see the sparkle in her eyes and knew that she was right.

"Had a nice evening dear?"

"The best," said Jessica. "Oh, Mum, I'm so happy." And she went to hug her mother, and then her father, who looked rather embarrassed at this unusual show of affection.

After that, the romance blossomed – films, dances, theatre, concerts; the only blot on the horizon was the prospect of being separated when they went off to University.

"Have you decided which Universities to apply to?" asked Jessica.

To her surprise, Ian said "I've decided not to go to University."

"Why not? You would get in, easily."

"But that's not the sort of life I want. It may sound a bit arrogant, but University wouldn't teach me what I need. I've decided I want to write, especially poetry. I don't want to spend three years hearing about what other people have written. If anything, that would just get in the way of what I want to do. I just have to write."

"But can you make a living out of writing?"

"Not easily, no. I realise I would need to get a job of some sort, but if I get a menial job, I would have lots of time for writing. The sort of job University would prepare me for would be much more demanding, and I'm afraid it would just swallow me up."

"But have you written any poems? Can you write poetry? Liking it, and knowing a lot about it, is not the same as being able to do it."

"I have written a few, but nothing yet published – not counting some juvenile efforts for the school magazine."

"Why haven't you shown me any?"

"I don't know. I suppose I've been frightened to. You might not like them."

"Try me."

****

Jessica stirred and looked again at the grave before her. She had no difficulty in remembering that poem, the first that he had ever shown her, or rather recited to her. She closed her eyes and spoke it out loud.

> When smoke and mist and evening hid
> Her light fruitfall in the crumbling leaves
> Night was her hair and the gorse was gold;
> A taunting melody she weaves.

> When cold winds clenched and snowflakes bloomed,
> And streams were laced with ice
> I kissed the girl with the night black hair
> And I sank in the seas of her eyes.

> When soft rain soothed the blue strewn wood
> The air was scented with birth;
> The sap was rising and the green buds swelled
> As I lay with her on the earth.

> In the lazy days, when curlews cried
> Purple heather was the sun.
> Larks were lost in a singing sky.
> And our song was sung.

> The tide has flown and the stars have turned
> And even-time is tolled
> But the earth still breathes and lovers still kiss
> Whenever the gorse is gold.

The memory of his words brought the tears back once again. She felt she could see him standing before her, just as he had done ten years earlier, reciting that poem and waiting anxiously for her opinion.

****

"Well." he asked. "What do you think?"

"I think it's lovely," she said. "But who is this girl?"

"Don't worry," he laughed. "She's not real. You're the only girl I love."

She caught her breath at that. He had never said before that he loved her. She hugged him and whispered "And I love you too."

"But what about the poem? I'm not really satisfied with it. Some of the images are too obvious, not subtle enough. I need to do some more work on it."

"Don't change any of it. It's my poem now. I love especially 'I sank in the seas of her eyes.' But what's the significance of the gorse?"

"Don't you know the old saying 'When the gorse is not in flower, kissing's out of season'? It's because gorse flowers all the year round."

"Have you written any other poems?"

"Only one, so far."

"Let's hear it then."

Ian hesitated. "It's not really ready."

"Perhaps it would help if you read it to me."

So Ian read.

"Until the day when the dust returns
And silence falls once more on the bell-streamed vale
And the wind-sighing hill
Where the clouds shout free to the sky and the sheep
And the bones of a dead sheep, white in the lake.

Until the day when the dust returns,
And blood and water cease to flow
In the veined meadows of the mind
And my once quick heart shall love no more
With every turn of the fresh sea breeze
And every spin of the stars

Until the day when the dust returns
I shall not mourn the dust,
As the sun grieves for the night and the sea for the shore.
But dreams shall grow green till that leaf-brown fall
When I will sit and watch them blaze
Around my death."

Ian stopped and looked anxiously at Jessica.

She said "Which bits are you are unhappy about?"

"I'd rather not say. I would prefer you to give your opinion first. Frankly and honestly. No punches pulled."

"OK," she decided. "But you must promise not to be upset."

He nodded.

She drew a deep breath and plunged in.

"I like the images, and I see where you are going with it. But I think there are too many words – reduces the impact. And some of it is rather too obvious. An unkind critic might say corny. Take the second line for example. The stream sounds like a bell, fine. But do you need to say it's a stream? If it's a valley, there's probably a stream. And is 'once more' needed? Why not just 'And silence falls on the belled vale'?"

"That loses the rhythm. How about 'ringing vale'?

"'And silence falls on the ringing vale'" Jessica repeated. "Yes, that's good. Then you could just have 'sighing hill'.

Leave the reader to decide if it is the wind sighing, or the hill itself. And cut the sheep, they don't add anything. OK, they are part of the picture, but not really part of the poem."

They carried on through the poem in this way until they came up with:

Until the day when the dust returns
And silence falls on the ringing vale
And the sighing hill
Where the clouds shout to the sky
And the white bones in the lake.

Until the day when the dust returns,
And blood and water cease to flow
In the veined meadows of the mind
And I shall love no more
With every twist of the breeze
And every spin of the stars

Until the day when the dust returns
I shall not mourn or moan,
As the sun for the night and the sea for the shore.
But dreams shall twine until that down fall
When I will watch them blaze
Around my death.

Ian gave a grunt of satisfaction. "Thanks, Jess. That's so much better. I can see that I will need to run all my poems past you."

Jessica decided to go to the nearby University, so she could live at home, which was cheaper – and also meant that she could carry on seeing Ian. His father's contacts got him a junior post in an office in Mydenbridge – a very junior post, a glorified office boy really. The work was of no interest to him, but it didn't involve much mental effort so he had plenty of opportunity to dream up new poems. He did read them all to Jessica before he finalised them. Sometimes he altered them a lot after her comments, while with others it was only a word here or there.

Eventually, he had enough material for a small book, which he managed to get published. It didn't sell many copies, but having it published at all was quite an achievement, and it brought him a certain amount of local recognition. A second book of poems followed soon. He started to get invitations to read his poems to poetry clubs around the region. That didn't bring in any money though. He was lucky if they paid his travelling expenses. But it all helped, when his father introduced him to the editor of a small-circulation magazine. They published a few of his poems, and he started writing articles for them, picking up the human interest behind stories that were in the local news. These went down well, and they actually paid him for them. They didn't pay much, but it was something. After a while, they started sending him further afield, still writing about the people who were caught up in things that were in the news.

When Jessica graduated, she did a further course to train as a teacher, and then got a job at a school in Mydenbridge. It was at that point that she said to Ian "I think the time has come for us to think about our future."

"What do you mean?"

"Well, I was wondering if you might be thinking of asking me to marry you."

"Oh, I see. And what would you say if I did?"

"There's only one way to find out!"

He really surprised her then. He did the job properly. He went down on one knee and said "Jessica. You are the love of my life. I can't live without you. Would you do me the honour, the very great honour, of consenting to be my wife?"

"Get up you fool! Yes, of course I will, yes, yes!"

After they had spent some time kissing one another, he broke away and looked serious.

"There are some problems, though, Jess. To start with, your parents might object, and quite rightly, that my finances will not allow me to keep you in the manner to which you have become accustomed."

She laughed. "Don't be ridiculous. They will be delighted. You know how much they like you. Anyway, we can live on my salary."

"Second problem then, where will we live? Even with your enormous salary, we couldn't afford to buy a house. Or even a garage."

"We don't need a garage. We haven't got a car."

"Now who's being silly? You know what I mean. We'll have to start saving up."

He did a quick mental calculation. "I reckon that, if we put aside, say, one third of your salary, we would be able to buy a small house in perhaps twenty years' time. Except that house prices would have gone up by then."

In the end, that problem disappeared. Ian's parents were so delighted by the news that they lent them the money to buy a house. They wanted to make it a gift, but Jessica insisted that it should be a loan, even though she knew that there was little prospect of being able to repay it. It wasn't much of a house, nothing fancy, just a two up, two-down mid-terrace house. But it was home.

They soon set to work to make it feel like their own home. They painted every room, mostly just white, but Jessica chose a pale lilac for their bedroom.

"What about the second bedroom?" asked Ian. "What colour shall we paint that?"

Jessica had plans for the second bedroom, plans that she didn't want to mention. Plans that involved wallpaper with teddy bears on it. She could imagine a cot in the corner, and mobiles hanging from the ceiling over the cot. Fish maybe, or butterflies?

Ian saw her hesitation, and thought he could understand the reason. "Let's just paint it white for the moment. We can do something else with it later on."

They made plans for the garden as well. It wasn't large – not more than a yard really – but there would be room for a small tree. Perhaps a flowering cherry? Jessica thought it would be nice for, well, for whoever was in that back bedroom, to be able to look out of the window and see the flowers. And perhaps birds would perch in the branches and sing? She realised that it might take five or ten years to get to that size, but it was nice to have plans for the future. She stood at the window, paintbrush in hand, looking out over the garden, and dreaming. Until Ian called her back, saying "Come on, Jess. We've got painting to do."

Then there was the wedding to arrange.

****

Jessica looked round at the old church, standing beside the graveyard. Memories of the funeral there, of course. Jessica forced herself instead to focus on memories of the wedding, also in the same church. Most of the memories were rather blurred, but she remembered the dress she had worn. She hadn't wanted a traditional wedding dress. She had gone instead for something she would be able to wear afterwards, for special occasions. It was still hanging in her wardrobe. She never had worn it again. And never would now, she thought. "How could I? What am I going to do with it now? I couldn't bear to throw it away, or even to give it away. Perhaps I could ask Mum to deal with it? Or Emily. Just get rid of it, quietly, without asking me about it, or even telling me what they'd done. But I would have to ask them, and I can't do that. Wouldn't it be nice if one of them would just do it?

One thing I do remember clearly though – what Eleanor said to me during the reception."

****

The reception was coming to an end. Guests were starting to drift away. Wedding presents, mostly unopened, were piled on top of the piano. Mrs Foster brought Jessica a glass of champagne and led her away into the garden.

"There's something I've been meaning to say to you, Jessica, and this seems the perfect moment. To start with, George and I are delighted to have you for a daughter – I won't say daughter-in-law, I prefer to think of you as a daughter. We never had a daughter, and it's lovely to be given a grown-up one. Secondly, I want to thank you for what you've done for Ian. For a long time, when he was at school, we couldn't see how he was going to make anything of his life. He was such a dreamer, he had to be pushed into doing anything at all. And then, he decided not to go to University. I have to say that we were very disappointed by that. We felt he was throwing away all his chances of getting anywhere. But he has shown that it was the right decision. Now he's going all over the world, and producing wonderful pieces of writing. We are so proud of him. And that's down to you. Before he met you, he was so shy, and was hopeless at talking to people. You've given him so much confidence, he's like a different person. It would never have happened without you. So, thank you, and welcome to the family."

****

Jessica remembered those words. They seemed to be engraved on her heart. "'It would never have happened without you.' If he hadn't met me, he would never have gone to those places, and then he would still be alive. It's all my fault. What have I done?" She knelt by the grave, weeping bitterly. But happier memories started to force their way through the tears. She remembered arriving at their little cottage after the reception, and how Ian had tried to pick her up to carry her over the threshold. He wasn't very strong – he had never been much of an athlete – but he did succeed in staggering a few steps before dropping her in the hall. They lay together in a heap, laughing. Jessica almost smiled, through her tears, at the recollection.

****

They had decided not to waste a lot of money on an expensive honeymoon. So they camped for a week in Wensleydale. It was a blissful time. Lying in each other's arms in the tent, listening to the rain on the canvas. Or, on days when the weather was better, wandering hand in hand through fields of buttercups, or over the wild hills. At the end of the day, supper in the pub near the campsite. They went in there every day that week. The landlord was really friendly, and on their last night, they were presented with a cake. Everyone in the pub joined in singing 'Happy Birthday' even though they knew it wasn't anyone's birthday. They felt they ought to sing something.

Ian was away for long periods, at times. When he came back, it was like being newly married all over again. Those few years were the happiest of their lives. Jessica worried about Ian's trips though. She knew that some of them involved dangerous places, but Ian assured her that he was very careful and that the risks weren't as bad as they were made out to be. But she watched the news carefully when he was away, in case there was an announcement that somebody from Britain had been hurt, or even killed, in a foreign country – always with the statement that the names had been withheld until next of kin had been informed. Her relief that it was not in the country that Ian had gone to was mixed with feelings of sadness for the unknown wives or mothers.

As well as the articles from his trips. He continued to write poems, all of which he read to Jessica. He returned from one trip abroad just in time for Jessica's birthday. When she came down for breakfast, she found a small parcel, carefully wrapped, on the table.

"Go on, Jess," said Ian. "Open it."

It was a book of Ian's poems. On the cover, the title. 'Jessica'.

"Oh, Ian. What a lovely birthday present. A book of poems, just for me." She put her arms round him and kissed him.

"Look inside," he said.

The dedication read 'To Jessica, who made everything possible.'

She looked at him. "That's lovely. But it's not really true. I haven't done anything. You would have written all these poems without me."

"Oh no I wouldn't. I was just dreaming about being a poet until I met you. You gave me the confidence to get started, and all your comments on my poems have been invaluable. But go on, look at the first page."

She turned the page and read.

Jessica

The stream laughs, the dream lives and flows – though still

The star in the East rose.

Here small blessings her smile blows,

Sun shines and leaves no shadows.

"That's lovely," she said. "It's not like anything else you've written. And you didn't show me this one before you published it."

"I wanted it to be a surprise. It's a bit of an experiment. It's called an *Englyn*, one of the forms of Welsh poetry. Probably not a very good one – it has to follow some complex rules, and I'm not very good at it. I had to force it rather, and I think it shows. It should read much more naturally." He tried to explain the rules governing *Cynghanedd*, and the patterns of the consonants. "If it's done well, the repeated pattern of consonants adds an extra rhythm to the poem. It was terribly difficult to do. I think it might be easier in Welsh."

"This is the best birthday present I've ever had."

Ian was only home for a few weeks before his next foreign assignment. Fortunately, it was the school holidays, so Jessica could spend all her time with Ian. They made the most of those few weeks. Walking over the hills, going to the theatre, or just lying in bed wrapped in each other's arms. But all too quickly came the moment when he had to leave, for a trip to Uganda. She drove him to the airport to see him off. "Do be careful," she said, as they paused by the security barrier at the airport. "I can't wait until you're safe home again. You know I couldn't live without you."

"Don't worry," he replied. "I always come back don't I?"

After he had been gone for a couple of weeks, Jessica was watching the news on the television. She heard that a British journalist had been killed in an explosion in Kenya. They thought it was a suicide bomb attack. As usual, the name had been withheld until next of kin had been informed. "Thank God that's not Ian," Jessica thought. "He's in Uganda; I had a letter from him yesterday. But how dreadful for the relatives. They might be watching this and wondering if this was their son, or their husband." She started to cry, combining relief for herself and Ian with sorrow for the bereaved loved ones.

The following morning, Jessica answered a knock at the door. Mrs Foster was there, together with a man Jessica didn't recognise.

"Hello, Eleanor," said Jessica. "Nice to see you. Come in." And she led the way into the living room. She was about to ask what brought her round when she saw the expression on Mrs Foster's face and stopped.

"Jessica," said Mrs Foster. "This is Mr Norton, the editor of the magazine Ian's been writing for."

"Oh, yes. Ian's told me a lot about you, and how helpful you've been."

"Sit down, dear" said Mrs Foster. "I'm afraid we've got some bad news. Very bad news."

Jessica turned pale. "It's not Ian, is it? What's happened?" She remembered the item on the news. "Not that bomb explosion? It can't be, there must be a mistake. He wasn't even in Kenya, he was in Uganda."

Mr Norton intervened. "He was following up a story, and it took him to Kenya. He had only just got there, so you won't have heard from him."

Mrs Foster added, her voice starting to break "I'm afraid it is true, Jessica. Ian is dead."

Jessica screamed and jumped to her feet. She started beating her fists on Mrs Foster's chest. "No, no, no, it can't be true, not Ian. No, no."

Mrs Foster put her arms round Jessica, and eventually managed to calm her down enough to explain to her that Ian had made a long-standing arrangement that, if anything should happen to him, Mr Norton would come to her first so that she could break the news to Jessica. "Now, dear, Mr Norton has some things he wants to say to you and I'll go upstairs and pack some things for you. You're coming to stay with us, for as long as you want. I'm not leaving you here on your own."

While she was upstairs, Mr Norton tried to explain to Jessica that the magazine would make all the arrangements to bring Ian's body home, and would meet all the costs, so she didn't have to worry about that. Jessica couldn't listen. She just kept sobbing "No, no, no."

Then he handed her an envelope. "Ian asked me to give you this."

Jessica took the envelope and stared blankly at it. Then she let it drop to the floor.

"Aren't you going to read it?" Mr Norton asked gently.

"I can't bear it," Jessica sobbed. "I can't believe it. I'll read it later, when I'm alone."

There was another soft knock at the door and Mrs Griffiths came in, making a valiant effort to control her tears. "Oh Jessica, love. Eleanor rang me with the news. She told me that you are going to stay with her for a while, which is good. She will need some company as well."

Jessica stared at her, and then realised what she meant. Just then, Mrs Foster came downstairs with a small bag. Jessica ran to her. "Oh Eleanor, I've been so, so selfish. I was only thinking about myself. I'm so, so, sorry." She threw her arms around her, and they wept on each other's shoulders.

Emily burst in, without knocking. "Jessica, Aunt Eleanor, I heard the news and had to come straight round." Unusually, Emily was at a loss for words. "I'm sorry doesn't even touch it. What can I say? If there's anything I can do – that's daft. Of course there isn't. But, well, you know. I'll go. I'm in the way here."

Jessica stopped her. "No of course you're not. Thanks for coming."

Eleanor added quietly "Jessica's going to need all the support you can give her over the next few weeks."

That night, after Eleanor had put Jessica to bed like a child, she sat with her until she thought she was asleep. Then she quietly left the room and went downstairs where Mr Foster was sitting staring at the fireplace. They sat together on the sofa, not saying anything, remembering all their hopes and dreams.

But Jessica wasn't asleep. She longed to feel Ian's arms around her. That was the only thing that could console her, and it would never happen again. How could she sleep? Would she ever sleep again? Then she remembered the envelope. She saw that Eleanor had put it on the bedside table. With trembling fingers she opened it, slowly. Two pieces of paper. She looked at the first. Not a letter, but a poem. She recognised straight away, Dylan Thomas' *A refusal to mourn the death, by fire, of a child in London*. She knew the poem well. She and Ian had often read it together and found it moving. But now, she was uncertain why he had wanted her to read it again. Was he telling her not to mourn? How could she not mourn? She turned to the second sheet. This wasn't a letter either, but another poem, one that she didn't recognise. It must be one of Ian's, she thought, but one that I haven't seen before. She tried to read it.

Do not mourn

I remember
Our first touch in the dark
And the walk home, raining
Our first kiss on the step
And the laced tongues shaming.
I remember
Our walks in the park
The shadowed moon waning
The poems we read
Your bright eyes waking
I remember
You in my arms in bed
And the quiet stars waiting
I remember.

You will remember now
As the tree remembers the fallen leaf
It does not mourn but feeds from it
And rejoices.
Do not mourn.
While you remember, I exist.
A line in time and space
Although now in a different place.

Remember
The rain on the tent
And the lightning fearing

The damp earth's scent
And the lost clouds clearing.
Me in your arms in bed
And the new sun nearing
Remember.

Do not mourn,
Though my writhing pen now rests. In pieces
Still unfinished, lie my dreams.
Though there are songs left unsung
And babies left unborn.
You shall still sing those songs,
And remember.

Do not mourn for me.
Why grieve? Our love still lives
While you have memories to dream
And dreams to live.

As she read it, over and over, it felt as though Ian was standing there, talking to her. At last, she did sleep, still holding Ian's poem.

****

Sitting by the grave, Jessica thought about that poem. She carried it with her everywhere, now rather crumpled and tear-stained, but she didn't need to take it out of her handbag to be able to recite every word. How typical of Ian, to put his thoughts into a poem rather than a letter.

And she thought, gratefully, of how kind Eleanor had been, especially at the funeral. Despite having her own grief to deal with. And of course her mother as well – it was like having two mothers at once.

****

At the funeral, Jessica was amazed at the number of people who had turned up. She recognised some of the people from the local Poetry Clubs that she had been to when Ian was reading his poems. Mr Norton was there, and he pointed out to her some of the other poets and writers, and literary critics, who had come. She hadn't realized quite how well respected Ian was as a writer.

"They all want to talk to you," Mr Norton had said. "Do you feel up to it? You won't have to say anything."

"I don't know. Perhaps I should, for Ian's sake?"

It wasn't as bad as she had feared. Mr Norton selected a few and steered them in her direction, and they made appropriate sympathetic comments, as well as saying how much they liked Ian's work, what a tragedy it was, and so on. She found she didn't even need to listen, but she thought how much Ian would have liked hearing his work praised by people he admired. But it was all so unreal. She hadn't even come properly to terms with the notion that Ian was dead; she wanted to go home and tell him all about it. It didn't help that she hadn't actually seen his body. She had asked to, but they wouldn't let her.

After the funeral, she said to her mother "Why wouldn't they let me see his body?"

"I told them that you should see it, but they said you weren't strong enough, it would upset you too much."

"Oh, God, was he that badly hurt?" She imagined the consequences of a bomb explosion, with his body being blown to pieces, and the stories you hear about scraping bits of flesh up off the road. Maybe it's not all there? Or, perhaps there are bits from someone else? How would they know which bits were Ian? The pictures that went through her mind were horrible.

"I know what you're thinking," said Mrs Griffiths. "But it's nothing like that. His body is all there, intact. But there was a fire after the explosion, and his body is horribly burnt."

"Oh, no, he must have suffered terribly." Jessica was weeping uncontrollably.

"No, he was killed instantly; the body was burned after he had died. I knew they should have let you see him." She held Jessica close until her crying had subsided.

The day after the funeral, she decided to go and visit Ian's grave. Eleanor went with her, and together they tidied up the wreaths that were lying on and around the grave. Then they sat on the bench, quietly, each in their own way thinking about Ian and re-living their memories.

When they got home again, Jessica said "Thanks for coming with me, Eleanor. It made it a lot easier. But I hope you won't be offended if I say that next time I would rather go by myself. I feel I want to be alone with Ian."

"Of course, dear. I quite understand. I feel a bit that way myself. We both want to remember Ian in our different ways."

So Jessica started making the journey up to the graveyard on the hill every day. She found the peacefulness of the graveyard soothing, and sitting on the bench by Ian's grave, she was able to recall all the times they had spent together. The wreaths on the grave soon faded and wilted and had to be thrown away, but she didn't mind. These tributes from other people were not important. But it did leave the grave a bit bare. That was when she decided to bring a pebble every day to put on the grave, to mark the passage of time, and as a symbol of her continuing grief. She first counted out the number of days since his death and put that number of stones on the grave. After that, it was one per day. Each stone with its own memories. At first, she collected stones from the stream she passed on the way up the hill. Later on, she made a trip to a shingle beach and collected a variety of pebbles, various sizes and shapes and colours, and started arranging them into some sort of pattern. Not a planned arrangement, she just let it grow, influenced by the nature of the stone that she had chosen that day.

After a couple of weeks, she decided to move back to her own house. That was not easy, living there without Ian. Every room, every piece of furniture reminded her of Ian. Sleeping in her own bed, without Ian by her side, was difficult. Even though he had been away quite a lot, so she was used to sleeping alone. But waking up without him, and knowing he would not come back, that was hard. The door to the back bedroom stayed closed. She started writing him letters to tell him of the things that had happened to her. Every letter, once she had finished it, she tore up and put the pieces in the bin.

She couldn't consider going back to work, facing her colleagues, and the children, with everyone being nice to her, it would be unbearable, so she resigned her position. The Head tried to talk her out of it, offering to keep the job open for her as long as she wanted, but she was adamant. So, she could spend as long as she wanted in the graveyard, talking to Ian and remembering the past.

A whole year went by. On the anniversary of his death, she made her usual journey, placed her chosen stone on the grave, and sat in the quiet graveyard with her memories. Before she left, she kissed the gravestone, as usual, and said "See you tomorrow, Ian my love."

The following day, she selected a beautiful purple stone, triangular, put it in her bag, and climbed up the hill. The sky was heavy with clouds and the wind was cold. She placed the stone carefully on the grave and admired the pattern. Then she sat on the bench as usual and closed her eyes to help the memories to come.

But it wasn't working as it usually did. She felt strangely anxious and tense. Something was not right. Then she heard a voice. Ian's voice.

"Jessica, what are you doing? Why have you come here? What do you want?"

"Ian? Is that you? I've so longed to hear your voice again. I've so longed to take you in my arms and kiss you again."

"That's not allowed," he said. "My lips are cold now, and one kiss from me would mean your life would not be long."

"Long or short, I don't care. My life without you is not worth living."

"You mustn't say that. There's so much that you need to do still – for your parents, for my parents, and for me as well. We all need you. We need the Jessica that we used to know and love."

"I can't just go back to how I was. I can't stop grieving for you. I've lost everything that matters to me."

"You must stop mourning like this. Didn't you read the poems I left you? Enough is more than enough. I can't rest while you are sitting here crying. Your tears are hot and they burn right through me. The best way of showing your love for me is to let me sleep now, and get on with your life. If you want a memorial, make your life my memorial."

Jessica sat there for a while, thinking about Ian's words, and remembering the poems he had left her. She remembered 'In pieces Still unfinished, lie my dreams' and 'You shall still sing those songs,'

Then she reached a decision. She thought she knew now what he meant, and what she had to do. She got up, kissed the gravestone, and said "OK, Ian, you win. But you'll allow me once a year I'm sure." As she left the graveyard, the clouds were clearing and the sun was starting to appear.

Instead of going home, she went straight round to the Foster's house. Eleanor looked at her in surprise. She seemed somehow different.

"I've been talking to Ian," she announced.

"To Ian?" Mrs Foster knew better than to argue that Ian was dead.

"Yes, and he has been telling me off. He says I need to get on with my life. And I know exactly where to start. Ian left a load of notebooks, and I'm going to sort through them and make a posthumous collection of his unpublished poems."

She rang Mr Norton and told him that she wanted to see him, and why. He sounded very pleased. "No need to come down here. I'll come up and see you. Then you can show me those notebooks."

It was the following week when Mr Norton came to Mydenbridge. Jessica showed him into the living room, where all Ian's notebooks were arranged on the table.

"I've been through them all," she said. "There are seven poems that are complete and ready for publication. I can be sure of them, because Ian always drew a carefully ruled line under a poem when he had finished it."

"That's a start," said Mr Norton. "But we can't make a book out of seven poems."

"That's true. But there are a lot of others that are very nearly finished. They just need a word or two here or there, and a bit of polishing, and I can do that."

Mr Norton looked doubtful. "I'm not sure we can present a book of Ian's poems if they aren't entirely his work."

Jessica disagreed. "It's no more than I did with all his other poems."

"You mean that all Ian's poems were partly your doing?"

"I wouldn't say that. I just suggested a word or two when Ian was stuck, or some minor changes. Most of it was so obvious that I often thought Ian deliberately left some bits for me to finish off, so that I would feel involved with what he was doing. All except one poem. There's one poem that I didn't see before he published it."

"I can guess which one. Jessica?"

She blushed. "That's right. He wanted it to be a surprise. I didn't even know the title he was proposing for that book, or the dedication. He thought I wouldn't let him do it, and he was right. But I was very flattered, and pleased, that he did it. Let me show you one of the poems I've finished off."

She read him one of them, and Mr Norton nodded. "That's a fine poem. And you say that some bits of it are what you've added? I wouldn't believe it. It sounds pure Ian Foster. I can't see the join."

She pointed out the words she had added or changed, and showed him the corresponding passage in Ian's notebook.

"Well, if you can do the job that well on enough poems, we would be able to make a book out of it."

"I've already done it. Enough, more than enough." She passed him a folder of poems.

He looked through it. That's fantastic. But we can't just say these are Ian's poems, if he hasn't approved the final version. We could say 'by Ian and Jessica Foster'."

Jessica objected vehemently. "No, these are Ian's poems, just as all the others are. They must be published as such."

"I know what we can do. We can make your role clear, in a sub-title or something like that. And we can put what Ian wrote on a website so that anyone can see exactly what you've done. Not only for ethical reasons, but also you need some credit for your role in it."

He paused and thought for a minute. "But there is one poem missing."

"Is there? I don't think so."

"Yes, there is. That envelope I gave you that day when ..." He stopped, unwilling to remind Jessica of that unhappy day.

"When you came to tell me that Ian was dead." Jessica finished his sentence for him.

"Yes. Ian told me that it contained a poem that he had written. It's not here."

"No, you're right. That one is too personal."

"Jessica. Don't you realise that all Ian's poems were personal? Every one of them was in some way a poem expressing his love for you? It must be included. The circumstances alone make it one of his most important poems."

Jessica reluctantly agreed, and drew a crumpled bit of paper from her handbag. "Here it is then. But let me copy it out. I want to keep this."

Her hand shook as she copied out Ian's last words to her. "I wouldn't have been able to do this a few weeks ago."

Mr Norton looked at her sympathetically. "What changed? Don't say if you don't want to."

"No, it's fine now. I had a talk with Ian, and he reminded me to take note of what he said in this poem, and the other he put in that envelope – '*A refusal to mourn the death, by fire, of a child in London*'. Dylan Thomas."

"I know it well. Yes, I can see what Ian was saying. This will make a great book now. And maybe the next book will be of your own poems?"

The next day, Jessica went up to the graveyard. She stood beside Ian's grave and looked at the pattern of pebbles. It seemed somehow complete now. "Don't worry, Ian," she whispered. "I've not come to disturb you again. I just wanted to tell you that I'm doing what you said. Your poems will be published. And maybe I'll start writing my own now." Did she imagine the sigh of approval from the grave?

Gwen

The Rose and Crown was crowded, as usual on a Friday night. As I pushed the door open and entered, I could see, in a corner away from the bar, a group of three men I knew sitting round a table. They waved to me, and I went over to join them. The three glasses on the table were all less than a quarter full. "The usual?" I asked. They nodded, and I went over to the bar. I came back with a tray, carefully balancing four pints of bitter. Real ale in this pub, hand-pulled; none of your tasteless pressurised stuff. I slid the tray onto the table and sat down.

"We were talking" said Evan "about coincidences and mistaken identity. Where brothers, or lovers, get separated, and meet up again years later and don't recognise one another. Like the *Comedy of Errors*."

Dai interjected "That's different. There, the twins get separated and years later they end up in the same town. Far-fetched coincidence, yes, but instead of not recognising each other, everyone in the town mistakes them for one another. Just the opposite in fact. For an example where twins don't recognise each other, there is Wagner's Ring cycle – *Die Walkure* I think. A pair of twins, after a long separation, don't recognise each other, and they fall in love. Not identical twins in that case, of course. Or there's *Cosi fan Tutte*, as an example of lovers not recognising each other."

"What happens there?" asked Evan.

"Well, it's actually impossibly complicated, but basically two pairs of lovers disguise themselves, and when they meet up, each of the men falls for the wrong woman."

Brian joined in "What I was thinking of was a situation where two lovers get parted for years, and when they meet they don't know each other. Sometimes the man disguises himself and tries to seduce the girl. She resists, and eventually he owns up and says 'Look it's me'. Common theme in traditional song; they often exchange tokens before they part – usually a ring broken in two."

Brian was something of an enthusiast for folk songs – not the Bob Dylan sort, still less the amplified folk-rock variety. He sang unaccompanied songs, in both Welsh and English. Quite well, actually. He'd made some CDs, but I don't know if anyone bought them. I had a copy of one of them, and I even played it occasionally. But not really my kind of music; I prefer something like Bach. Or Handel – now *Messiah*, there's a real masterpiece.

"It's all ridiculous" said Evan. "Surely in that case her response would be to slap his face and walk away, if he tried such a mean trick. Anyway, I would recognise my brother, or my wife, however long we'd been apart – let alone twins."

"But it does happen", said Dai. "I know a real example, if you've got the time to listen."

We all sat back to hear the story. Dai always had a good story to illustrate any point you care to mention. As a teacher, it must have been a great asset. We could imagine him, tall and grey haired, with a class of schoolchildren clustered round him, spellbound, while he recounted one of his tales. Whether you believed them or not was up to you.

He began "It all started about twenty-five years ago, when I was living in the Neath valley. A beautiful part of the world. The waterfalls are superb." We all nodded. We knew it well, but we were anxious for him to get on with the tale rather than getting distracted by the attractions of the Neath Valley. "Well, I was about sixteen at the time, and a group of us, all about the same age, boys and girls, used to go out most weekends, exploring the cave, Porth yr Ogof, at Ystradfellte or walking in the Brecon Beacons. We loved it up there – the wildness, the freedom, being able to wander for hours without seeing any houses, or people either. And the silence. If the wind isn't blowing, and the skylarks aren't singing, you can just stand still and listen to the blood pumping through your ears. It can feel like your head is going to explode, or implode rather. It's different now, of course. People everywhere."

"I know," said Evan. "I was there last summer, and it was quite crowded on the top of Pen y Fan. I prefer the Black Mountain. It's a lot quieter. But do get on with the story."

"Well," said Dai. "One of the girls, Gwen, was a real beauty, and one of the lads, Alun, fell for her in a big way. It rather broke the group up in fact. The rest would be larking about, and those two would just walk along hand in hand, taking no notice of anything else. When we were down the cave, they would just sit outside gazing into each other's eyes. Or doing I don't know what. But really, what broke the group up was when we all went off to University and so on. Gwen went to London to train to be a nurse, but not before she and Alun had sworn undying love for one another. Before they parted, Alun had a tattoo done on his arm – you know the sort of thing, Gwen and a heart with it. Alun went off to University in Newcastle. But they kept in contact, and would meet up again when they came back to Wales for holidays. So the relationship kept going, in a sort of way, and they fully intended to get married when the time was right.

But it didn't work out like that. At University, Alun had got really involved with voluntary work, and when he graduated, he felt he should do something useful with his life. So, he volunteered for disaster relief work with an NGO. Initially, he didn't really know what he was doing, but his University experience had at least equipped him to deal with problems as they arose, so he gradually built up a useful level of expertise. He had intended to only do this for a year or so, and then come back to settle down, get a proper job, marry Gwen, set up house and raise a family – all that sort of thing. But he found himself sucked into it. One year became two, and then three. Eventually, he became a valued member of a relief team, and he got sent to all parts of the world – earthquakes, floods, famines, he was there, setting up camps, digging out bodies, sorting out food and water supplies, whatever was needed.

For a while Gwen and Alun would write to each other regularly (this was before the days when everyone used e-mail), but it was difficult for him to keep it up. He was often in such remote areas, that sending letters was difficult if not impossible. During this time, Gwen stayed faithful to the memory of Alun, although there was a procession of men asking her out. But she was conscious of the years passing by and often wondered how long she could keep going like that. As the intervals between Alun's letters got longer and longer, the memory got weaker and she felt progressively less able to resist the temptation.

Then she met Paul. She was quite taken with Paul. He was not just good-looking, but he was kind and gentle, and good company. So she agreed to a date with him – this was about four years after Alun had gone away, and a whole year since she had heard anything from him at all. After a few dates, one Saturday she asked Paul back to the flat that she shared with a girl called Claire. It was a decent sized flat, and they had their own bedrooms, so it was easy to entertain friends there. Claire frequently had friends there overnight – Gwen was intrigued by this, as they were always female friends. On this occasion, Claire wasn't entertaining anyone, and the three of them shared a bottle of wine, and had a great time, listening to music, talking about all sorts of things, opening another bottle, and ending up with Paul staying the night in Gwen's bed. Gwen was nervous about this, as she had not slept with anyone before, not even Alun. But she needn't have worried. Paul proved to be an experienced lover, and knew exactly what to do to make it good for her. And she did enjoy it. Except that all the time the thought was in her mind "Will it be like this with Alun when he comes back?"

When she woke up the following morning, it was nice to find Paul lying by her side, snoring gently. She propped herself up on one elbow and gazed down at him, gently stroking the hairs on his chest. Then she got up, put on a dressing gown and went through to the living room, where she found Claire already having breakfast. "Well," said Claire. "How did it go?" But one look at Gwen's face told her. "Was it your first time?"

Gwen blushed, and admitted that it was. "I thought so," said Claire. "You look, well, sort of different. Radiant, I think is the word. Or, somehow, fulfilled. I'm so glad. He seems a lovely lad. I'm sure he will make you happy."

Gwen thought so too, although she couldn't help feeling that Alun would have made her even happier. Paul put his head round the door, saw Claire and retreated hastily, re-emerging a few minutes later with some clothes on. After breakfast, they went for a walk on the Heath, hand in hand. "It's strange," she thought. "When I'm walking like this with Paul, I barely think about Alun at all. But last night, in bed, I thought about him all the time."

Over the next six months, Paul became a regular visitor to the flat, and their friends started to regard them as an item. But Gwen couldn't stop thinking about Alun, especially when she was in bed with Paul. On one occasion she even called out Alun's name at a crucial moment. Then, one evening, just as Gwen was thinking about bed, Paul said "We can't go on like this."

Gwen was taken aback. "What do you mean?"

"You're always thinking about this Alun character. Even when I'm making love to you, it's him you're thinking of. I want to be a first-team player, not a substitute, not a replacement, not a, a, what do you call it in the theatre?"

"Understudy?" Gwen suggested, helpfully.

"That's it. It's no good. I can't do it. I need a relationship with some future to it." And he picked up his bag and walked out of the door.

Gwen was distraught. She was still standing there, in tears, when Claire came home.

"What's happened? Where's Paul?"

"Gone. It's over."

"You poor thing," said Claire. "Come here." And she put her arms round Gwen and held her tight.

Gwen wasn't sure how it happened, whether she had started kissing Claire or the other way round, but somehow she found herself in Claire's bed that night. It was strange, she thought. She had never been sexually attracted by girls, but it was a comforting experience, without the urgency of Paul's love-making.

But it wasn't a turning point in Gwen's life. She continued to have other men friends, which she found somehow more satisfying, although none of them became as established as Paul was. And in between, she would, at intervals, share Claire's bed instead.

But none of this completely removed the memory of Alun. Gwen often wondered what had happened to him. She went down to South Wales from time to time, to see her parents. While she was there, she usually visited Alun's parents as well, to see it they had any news of him, but they also had lost touch with him, so she had no way of contacting him. He had become a sort of freelancer, working with whichever organisation seemed to need him most, so even the people he had originally been working for had no idea where he was. During these visits she also met up with other members of the gang. They noticed that she seemed quite distressed about losing contact with Alun. Although when she was in London, her other activities pushed old memories to one side; when she came back to Wales the contact with old friends brought back these memories, painfully."

Dai paused and looked at his glass. It was almost empty.

"Thirsty work, this story-telling. Whose round is it?"

"It must be my turn" said Brian, and got up to go the bar, carrying the tray with three empty glasses on it. Evan's was still a quarter full. He was always a slow drinker.

"How's the work on your house going, Evan?" I asked. He had quite a small house, and now his family was growing up, and the kids wanted separate bedrooms, he was getting short of space, so he was having an extension built.

He groaned. "Slowly. They come and do a bit and then go away again. I have to keep chasing them to get on with it. I'm glad I made sure we got a proper contract for the work, so they only get paid for what they have done."

Evan was a solicitor, so he was bound to make sure things were done properly.

"It must be months ago they started. Where have they got to now?"

"Let me see. Yes, it must be six months ago that they started. At least they got the roof on last week, so there won't be the same problems with the weather holding them up. All the work's inside now – wiring, plastering and so on."

Brian came back with the tray and four pints of beer, spilling some of it on the way. We picked up our glasses and looked at the pool of beer left on the tray.

"Your hands are getting rather shaky," said Dai. "You ought to go to see a doctor about that."

We all laughed. Brian was a GP, so he only had to sneeze, or complain about a headache, or a pain in his leg, and we would suggest he should visit his doctor.

"Now," said Dai. "Where had I got to?"

"You were saying about Gwen and Alun losing contact with one another."

Evan added, "This Gwen sounds a real go-er. All these men friends, and sleeping with Claire as well. Did she sleep with other girls too?"

"Don't get the wrong impression," said Dai. "The story is very compressed. There were lots of gaps between, so there weren't that many men friends. And she only slept with Claire occasionally. As for other girls, she never felt in the least tempted in that way. Although there was one occasion when one of Claire's friends, Lynne, suggested a threesome. Gwen actually found that very embarrassing, even quite disgusting, some of the things Lynne wanted to do."

"Come off it," said Evan. "You're making all this up. How could you possibly know so much about what went on in their bedroom?"

"I have my sources. Although I confess to embellishing some of the details."

"What was Alun doing all this time?" asked Brian. "Was he having it off as well?"

"Well, he was no saint, but his opportunities were much more limited. The local girls were, by and large, strictly off-limits, but some of the female aid workers were not averse to a bit of male company occasionally, when they had some time off."

"Get back to the story," I said.

"Ah, yes. Well, about five years after they had finally lost touch completely, news came through of a massive disaster in Pakistan. There had been an earthquake that had caused a lot of deaths, and destruction of houses. Relief teams had been sent, and were hard at work setting up camps and dealing with all the injured. Then there was a second earthquake, which caused a landslide, right above the site where the relief teams were working. Many of the aid workers were caught up in this, so there was an urgent need for more volunteers, to rescue the aid workers as well as thousands more of the local inhabitants. The hospital where Gwen was working circulated an appeal for nurses and medical staff to go out to Pakistan to help the rescue effort. Gwen saw the appeal and decided that she ought to go.

When she got there, she was horrified by the conditions under which they were expected to work. This was nothing like the work she was used to in her hospital in London. An emergency hospital had been set up in a school, some distance from the site of the disaster. The facilities there were basic, at best. They were using an emergency generator for electricity, which kept breaking down. The water supply was suspect, and sanitation was almost non-existent. Gwen was amazed to see lizards crawling up the walls. And the flies were terrible. Although they had screens over the windows, it wasn't very effective – many of them had large gaps in them. However, this was luxury compared to the conditions at the field hospitals that operated at the disaster site itself, where they were working under canvas, with many – indeed most, of the patients lying on the ground. The system was that the field hospitals would administer first aid to the less serious cases. Those that needed more treatment than that would be patched up and sent down to the hospital where Gwen was working. Those casualties assessed as having no chance of survival would be left to die. Harsh, but they had to give absolute priority to those that could be helped.

Of course, most of the casualties were local people, but the nature of the disaster meant that there was a small minority of aid workers amongst the injured. So it was no surprise to Gwen when she received an obviously European patient, heavily bandaged and unconscious. She did what she could for him, and gradually he regained consciousness. She tried talking to him, but he had no recollection of what had happened. Nor even of who he was. There was nothing on him to identify him, although she could tell straight away, from his accent, that he was Welsh. She tried talking to him about Wales, and where she grew up, and that seemed to stir some sort of response. As he slowly recovered, he began to take notice of the pretty nurse who was looking after him.

"What's your name?" he asked.

"You can call me Nurse Jones." she said. "What's your name?"

He sighed. "I can't remember."

"What about where you come from? I can tell you're Welsh."

"I don't know. I do remember something about hills and valleys, and waterfalls."

She laughed. That doesn't narrow it down much!"

He looked at her again. "You've got lovely eyes. If I wasn't lying here like this, I'd ask you for a date."

She laughed again. "Now, that's enough of that. We nurses aren't allowed to get too friendly with our patients."

"I like it when you laugh. Your face sort of curls up. We don't hear much laughter in here."

Over the next few days, under her careful nursing, somewhat to the detriment of her other patients it has to be said, his strength returned. As it did so, they talked more and more. Or rather, she talked and he listened. He got her to tell him about her life growing up in the Neath Valley, and he felt some sort of memory stirring deep inside him.

She could see him struggling with his thoughts. Then he said "You know, I think you remind me of someone. A girl who used to smile like you do. But the memory keeps coming and going. Every time that I think I'm getting near it, it fades away again. Shit, I wish I could remember."

Gwen could see that the effort was starting to disturb him. "There, now," she said. "That's enough talking for the moment. I'll make you comfortable and you can have some sleep. That's what you need."

She plumped his pillow, and gently laid him back down. She paused for a moment, gazing at him as he closed his eyes. Then she hurried away to deal with other patients.

She felt strangely attracted to this anonymous man in bandages. She couldn't really be falling in love with a stranger? But as they talked, she still remembered Alun, and thought with sorrow of those happy days, now long past – but still getting in the way of forming new relationships. But every time she took his pulse he would take hold of her hand and she found it more and more difficult to bring herself to pull it away.

Dai paused again, and looked pointedly at his empty glass.

"My round," said Evan, and went to get the drinks, although he still had most of his previous pint left.

"Did you see the rugby on Saturday?" I asked.

Brian groaned. "Terrible, wasn't it? I don't understand Wales' tactics. They kept kicking the ball away, just playing to England's strengths."

Dai agreed. "When they've got all those strong backs, why didn't they try running at them more? We've lost all chance of the Championship now, unless Italy beat France by a big margin. Unlikely."

"But that try should never have been disallowed," I said. "The replay clearly showed he'd grounded the ball before he lost it. I don't know what they were thinking of. It would have made all the difference, at such a key moment in the game."

"But that wasn't the point," retorted Brian. "I thought he had his foot in touch before that, although I hate to say it."

Evan came back with the drinks, three pints, with just a half for him.

We looked at the drinks. "Still a slow drinker then, Evan? Missus giving you a hard time?"

He looked sheepish. "She does go on a bit about the amount I drink. Last time, I went to sleep on the sofa when I got home and didn't wake up until three o'clock. Anyway, I've got some important work to do in the morning, and I want to have a clear head for it."

Dai took a deep drink and resumed his story. "As I was saying, Alun, lying in bed, all bandaged up, kept trying to chat up Gwen, who still didn't know who he was, but thought she might be falling in love with him. Eventually a senior nurse came round to look at him. "I think it's time we took those bandages off. Let's have a good look at how he's getting on with his injuries." She called a doctor over.

When they removed the bandages from his face, Gwen thought he looked vaguely familiar, but his injuries were so severe that she couldn't be sure if she had really seen him before somewhere. But when they removed the bandages from his arms, Gwen gave a gasp. There on his arm, was the familiar tattoo. "Alun! It's Alun! Don't you recognise me? I'm Gwen!" His eyes flickered as though, deep down inside somewhere, he did remember. "Gwen? Do I know someone called Gwen? It does sound familiar, but, no it's gone again. I just can't hold on to it."

"Nurse! Do you know this patient?" the doctor demanded. "Who is he?"

Gwen explained about their past history, and how she recognised him by the tattoo.

"That's good," said the doctor. "I hate having unknown patients, not knowing who to inform. We'll let his parents know straight away. Do you have their address?"

"They'll be so pleased." Gwen paused. "Actually, they didn't even know he was here at all. They haven't heard from him for ages. So it'll be a double surprise, finding out where he is, and that he is safe. I know they worried about him."

But Alun still didn't remember her, or anything of the past. So, she talked to him for hours, telling him all about their youth in the Neath Valley, the cave at Ystradfellte, the walks in the Brecon Beacons, the waterfalls. And of course, about his parents. And she told him all about what she had been doing since, or rather the part of it that she wanted him to hear, and as far as she knew it, the things that he had done since then. It was a long time before Alun recovered any memory of the past, and even then he couldn't be sure how much of it he really remembered, and how much he was just re-inventing from what she had said. But he still couldn't remember anything of the disaster itself – and can't to this day. As soon as he was well enough, he was sent back to the UK to finish his recuperation. As the immediate crisis of the disaster was passed by that time, and the volunteer nurses were no longer needed, Gwen was allowed to accompany him. A year later, they were married.

Dai stopped, and drained the final half of his pint in one go. "That's the story. So these things can happen."

"I don't believe a word of it," said Evan. "You're making it all up. I can't believe in such a far-fetched coincidence."

Brian looked at Dai. "Is it really true?"

Dai hesitated "Every word," he said. "Well, almost. His name was Dafydd, not Alun. The rest is true though, essentially."

There was a pause. Slowly, a thought occurred to me. "Dai, or Dafydd. Your wife's name is Gwen, and she's a nurse, isn't she?" He nodded.

"Let's have a look at your arm."

He rolled up his sleeve. "The other one," I said.

There on his left arm, immediately above the scar of some terrible past injury, was a tattoo. Gwen and a heart, just as he had described.

Hugh Bateman

Hugh Bateman was in trouble. Not for the first time, it must be said. He'd had a history of minor indiscretions, thoughtlessness, carelessness. But this time it was serious. As the younger son of wealthy parents, he'd always had access to more money than was good for him. And without the prospect of taking over the family business, he had not seen any need to behave in a responsible manner. He liked that carefree way of life. So when, two years earlier, Rupert, his older brother, was killed in a road accident, he resented being told that he should now behave more responsibly, and start preparing to inherit the business. He hadn't noticeably moderated his behaviour.

His parents were devastated by Rupert's death. He had been everything that they could have wished for in a son – steady, thoughtful, respectful towards his parents, and, above all, showing every sign of becoming a real asset to the family firm. He was engaged to a lovely girl, and they dreamed of becoming grandparents before very long. Now, all their hopes and dreams had to be transferred to Hugh, the black sheep of the family.

When the funeral was over, his father said to Hugh "Come into the library. We need to have a serious talk about your future."

In the library, he poured them each a large glass of scotch. Hugh sighed. Being called into the library was bad enough, but whisky as well – that must mean a serious lecture. Mr Bateman's first words confirmed his fears. "You must know how much of a disappointment, and a worry, you've been to us, and such an unpleasant contrast to your brother. You've been frittering away your life, and my money. You must realise that the situation has changed now. You are now our only son, and all our hopes rest on you. I know it's a long shot, but people can change, and we have no choice but to trust in you to change your behaviour. When I've gone, you know that you will inherit a large fortune. I have built this business up from nothing, and I want to do what I can to make sure that I will leave it in good hands. So, I expect, no I demand that you now turn over a new leaf and take Rupert's place in the firm. Starting tomorrow, I want you in the office at nine o'clock, and I'll go through the books with you, so you can see how it all works. We can also discuss our plans for further expansion. Then I want you to meet the key people in the firm – the shop hands as well as the office staff. They need to know you and trust you. A good working relationship has been a major factor in our success, and you need to set them a good example. So, no more philandering and no more trouble with the police. That's important. Do you understand that?"

Hugh nodded, without enthusiasm.

"It would help if you could find yourself a nice steady girl and marry her. Diana Johnson would be an excellent choice. You met her at our party last year. They're a good family. Not aristocracy, unfortunately, but at least they're old money. So it will be a step up for you, socially. Your mother has talked to Mrs Johnson, and she has no objection to the match, in fact she thinks it is an excellent idea." He sat back in his chair and waited for Hugh's response.

Hugh paused before replying. Then he said, "Well, father, you must realise that my heart's not in it. All that paperwork, spreadsheets, budgets, and I don't know what – it's all so boring. I really wouldn't be any good at it. There must be another way."

His father started to lose his composure. "No, there isn't. You've always been very willing to spend my money. Now the time has come for you to earn some of it. If you refuse, that's an end of it. No more money from me. Either do what I say, or find yourself a job to support yourself."

"In that case, I suppose I have no choice. I'll have to try to make a go of it. But not Diana Johnson, please. I don't love her – I don't even like her. Can't I try to find a girl for myself?"

His father paused, before agreeing. "That's a deal then. You pull your weight in the firm, and I'll give you a year to find someone to marry. We'll say no more about Diana till then. But it must be someone suitable. No more of those floozies from the town."

So it was settled. Hugh did his best to get interested in the firm, but he found the office side a real chore. On the other hand, he was good at talking to the workers in the factory. He liked walking around the plant, chatting to them, and they responded to his free and easy manner. He found out that the 'good working relationship' that his father had boasted of was not entirely true. There weren't any real problems, but they felt that his father, and Rupert, were rather remote figures. He quickly got to know all the workers by name, and their home background as well. He found out that some of the women were having problems arranging child care, so he got his father to agree to allow flexible work times, and even to have a crèche on site. There was soon a happier atmosphere on the shop floor, and a corresponding increase in productivity. His father was delighted. He could overlook Hugh's lack of interest in the office paperwork – after all they could, and did, employ an accountant to deal with that sort of stuff. The only fly in the ointment, from his father's perspective, was the absence of a prospective bride. If Hugh was seeing any girl, or girls, it was without his parents' knowledge. He hadn't brought any home to be vetted.

This situation continued for a year or so. Things seemed to be going so well that his father started to relax. He even decided not to resurrect the idea of marrying Diana Johnson, although she was still available. "Let's give him some more time," he said to his wife. "He'll find the right girl eventually."

"We could try to help it along a bit," she replied. "Let's have another party. We can draw up a list of likely candidates and make sure we invite them all."

But it didn't work. Hugh showed no interest in any of them.

The turning point came soon after that. Richard, one of Hugh's closest friends, was about to get married, and of course Hugh was invited to the stag night. He didn't come home at all that night. At breakfast next morning, Mrs Bateman was worried. "Where do you think Hugh has got to?"

"Oh, don't worry. You know what these stag nights are like. He probably slept on Richard's floor. He'll turn up in a minute. He'll need to be quick though, if he's to get to the wedding on time."

The phone rang. Mr Bateman answered. "Hello. Bateman here."

"Good morning Mr Bateman. Sergeant Wilson here. We've got your son Hugh down at the station. Can you come and get him? He's saying something about needing to get to a wedding."

"What's he done?"

"The usual sort of thing, drunk and disorderly, criminal damage, and so on."

"Criminal damage?"

"Yes. It seems that he tried to climb up a traffic light to put some trousers on it, and it broke."

Mr Bateman sighed. "OK, I'll come and get him." He put the phone down and turned to his wife. "I hope I'm wrong, but this might mean that he's slipping back into his old ways. I was afraid it would happen, sooner or later, once he got together with his old friends."

Time showed that his fears were well founded. Over the next few months, trips to the police station to bail him out became a regular occurrence. Fortunately, there was nothing very serious, but it was a nuisance. And, to make matters worse, Hugh started to neglect his work with the firm.

After a few months of this, Mr Bateman made a decision. Something needed to be done to break this cycle of behaviour. He called Hugh into the library. Hugh saw that he had poured them each a glass of whisky and his heart sank. That meant another lecture. But this time, it was more than a lecture.

"You know that we've got a number of agents who deal with our exports in a range of countries?"

"Of course."

"Well, it's about time someone paid them a visit. Just showing the flag, really. Making sure they know that we appreciate what they do for us. And to see what opportunities there might be for expansion. In some cases, the agents are covering a lot of countries – possibly too many. See if there are areas where we could do with a few more agents. That sort of thing. Quite an open brief really."

"And you want me to do this?" Hugh was flattered. "Seems like the old man trusts me, even after all the recent troubles," he thought. "A trip round the world, at the firm's expense! Sounds too good to be true."

"When do you want me to go? And for how long?"

"As long as it takes. I think you should go in, say, a week's time. My secretary will make all the arrangements."

Then Mr Bateman looked serious. "One thing though. Many of these countries have different cultures from ours, and they can be very strict. So, no boozing, no girls, and absolutely no drugs. I won't be able to bail you out from there. And, let's be quite clear, I wouldn't even if I could. If you get into trouble out there, you're on your own."

Hugh set off with the best of intentions. At first, everything went well. He enjoyed meeting the agents – talking to people was what he did best. Some of the agents were rather odd characters, but in general they responded well to his suggestions, and they made useful comments, like changing the colour of the packaging. He sent regular reports back to his father. But after a few weeks, he started yielding to temptation. Smuggling bottles of whisky back to his hotel room, to start with. Then, taking girls back to his room. And now, he was in trouble with the police. And this time, it looked serious. He wasn't even sure what the trouble was. Maybe it was that package one of the agents had asked him to take to someone in the next country he was visiting? He hadn't even thought to ask what was in it. Whatever it was, here he was, dumped in a cell.

He looked around. A bare plank by the wall which he supposed must be his bed. He picked up the threadbare blanket with disgust. It was filthy, and no doubt crawling with lice. And the bucket in the corner smelled as though it had not been emptied, let alone cleaned, after the previous occupant had used it. He sat on the edge of the bed, put his head in his hands, and sighed. "How am I going to get out of this one?"

The door of the cell opened. "Visitor for you!" someone shouted, or at least that's what he thought they said. He had some knowledge of the local language, but only rudimentary. A slim, dark-haired, young woman entered, dressed in a long narrow turquoise dress, buttoned up to the neck, and with long sleeves, in the fashion of the country. She was carrying a bundle of papers.

"Who are you?" he asked.

"I've been sent by the British Consulate to represent you. You won't be able to pronounce my real name, but you can call me Susan. It's common here, especially for anyone working with foreigners, to adopt an English name." She smiled at him, and he noticed her grey eyes. She looked nice. "Things are looking up" he thought.

"I'm sorry about this cell. It's a shit-hole", he stopped and chuckled. "Literally."

"You're lucky" she said. "The consulate moved unusually quickly to get you a better cell. Otherwise you'd have been in a cage with twenty others. At least they start off with twenty. Sometimes there's one or two less by the time the morning comes."

"You mean they escape?"

She laughed. "No chance. No, if you put a mixture of criminals, some of them extremely violent, in a close space, you must expect to get a lot of fights. Some of them don't survive."

She asked him about his case, and she made notes in a little book. She wasn't smiling now. "This is going to be a difficult one. I have to say that the chances of you getting off are very small indeed. The best we can realistically hope for is to get a light sentence, say five years, maybe ten."

He was aghast. Ten years in a place like this? After she left, he felt even more despondent than before. He tried, with a small amount of success, to console himself by thinking of further visits from his pretty young lawyer.

After he had been in prison for about a month, he had a letter from his father. It told him that his mother had been devastated by the news that he was in jail, and she had never recovered from the shock, and the grief. She had just faded away and died. His father clearly blamed him for this, although not in so many words, and repeated what he had said at the outset – that he would not bail him out. And he ended by saying that Hugh should not expect to hear from him again. Hugh was deeply affected by the news. Although he had never been really close to his parents – Rupert was always the favourite – he was grieved that he should be the cause of such suffering. But being cast off like that had more effect than all his father's lectures. He resolved to put his past behind him, and become a different person, if, no, when, he got out of there. He would show his father that he was just as good as Rupert would have been.

The case dragged on for months. He began to look forward to the visits from his lawyer. Each time, when they had finished discussing the progress of his case, or the lack of it, they went on to talk about more personal things. He told her about his life in England – the good job that he had (or used to have) with his father's firm, his mother's death, the tragic accident that had killed his elder brother, and how that made him the heir who would eventually inherit a lot of money and property. And she told him about her family, how strict her parents were, although they were kind really. He found out that she wasn't married, and that she was trying to build a good career for herself. Women lawyers were still quite rare, so she was having a hard time of it, but there were some cases where she had an advantage, especially in representing women clients, who didn't like discussing their cases with a man. He felt that they were building up quite a relationship. If he wasn't banged up in this cell, he would try asking her out on a date. Would such a thing even be possible here? He would sit in his cell, after she had gone, and dream for hours about what it would be like to hold her in his arms and kiss her. And he started to believe that she felt the same way about him. He couldn't quite put his finger on it; maybe it was the way those grey eyes smiled at him when she entered his cell. The anticipation of her visits helped to keep him going. That, and the thought that he might be able to convince the court that he wasn't guilty.

And then, one day, the eyes weren't smiling. She looked serious. "I'll come straight to the point. It's bad news, I'm afraid. I've been trying to get them to fix a date for a hearing. Up to yesterday, they just dodged the issue, I couldn't get a straight answer out of anyone. Then, yesterday, someone let slip that it would be at least a year before we get to court."

"A year! A whole year before I even get a chance to put across my side of the story?"

She nodded. "But they will take it off your sentence in the end. Probably."

"So you believe that I'm guilty?"

"No, of course not. I know you're not. But as I said at the start, it will be difficult to convince the court of that." She thought for a moment. "There is one possibility."

"Go on."

"Now we know that it will be a long time before a hearing, I could put in an application for bail. Then at least you would be able to live somewhere more comfortable. You wouldn't be allowed to leave the country of course."

That sounded better than nothing. Sleeping in a proper bed, having a shower whenever he wanted. And, he suddenly realised, he would be able to ask Susan out for dates. He closed his eyes and tried to picture it. Blissful. Even if he couldn't go home for ages yet.

"But what about the money?" He said, coming down to earth again. "Won't I have to put up some money as a surety or something? My father expressly said that he wouldn't bail me out if I got into trouble, and he repeated that when he wrote to tell me of my mother's death. I might be able to get my friends back in England to send me some, but it would take time. How much would I need?"

"Don't worry about that. I can put up the money." Her eyes were smiling again now.

"Really?" What a treasure Susan was.

The bail application was successful. When he came out of prison, he moved into a small hotel that Susan had found for him – cheap but clean. He revelled in his newly regained freedom, being able to walk the streets, do some shopping to replace the clothes that had got decidedly worn and dirty during his incarceration. And he did pluck up the courage to ask Susan out for a date. Much to his surprise, she agreed.

"But we have to be very discreet," she said. "Lawyers aren't supposed to socialise with their clients. But we could go to a restaurant and make it look as though we are discussing your case."

One date led to another, and soon they were going out together once or twice a week. But the constraints started to prove irksome for him.

"I wish I could take you back to England with me, now" he said. "But I suppose I can last out another six months."

She looked serious again. "I didn't want to tell you this," she said "But there's been another delay. It's likely to be longer than that."

He put his head in his hands. "I can't bear it." he said. "I'll go mad if I can't hold you in my arms. I want us to get married and go back to England. And there's another thing. I had a letter from home last week."

Susan was surprised. "I thought your father had said he wasn't going to write to you again?"

"Not from my father. From his lawyers. He died a month ago, quite suddenly."

"Oh, I am sorry. Now you've lost both parents while you have been here. Without being able to go back to see them. Without saying goodbye."

"And without being able to show my father that I can change. But I will do it anyway."

"But what about the company? How will that go on without your father?"

"The lawyers say that the manager is carrying on, for the moment. He can keep things ticking over. But I really have to get back to England now, to take over the reins."

"There is a way out," Susan said, after some hesitation. "You can't leave the country legally, of course. But there are ways of getting out. You could do that. I can arrange it."

"But if I skip bail, you would lose your money?"

"I know."

"You would really do that for me? Why?"

She smiled at him. Those grey eyes again. "I think you know the answer to that question by now."

"And you would come with me?

"No, sorry. That's not possible. It's not only my career that's on the line, but my parents need me. They're getting old, and I need to look after them. In our country, children have a duty to look after their parents, and I can't just leave them. They would be heartbroken, and destitute as well."

"So then I would never see you again?"

"I wouldn't say that. It's just a question of time. Let's say five years. If by that time, you still want me, and if you haven't found someone else in England, I'll come."

He sighed, but didn't see any option but to agree. "I suppose it might even be an advantage. I will have some time to get the firm running properly again before we get married. And we can e-mail one another."

"No" she said firmly. "Write to me instead. They can easily monitor my e-mails and it wouldn't look good if I was getting regular e-mails from you after you've jumped bail. But we can write to each other, as long as you're careful in what you say. They might intercept my post, but there's less risk than with e-mails. And before you go, which will be in several weeks' time, we mustn't see each other again. I can't take the risk of being part of your escape plan. So this is good-bye now. No tearful farewells."

So he went, with a heavy heart. Discretion forbids me disclosing the details of his escape route; suffice it to say that it was long and arduous, but he eventually reached England safely. He lived up to the resolution he had made when he had heard of his mother's death, even though his father was no longer around to see how successful he could be. He was a changed man, older and wiser now, so he could put the dissipations of his youth firmly behind him. He found that the manager who had been keeping the firm going had done a reasonably competent job, but the company was really just treading water. No new ideas, no new products. He set to work to re-invigorate and diversify it, and he found that once he got into this work, it became more interesting. The money that he had inherited from his parents he used shrewdly, and built the business up until he was extremely wealthy, much more so than his father had been. He didn't forget Susan, at least not completely, and not straight away. For a while, they corresponded regularly. But as he became more involved in his work, and with the people that he met through his work, there seemed to be less time available for writing letters. As the frequency decreased, it became more and more difficult to continue. Each letter seemed to be taken up with apologising for the length of time since he last wrote. Then he met Diana again.

He remembered his reaction to his father's suggestion that she would be a suitable girl to marry, and was surprised to find that now she wasn't at all like his impression at that time. She was everything that Susan wasn't. Long blonde hair, blue eyes, and not what you would call slim. I don't mean she was fat, but there was plenty of shape to her. Beautiful in fact, but in a completely different way. Maybe that was what he found attractive: she didn't remind him of Susan at all.

She was certainly good company, lively and talkative. They shared many interests, and they started going to concerts, or to the theatre, together, although he didn't think of them as being an item. The memory of Susan was becoming fainter, although sometimes he was haunted by a recollection of those grey eyes.

This went on for about a year – seeing each other regularly, but not progressing further than simple friendship. Until he was invited to dinner by Diana's parents, the Johnsons. Hugh was surprised by this, and wondered what was behind it. But he didn't see how he could get out of it, so he accepted the invitation. For the most part, the evening was quite innocuous. Over dinner, they talked about the plays they had seen, books they had read, how his business was going. Steering well clear of contentious issues like politics, although

Hugh would have liked to see where Mr Johnson stood on the issues of the day. That might have livened things up a bit, he thought. After the meal was over, Mrs Johnson made some sort of excuse to take Diana off elsewhere, leaving her husband alone with Hugh.

Mr Johnson stood by the fireplace and cleared his throat. "My wife says that I need to have a chat with you about Diana."

"What about her?"

"Well, Mrs Johnson says that you have been going out together for over a year, and I ought to ask you what your relationship is with her." He looked very nervous about saying this.

Hugh grinned. "I take it that you are asking me about my intentions with your daughter. That seems a very old-fashioned thing to do?"

"I suppose it is. But my wife pointed out that Diana is not getting any younger, and frankly, well, she says that we need to find her a good husband soon. "

"Surely that is up to Diana to sort out?"

"Well, yes, I suppose that is true. But, as my wife says, while you two are going out together, no-one else is going to get a look in. Mrs Johnson says that if you two don't end up getting married, then she might end up left on the shelf. And she, well, we, don't want that to happen."

He moved away from the fireplace and started pacing up and down the room. "Now, I don't need to ask you about your prospects. I know that you are very well off, and would have no difficulty in providing for my daughter. Mrs Johnson would be delighted at such a good match for Diana." He didn't say how much his wife was looking forward to mixing with rich and famous people. "The question my wife wants answered – and I do too – is whether you have any intention of marrying her."

Hugh was taken by surprise at the question. "I don't really know the answer to that. I haven't thought of her in that way –

it might sound trite, but we are really just good friends." He paused. They really did get on very well together, and that new house he had bought seemed much too big to live in all by himself. And she was very beautiful. She would be quite an asset at entertaining important clients. He remembered also that his father had said that she would be a good match, socially, and reflected that the boot was, if anything, now on the other foot. He knew enough about the Johnsons to realise that their fortune had declined considerably, and that he was now much better off than they were. "What does Diana think about it?"

This time, Mr Johnson hesitated. "Well, I think you can leave that to us. My wife assures me that Diana would raise no objections."

"Then, "said Hugh. "I suppose we could do it."

Mr Johnson sighed with relief. "Good, let's shake hands on it then. I'll go and tell my wife. And Diana, of course."

So it was arranged. They were engaged to be married, although Hugh felt that the process was a bit odd, and that he seemed to have been steam-rollered, and by remote control. And somewhere, in the back of his mind, he still had something of a memory of the girl with the grey eyes who had got him out of prison.

Meanwhile, on the other side of the world, Susan had not forgotten him at all. When Hugh's letters stopped coming, it did hurt. She wrote to him several times after that, but there was no reply. The worst thing was that she didn't know what had happened. Of course, the most likely reason was that he had got tired of writing to her, had met someone else, and forgotten her completely. On the other hand, he might be ill and needing her to look after him. He might even be dead. She just didn't know. She thought about going to England to find out. She could do that now. Her father had died from a heart attack about a year after Hugh had left. Her mother had gone slowly downhill after that, and eventually she had died too. So now there was nothing overwhelming to keep Susan from going.

But she hesitated. Part of her thought it might be better not to know. Giving up her job and travelling all that way, just to find out when she got there that he was married to someone else and didn't want to see her. She couldn't bear that. But, if he was ill and needed her. He might even be too ill to write to her to tell her that. And he might not have told his friends about her, so no-one would know to get in touch with her.

After weeks of hesitation and indecision, she eventually realised that she had to find out. In the long run, it was better to know than to face this uncertainty indefinitely. It would nag at her for the rest of her life. So she resigned from her job, drew her money out of the bank, and bought a plane ticket. A week later, she found herself at Heathrow.

She had done some research on the internet, and found out that his house, Bleadale Park, was near Oldwick, a small country town in the north-east of England, and that she could get there by train. It was a small station – a waiting room and ticket office, some flower beds, and not much else. A single taxi was waiting in the rank outside. She asked the driver if he knew where Bleadale Park was. "Mr Bateman's house? Of course I do. Hop in."

They were soon out of the town and driving through a green landscape of rolling fields and trees. "You going to this party then?" the driver asked.

"Party?"

"Yes, a big do it must be. Celebrating his engagement. Nice girl she is, but she's really fallen on her feet there. A good catch."

Her heart sank. So she had come all this way for nothing. A lifetime of regrets to look forward to. She nearly asked the driver to turn round so she could go straight back home. But then she realised that she must go through with it, and see him for one last time.

The driver went on. "Big man in these parts, is Mr Bateman. He owns all this land around here. Bought it when Lord Furlingham died and they had to sell up the estate. They wanted him to stand in the last election, and he would have got in. No problem. Most of the people around here depend on him for their living, one way or another. They reckon he's up for a title in the next honours list – maybe a knighthood, possibly a peerage. So his new wife is likely to be Lady Bateman."

She looked around. All these fields with cows and sheep. "I didn't know he was a farmer?"

The driver chuckled. "Bless your life, no. He doesn't farm the land. He owns the farms but there's tenant farmers do all the work. He just collects the money. Must be rolling in it."

The landscape was changing now. No more cows and sheep, but an expanse of grass with trees dotted in it, and railings around it.

"Getting near now. This is the park. See the deer over there? He's got some sort of rare cattle around as well."

The taxi pulled off the road and through a huge pair of wrought-iron gates. She could see the house now – it looked enormous. She wondered why he would want such a large house. They swept round the circle in front of the house and stopped before the imposing front entrance. A man in uniform came down the steps and opened the door for her. As she walked up the steps and in through the door, she could hear the sound of music and laughter coming from somewhere inside the house. Another uniformed man came up to her, took her coat and said "This way, miss. Who shall I say?"

That threw her. She hadn't even been invited to this party. She couldn't just be introduced as yet another guest.

"Wait a moment," she said. "I want to send in a note first."

"Certainly, miss." He produced, as if by magic, a notepad and a pencil. She thought for a moment and then wrote:

Please send me out a glass of wine and a slice of bread. Don't forget the girl who set you free.

She folded the note. "Please give this to Mr Bateman."

"Certainly, miss," the man said again, and disappeared down the corridor with the note. She waited, and paced up and down the marbled hall, with her heart pounding

Suddenly, the music stopped and the laughter died away. All was silent – a stunned silence it seemed, if such a thing exists. Then he was there, running down the corridor towards her. "Susan!" he said, and took her in his arms and kissed her long and hard. "That's the first time we've kissed" she thought with amazement. Then he drew back, still holding her hands, and gazed at her. "It's so good to see you again," he said. "I thought I never would."

"And it will be the last time," she said, with tears in her eyes. "You're about to get married."

"Oh no I'm not. Not now that you're here. Unless, well, unless *you* will marry me?"

That's the strangest proposal a girl ever had, she thought.

"Who is this girl?"

Susan looked round. There was a very cross-looking woman standing there, with a beautiful blonde girl beside her, who also looked on the verge of tears.

"Oh, Mrs Johnson, Diana, this is Susan, who got me out of prison five years ago. She's the girl I'm going to marry."

Mrs Johnson was vitriolic. "You cannot do this! You promised to marry my daughter, and that's what you will do."

"No, mother. I wouldn't marry him now if he was the last man on Earth." Diana fled from the room.

"Well, then, Mr Bateman. I will sue you for every penny you've got."

Hugh took her to one side and said calmly. "Mrs Johnson. I know, and you know, that Diana doesn't love me, and never did. This pretence of a marriage was your idea alone. Diana was just doing what you told her to do. Frankly, so was I. I never loved her either. I don't know why I agreed to marry her; I guess I was just lonely. But as for you, the only thought in your head was to make a good match for your daughter. It's clear to me that you were attracted by the prospect of mixing with rich and famous people, and seeing your daughter living in grand style. Well, I can't promise you rich and famous people, but I can do something about the money. With what I will settle on her, Diana will be a wealthy young woman. She will have suitors queuing up at her door. And really you know she will be better off without me. As a starting gift, she can have that Rolls that's sitting outside. Here are the keys. My secretary will deal with the paperwork."

Mrs Johnson stood there, open-mouthed. What a cheek, she thought – but then her avaricious nature took over. The thought of travelling home in style had its attractions. It might help to silence the neighbours. "Well," she said coldly. "You'll be hearing from me." And she went in search of Diana to take her home.

By now, the guests had realised that the party was over, and they slowly left, whispering to each other, casting sideways glances at the couple standing, oblivious, by the window in the hall, locked in each other's arms.

Lady Geraldine

Geraldine stood on top of the tower and surveyed the country around. Although the house was always referred to locally as 'the Castle', in reality it was no such thing. Old, certainly – some of it dating back to the seventeenth century – but the only bit that looked at all like a castle was this tower. And that wasn't old at all. It was added in Victorian times, for the prosaic purpose of housing a water tank, when running water was installed. Someone had thought it would be a good idea to make a feature of it, so they had added battlements, enclosing a flat roof, which was accessed by a door at the side of the tank. The water tank was originally necessary because the spring, higher up the hill, which provided their water at that time, was only a small one, but it ran reliably, 24 hours a day, and the tank would fill up overnight to provide all their water for the daytime. Even now, when they had mains water, the tank was still in use.

Geraldine liked to come up here, whenever she could get away. She imagined Thornfield would have looked just like this, with Bertha locked up in a room in the tower. She felt an affinity with Bertha. "At least she had some spirit in her," she thought. "Not like that milksop Jane. But I can't imagine Marcus locking me away in the tower!" As she gazed at the fields and woods all round, she tried to imagine what it would be like to be shut away up there. "At least I wouldn't have to make small talk with Marcus' dreadful friends. And I wouldn't have to wear these horrible formal clothes. But it would be terrible just looking at the fields and woods, without being able to get out there and roam around. Hello, I wonder what's going on over there?" From one part of the woods, a thin column of bluish-grey smoke was rising, eddying through the trees. "Looks like someone's camping in the woods."

The door opened and a man came out, carrying a tray with a glass on it. He coughed. "Your Dubonnet, m'lady."

"Thank you, Scroggs," she said.

He flinched, imperceptibly. He didn't like being thanked. It was his job, his purpose in life. All this 'please' and 'thank you' was rather demeaning. To him, it showed that she wasn't a real lady, not used to having servants.

"Tell me, Scroggs, what's that smoke coming up from the woods over there?"

"Ah," he said, "I believe that is coming from the people, er, hippies I think you would call them. His lordship said they could camp in the woods for a while, as long as they didn't make a nuisance of themselves. I think it's a sort of commune." His voice made it clear that he did not approve at all. He stood there a while, waiting. Then he coughed again. "Will there be anything else, m'lady?"

"Oh, no thank you, Scroggs. That will be all."

With an almost perceptible sigh, he withdrew.

Geraldine leant against a turret, sipping her Dubonnet, wondering why she had married Marcus. "I suppose I thought it would be a bit of an adventure, marrying a lord?" she thought. "And Mum was all for it, of course. She revelled in it, her only daughter getting married to a member of the aristocracy. But now, the reality of it, the title is a burden, I hate being called Lady Gravesby, Was I in love with him at the time? I must have thought I was, but looking back on it now, it must have been just the romance of it. The wedding must have set someone back a packet; I suppose Marcus must have paid for at least some of it. Mum and Dad could never have afforded it. I was supposed to enjoy it – the best day of my life, they said – but actually it was torture. All that dressing up, all those speeches. And the photographs, that was the worst of all. Not just the official photographer, and of course lots of the guests snapping away, but some magazine had sent a photographer as well. Posing here, there and everywhere – on the terrace, by the lake, in front of the rotunda, on the tennis court. That was really ridiculous, waving a racket about as though I was about to play tennis in a wedding dress with a train! And they published some of them too, which was really embarrassing. And now, here I am, stuck in this marriage, and this house, with all the servants doing their best to make me feel out of place – which I am, of course. I feel a bit like Rebecca must have felt – no, hang on, she was the first Mrs de Winter. I mean the other one, the one with no name. Strange to have a central character without a name. At least I haven't broken anything valuable, yet. I would probably hide the bits, just like what's-her-name did."

She finished her drink and made a decision. "Off with these clothes and get into something more comfortable. Then I'll go for a walk in the woods. Maybe I'll see what those hippies are up to."

Then she remembered. "Blast. Before I do that, I'd better go and see how Cook is getting on with tonight's dinner. Yet another of those tedious dinners."

Her presence in the kitchen was not welcomed. Cook had everything under control of course, as usual, and she couldn't see why her ladyship kept poking around. There was nothing useful she could do or say, and she just got in the way, asking about the menu, lifting lids of saucepans, sticking her nose in where she wasn't wanted.

There was a knock at the back door.

"I'll get it," said Geraldine. Cook muttered something under her breath. When Geraldine opened the door, she found a man standing there. She looked him up and down. Tall, dark complexion – swarthy, it might say in novels. Heathcliff came into her mind.

"Oh," he said. "Who are you? You look a bit posh to be answering the kitchen door."

Cook called out, without leaving her work "Hello, Jack. This is her ladyship."

"Very democratic household, I see, to have the mistress helping out in the kitchen."

Geraldine ignored the comment. "What do you want?"

Jack explained "I'm from the group who are camping in the woods – your woods, I suppose I should say. Cook very kindly lets us have some water from time to time."

"Don't you get your water from the stream?"

"We do, for most purposes – washing and so on. But we have doubts as to whether it's fit for drinking, so it's handy to get some from here." He produced a small barrel, on wheels. "If I can just fill this up from the tap?"

"Of course, come in."

Geraldine watched him fill it, with her curiosity growing. "I wonder what it's like?" she thought. "Living out there in the woods, cooking on an open fire, hearing the birds singing around you when you wake up?" She wanted to ask, but somehow it didn't seem the right time. Maybe when she took that walk in the woods she could call in and talk to them. But there wasn't time now. The guests would be arriving soon, and before long she would have to go and dress for dinner.

Next day, over breakfast, Marcus said "I've got to go up to town for a couple of days. So you'll have the place to yourself. I'm sure you can find something with which to amuse yourself?"

"Oh, yes. I'll be OK. You go and enjoy yourself."

He looked at her. "I'm not going for fun, you know. This is a business trip."

"Of course, I didn't mean... Well, I hope it goes well then." Secretly, she was pleased, although feeling rather guilty at her reaction. But it would be nice for a couple of days to do what she liked, wear what she liked, eat what she liked – although she anticipated a problem in persuading Cook not to prepare lavish three course meals. Soup and a salad were not Cook's idea of a meal. Geraldine knew without recourse to the scales, that she had put on weight in the three months since they were married. All those big meals – she hadn't yet got used to the idea of not eating everything put in front of her – and the lack of exercise. "What am I expected to do all day? Sit around reading? Much as I love reading a good book at bedtime, I can't spend all day doing it. What else do they do in novels? Embroidery? Writing letters? They certainly don't expect me to go for long walks over the moors, like Cathy did. Now I've got two days to do my own thing. The first thing I'll do is find out what those hippies are doing, what they're like." But she didn't say that to Marcus. She knew he wouldn't approve.

As soon as Marcus had left, she went upstairs, removed her tweed skirt and cashmere jumper and put on an old pair of jeans and T shirt that she retrieved from a secret place at the back of the wardrobe. Now more suitably dressed, she set off for her walk in the woods. She didn't go directly to the camp site. She pretended to herself that she was just going out for a walk, and she would, apparently accidentally, encounter the camp site during her walk. So she set off in the opposite direction, down towards the lake. "Good idea," she thought. "If anyone's watching from the house, they won't guess where I'm going." She watched the ducks for a while, and noticed that some of them were putting their heads under water and sticking their tails in the air, while others were going completely underwater and staying down for a while. "Maybe there are two different sorts of ducks?" She looked more closely. "Yes, they are different colours. I wonder if we've got a book about birds? Maybe I should take that up as a hobby. Something to pass the time, and it would make a good excuse to get out of the house."

Leaving the lake, she walked to the edge of the park and let herself out through a small gate that lead directly onto the moor. The sun was shining, and some white cumulus clouds were hurrying across the sky as she climbed the hill, through the heather, just coming into flower. When she reached the top of the slope, she could see the expanse of moor, rolling and rising as far as she could see, up to the heights of Kinder Scout and Bleaklow in the distance. Behind her, the house and park looked quite small in the valley. She thought she could hear a lark singing high overhead. She lay down in the heather and squinted up into the sun to try to see it, but it was too high and too small. "What a lot of effort," she thought, "to fly up so high. And why sing?" She closed her eyes to hear it better. Somewhere, not far away, a grouse flew up with a startled "Go back! Go back!". "Something must have disturbed it," she thought. "But not as much as in a few weeks when Marcus and his friends come up here with their guns. Poor things."

"Hello, again," said a voice.

She opened her eyes. Standing before her was Jack, looking even more like Heathcliff, silhouetted against the sky. He must have known what she was thinking. "Cathy, I presume?"

"No, Geraldine, actually. Or I suppose it should be Lady Gravesby to you."

"I think I'll call you Cathy, anyway," he said, flopping down in the heather beside her. "Geraldine sounds much too posh."

She laughed. "And I expect you think of yourself as Heathcliff, then."

"I could be, if you want."

She stopped laughing. There seemed to be more meaning in that remark than she liked to think about. "What are you doing up here anyway?"

"Same as you, I guess. Enjoying the moors and the sunshine. I don't need your permission to walk here. At least, not until your husband starts murdering these poor birds." He glanced at her inquisitively. "Or do you do that as well?"

"No, I certainly do not. I've never touched a gun in my life. Never killed anything either – unless you count wasps and slugs. But I expect I'll have to do my bit entertaining the guests."

He could tell that she wasn't looking forward to that at all.

"Tell me," she said. "What's it like, being a hippie?"

"Who said I was a hippie?"

"That's what Scroggs said."

"Who's Scroggs?"

"Our butler."

"I suppose he would be, with a name like that. Is it his real name, or do you just call all your butlers Scroggs, to save remembering the real names of new ones?"

"I think it's his real name. And he's been there for ages, as far as I know; we don't keep changing them."

"I've never met anyone with a butler before. But I suppose it's to be expected – big house like that."

"He's not just a butler – valet, chauffeur, footman, even does minor odd jobs round the house. But he likes to be called a butler. Sounds better than odd job man. Anyway, tell me about hippies."

"Well, to start with, he's wrong about that. We don't think of ourselves as hippies – rather old-fashioned concept, really."

"What are you then? Gypsies?"

"We don't like labels. That's partly what we're trying to get away from. We're certainly not 'gypsies' as you call them, nor travellers of any sort. No, we're just a group of people who have rejected the way society is organised at the moment, and we're trying to live in a different, more sustainable, way. Carbon neutral – cutting down on the use of energy, and generating our own for what we need, for a start. And growing our own food, as much as possible."

"You're not going to be able to grow much food in the wood you're in. And I've seen the smoke from your fire – that's hardly 'carbon-neutral'."

"It's actually better than it looks. We're not cutting down trees or anything like that. We just gather up fallen branches.

But anyway, this is just a temporary camp while we get things set up. We're planning to have a more permanent base, in Wales, near Tregaron. Rhiannon is from round there, and she has lots of contacts. She's identified a suitable site, and we'll be moving there before long. Then we can start to get things set up properly. There's a waterfall which will help with power, and we'll have solar heating and a wind turbine. And we'll have compostable toilets and things like that. And there's a good patch of land for growing vegetables. No meat, of course. Strictly vegetarian. Some of us are vegetarians for ethical reasons, but even those who aren't, agree that we can only really be self-sufficient in food as vegetarians. We will have some goats, but only for milk. And some hens for eggs."

"Do vegetarians eat things like eggs and milk? They're animal products too."

"You're thinking of vegans. None of us are vegans, at the moment. But if any vegans join us we would need to adjust what we grow, to produce enough protein and vitamins."

"But you can't really be completely self-sufficient can you? Won't you have to buy some things – clothes for example?"

"We did think about making our own clothes, but it's too complicated. And we'll need money for other things – Council Tax, costs of running the van, and so on. We're not planning to be hermits. Some of us do on-line work – so we'll need money for internet connections – and others will get jobs locally. We want to be a real part of the local community, using the shops, drinking in the pub, and so on."

"Will the locals accept you? Don't they all speak Welsh for a start?"

"You're right, that's an important factor. They've had unpleasant experiences with some of the types who've moved in – stealing chickens and crops from the fields, or even worse, to pay for drugs. We have a 'no hard drugs' policy. And Rhiannon knows many of the people already, which will be a great help. She speaks some Welsh, and the rest of us plan to learn it, so we can talk to them in their own language."

Geraldine said nothing for a while. She just lay there, looking up at the sky and thinking how good, how honest, such as life sounded, compared to the artificiality of her current existence. How tedious it all seemed – endless dinner parties, entertaining Marcus' friends. Nothing to do all day, at least nothing of significance. To say nothing of enduring the thinly disguised contempt of the servants. Then, thinking about her existence, she remembered the time. "I must get back, they'll be wondering where I've got to."

"Does that matter? Aren't you the mistress? Don't they just do what they're told?"

"It's not as easy as that. And Marcus will want to know what I've been doing while he's away. Help me up."

Jack got to his feet and held out a hand. Geraldine took it and lifted herself up from the ground. They stood like that for a moment until she recollected herself and reclaimed her hand.

"Anyway, you can come and see our camp on your way back to the house."

When they got to the camp site, Jack clapped his hands and said "Gather round, people, we've got a distinguished visitor. Our hostess has come to see how we live. Officially she's Lady Gravesby, but I call her Cathy. "

He turned to Geraldine. "Over here, cooking our supper, is Rhiannon. I told you about her. And here we've got Poppy, Gustav and Benvenuto – we call him Ben."

"Hi, Cathy," they chorused.

"Where are the others?" Jack asked.

Rhiannon looked up from her cooking pot over the fire. "Alex is out collecting wood, and Carlo's gone down to the stream to fetch some more water."

Geraldine looked round the site, fascinated. "You've got a wigwam, like the Red Indians. Is that where you sleep? All of you together?"

Jack pretended to be shocked. "You mustn't call them Red Indians, that's derogatory. You should say 'native Americans'. Or, if they're from Canada, 'Aboriginal people'. And, technically, it's not a wigwam but a tipi. Or a tepee if you like. A wigwam is a different sort of structure altogether."

"I stand corrected. But whatever it is, do you all sleep together in it?"

"Of course."

"But what about privacy? I mean, getting dressed and undressed? In front of each other?"

Jack laughed. "We don't have anything to be ashamed of. Actually, you get used to it very quickly. And it's great being all in there together. We don't need any heating at all."

Geraldine wanted to ask what happened if a couple wanted to make love to each other; it surely must be very inhibiting – but she didn't know how to say it. Were any of them 'couples' in that sense? Or perhaps they shared everything, even partners. But she certainly felt she couldn't ask that. Instead, she asked about the toilet arrangements.

"We have a pit latrine," He pointed to a small shelter just beyond the edge of the site.

"You mean, just a hole in the ground?" She shuddered. "That sounds disgusting."

"It's not that bad, if managed properly. But you must remember that this is only a temporary set-up. When we get to Tregaron, we will be renovating, or rebuilding, some derelict houses. You will probably think that sounds a lot more civilized. As I said, we will be leaving here soon – Rhiannon, how are the arrangements going?"

Rhiannon looked up from her pot again. "It's good. All virtually ready. We could leave in a couple of days, even tomorrow if you want. Supper's ready, by the way. Is Cathy staying for supper? There's plenty of it."

Geraldine hesitated. "I didn't give Cook any instructions. I expect she'll have prepared supper for me."

Jack looked at her in disbelief. "Who's the boss in your house, you or the servants? Why do you keep worrying about what they think?"

"I do sound a bit like what's her name in *Rebecca*, don't I? Maybe I should be more like Dona St Columb and order the servants about, even if it means the horses don't have a chance for a proper rest and a drink."

Rhiannon said "I'm not sure what you're talking about, but it sounds like you're staying for supper?"

"Yes, I will" Geraldine said decisively.

As they sat round the fire, talking, laughing, and singing, Geraldine was thinking what a contrast it made with the stuffy dinner parties at home. Here, she felt relaxed, free, and able to enjoy herself, totally uninhibited. Her misgivings about pit latrines and lack of privacy now seemed quite insignificant. "Wouldn't it be nice," she thought "to be able to share properly in such a life? To be able to be so spontaneous, and not worry about what people think of you. Totally impossible, of course. What would Marcus think? Or the servants? I can't just run away and leave them. What a mad idea!"

When Geraldine eventually got home, she found Cook in a foul temper. "Your dinner's ruined you know. Where have you been until this time?"

"Minding my own business," snapped Geraldine, and went upstairs, leaving Cook standing in the kitchen muttering something about his Lordship having something to say about this. "I've a good mind to give in my notice. I've never been spoken to like that in all the years I've been here, 'Lady Gravesby' indeed, Lady Muck more like. Cheap upstart!"

But Geraldine didn't hear any of that. She almost danced upstairs, and got ready for bed, singing *The Raggle-taggle Gypsies* to herself. She picked up her copy of *Frenchman's Creek* and lay in bed reading it from where she had left off. But the events of the day had been so exhilarating, and tiring, that she soon drifted off to sleep. In her dreams, Jack became a suave French pirate, and the woods contained not a camp site but a painted sloop lying at anchor in a creek.

The next day, her mind was made up. She put on her old jeans and T-shirt again, gave Cook a note for Marcus and told her that she was going away for a while and didn't know when she would be back. Carrying nothing except two of her favourite books, she walked out across the park, taking again the circuitous route to the woods, via the lake.

Marcus arrived home late the following morning. Scroggs heard the car coming up the drive, and went out to meet him. As he took the luggage from the boot, Marcus said, "Everything all right here, Scroggs?"

He noticed Scroggs' hesitation. "Is something the matter?"

"Well, it's Lady Gravesby. She's, er, disappeared."

"Disappeared? What do you mean?"

"Cook says she went out yesterday morning and told her she didn't know when she would be back. Cook thought it was strange. And she left a note for you." He handed over the envelope. Marcus tore it open and read the two words inside – 'Sorry. Good-bye'.

"Hells bells," he said. "What does that mean? What's she got into her head? Where's she gone?"

Scroggs coughed. "It's not my place to speculate, sir, but there was some talk that she'd been seen talking to those hippies that are camping in the woods."

Marcus stared at him. "You think she's gone off to join that band of ne'er-do-wells? We'll soon see about that. I'll send them packing with a flea in their ear." He strode off towards the wood, muttering to himself and getting angrier and angrier.

When he reached the camp site, Jack was the first person he saw.

"Well," said Jack. "This is an honour. His lordship himself paying us a visit. What brings you up here?"

"Cut it out," Marcus spluttered. "Where's my wife? What have you done with her?"

Before he could answer, Geraldine emerged from the tepee, wearing a battered pair of jeans and an old T shirt. "Hello, Marcus. You found me quickly."

"It wasn't difficult. Now, no more of this nonsense, you're coming home with me right now. And this band of brigands can pack up and leave my land. And bring with you all the valuables you've taken from the house. I know what they're up to; they're just using you to get their filthy hands on my possessions."

"You're wrong on all counts. Firstly, I didn't bring anything with me, only what you see me wearing now. No, that's not quite true – I did bring a couple of books. Do you want them back?" She produced well-thumbed copies of *Frenchman's Creek* and *Lady Chatterley's Lover.* Marcus waved them away, angrily.

She went on. "Secondly, they're not a band of brigands, and they're not out to rob you of anything. They're good honest and friendly people who are just trying to live a better sort of life. And finally, I am not coming back with you; I'm staying with them."

Jack clapped his hands. "Well said, Cathy."

Marcus rounded on him. "Keep quiet you, I'll deal with you later. This is between me and my wife. And what's this 'Cathy'? Her name's Geraldine, if you must know."

Jack smiled. "I prefer to call her Cathy."

Marcus ignored him. "You can't really mean it? Sleeping rough out here, instead of in a comfortable bed at home? Cold and wet, instead of a comfortable warm house? Doing everything for yourself, instead of having servants to look after you? You've taken leave of your senses."

"I mean exactly that. I hate all those dinner parties, all that comfort, all that business with servants. You can't make a wild bird happy by giving it a gilded cage. I want to fly, and with Jack and the others that's what I feel like, like I'm free again."

"Look, I'll be generous. Come back with me now, and I'll say no more about it. Even after you've been sleeping with that man. Lots of people wouldn't take you back, you know. 'Damaged goods' they'd say."

"Wrong again. Yes, I slept last night in the tepee with Jack and the others, but nothing like that happened. But I don't say that it won't, if Jack wants to." And she smiled at Jack. "And now, I think you'd better go home. Arguing like this is not going to get you anywhere, and it's bad for your blood pressure." With that, she disappeared back into the tepee.

Marcus was thunderstruck, but there was obviously nothing he could do. He turned on his heel and marched back to the house, after shouting over his shoulder "I want you off my land by tomorrow morning!"

After he had gone, Marcus joined Geraldine inside the tepee. "Did you really mean what you said to him?"

"All of it, yes."

"Including the bit about, well about us, you and me, er, you know..."

Geraldine giggled at his hesitation, almost prudish, and so out of character.

"Mellors wouldn't have put it like that! He would have come straight out with it. Yes." she whispered in his ear. "I've never used this word before, but now is a good time. I want you to fuck me!"

When Marcus woke up the following morning, he automatically reached out with his arm to touch Geraldine. Finding nothing, he remembered what had happened. "Damn! I handled that badly yesterday. I see now it's no use trying to bully her. Perhaps I could try a softer approach, tell her how much I need her and so on. I'll go up there after breakfast and have another go. Damn again. I told them to pack up and go, I'd better go up straight away, before they've left."

So he set off, not in the best of moods; he never liked missing his breakfast. On the way, he rehearsed the things he would say – offer to buy her some nice clothes, take her on a trip somewhere, even telling her he loved her. But when he got to the campsite, he found it empty. The tepee had gone, all signs of occupation had been removed, even the ashes of the fire had been carefully scattered in the bushes. Marcus sat disconsolately on a log, staring at the bare patch of burned ground in the centre of the clearing.

Soap, starch and candles

From Swansea, you can see Devon. On a clear day anyway, when you can just make out the hills above Lynmouth. They say that if you can see Devon, it's going to rain. On the other hand, if you can't see it, it's already raining. I think lots of cities must have similar sayings – in Manchester it's the hills of the Peak District. To my mind, seeing all that way across the sea was an added attraction to a ride on the Mumbles train. That of course is long gone now, which is a pity. It was the oldest passenger-carrying railway in the world, and would now be a major tourist attraction. People would come from all over the world to ride on it. But someone thought buses would pay better. That's progress for you. Although it was properly called a railway, we always referred to them as trams, which was what they looked like, with their upper and lower decks. You needed to go upstairs to get the best of the view, especially for the first part of the journey when it ran behind the sand dunes around Swansea Bay. Of course as a child I always wanted to go upstairs anyway. I remember the reversible seats, which meant you could face forwards whichever way the tram was going – you just had to tip the back of the seat in the opposite direction. Beyond Blackpill, the sand dunes ended, so the tram was running along the edge of the sea; if the tide was in, it seemed that the water was lapping against the wheels. Of course if the tide was out, you just had a good view of miles of mud. And, beyond the mud, a queue of oil tankers waiting for the tide so they could get into the docks. In those days, Swansea was a major port. Now, I suppose they all go to Milford Haven instead; that's a real deep water port, so they don't have to wait for the tide. And I guess Swansea couldn't take the huge tankers they use these days.

Further round the coast, beyond Oystermouth, the cliffs closed in so there was just room for the tracks and the road; further still, the road gave up and went inland, over to Bracelet Bay with its ice cream stall in the shape of a giant apple, leaving the tram on its own for the final part of the journey under the cliffs to Mumbles Pier.

That's where the story really starts. Mumbles Pier, not just arcades and amusements, and of course the Lifeboat Station – another treat for a child – but also a working pier where you could board the paddle steamers for the trip across the Bristol Channel to Ilfracombe. Sometimes, if the weather was good enough (which it rarely was), you could go on to Lundy Island. As a child, this trip was marvellous, mainly because you could go below, to the viewing gallery around the engine room and gaze at all that gleaming brass, dials and gauges, hissing steam, and the well-oiled pistons sliding, apparently effortlessly, in and out, driving the massive paddles at the side of the ship.

Actually, the story really starts much later on. As a teenager, without the encumbrance of parents, the trip to Ilfracombe presented all sorts of opportunities. Somehow, the combination of being away for the day plus the relative comfort of the seats in the lounge released our inhibitions, especially in regard to meeting girls. Those of us with steady girlfriends, or even temporary ones, would spend the trip in the lounge, necking. We even had kissing competitions – seeing how long you could maintain a kiss. Proper mouth on mouth kissing. It required a special technique so you could breathe without breaking contact. Done properly, you could maintain it virtually indefinitely.

Finally, I can get round to the proper start of the story, which was one Easter Monday. I was without a steady girlfriend at the time, since I had finished with Marilyn. Actually, that's not quite true. I had sort of stopped seeing her;

I guess I must have got a bit bored with our relationship. And there always seemed to be something else to do, so I just stopped asking her out. At times I felt rather guilty about this. I should have said something to her, but that would have involved making a decision, and that was a big step to take. So I just drifted out of it. I hope she didn't feel hurt about it. I have to confess that it wasn't the first time I'd done that. But I don't flatter myself that I left a trail of broken hearts behind. I wasn't that special. They would soon get over it.

Anyway, on this trip, I was looking around. That makes it sound a bit like a cattle market, and indeed it was. Many of the girls were on the same errand, or so it seemed to me. As I viewed the talent, I wasn't encouraged. Not at first. They all seemed to be huddled in groups, giggling about some sort of girly in-jokes. Totally impenetrable. Then I saw her. Sitting quietly and thoughtfully, on the edge of one of the groups, but not really joining in whatever it was they were giggling about. I eyed her up. Pretty enough, but not stunningly beautiful. Rather plump it has to be said. Nondescript sort of brownish hair. To this day, I have no idea what colour her eyes are. But she'd a sort of friendly face. After studying her for a while, I made up my mind to try to chat her up. I went over.

"Hi!" I said. "I'm Jeff."

She smiled up at me and moved over a bit so I could sit down. "I'm Jean." she said. Then we chatted a bit, about this and that, and I told her that my father was a train driver. (This wasn't actually true. He was a teacher, but that didn't sound very cool. I thought a train driver was much more interesting.)

"Wow," she said. "That's much more exciting than my Dad. He has a shop."

"What sort of shop?"

"Oh, it's just a corner shop. Sells all sorts of stuff, from soap to sealing wax, turpentine to treacle, creosote to clothes pegs. "

"That sounds fantastic!" I closed my eyes and imagined the mixture of smells in such a shop.

Out of the corner of my eye, I could see the other girls in the groups glancing round at us, whispering, and giggling a bit more. Really embarrassing.

By now, a few other boys had joined the group, although they seemed to be mainly talking to each other rather than attempting to chat up any particular girl. Suddenly, one of the girls said "Let's play 'Catch and Kiss!'". The others assented enthusiastically, so there was nothing for it but to join in, although playing games seemed rather childish. The game involved the boys standing more or less in a line while the girls formed a line on the other side of the lounge. One of the girls would throw something, and whichever boy caught it, or was hit by it, had to kiss the girl who had thrown it. "What shall we throw? Has anyone got a ball?" No-one had. Then one of the boys produced a rolled up cap from his pocket. "Will this do?" he asked.

Most of the girls were rubbish at throwing anything, so it often never even reached the line of boys. If it did, their aim was so poor that it didn't hit the intended target, so there was much random kissing, of a very perfunctory nature. But somehow Jean always seemed to be able to hit me with the cap. And the kisses that followed were far from perfunctory. That was blissful – not just holding her firmly against me, but kissing those lips that tasted of liquorice, cod liver oil, pepper, and everything else that was sold in their shop. This was noticed by all the others in the group. "Go it, Jeff," encouraged the boys. "Ooh, Jean," called the girls. "You've got a catch there!" I could feel my face going redder and redder. Eventually, it was all too much, so we broke away from the group and went off to wander round the boat, hand-in-hand, followed by cat-calls from both boys and girls.

Our relationship flourished after that. We often went to the cinema, or just walked along the beach. As the weather got warmer, with the summer coming on, we started going out to the Gower. Once our exams were over, we had days on end free of anything except spending time together. Nicholaston

Burrows was a favourite place – far enough from the crowds at the other end of Oxwich Bay, where the car park was, that it was easy to find a secluded spot in the extensive sand dunes where we could lie in each other's arms without any risk of being interrupted – except occasionally by an inquisitive dog searching for its owner. If we got tired of kissing, which wasn't often, we could lie on our backs and look up at the seagulls wheeling and calling in a cloudless sky. In those days, the sky was always cloudless, and the sun was always hot.

Or there was Brandy Cove. A mile down a muddy path was enough to put off most visitors. And at the end, a tiny secluded beach. Underneath the cliffs at the side, we were hidden even from the walkers on the cliff path. And we went swimming there. Jean wasn't much of a swimmer, so she would often just stand up to her waist in the water and watch me. Sometimes, I would swim towards her underwater so she couldn't see me, and I would surprise her by grabbing her legs. Occasionally my aim wasn't too good, and I would touch her in places that I thought were forbidden, but she didn't seem to mind. That encouraged me to be rather more experimental in our embraces, and I wasn't rebuffed.

So, the summer flew by, and then it was autumn, and back to school. My last year, I thought, with relief. Just the exams in June to deal with, and then, freedom. Or so I thought, forgetting that leaving school meant getting a job of some sort. I had long ago ruled out the possibility of University; I found all that sort of stuff irksome. And I had no particular ambitions about a job. Anything would do, as long as it brought in some money. But my parents had managed to convince me that it was worth trying to get decent grades in my exams – better prospects. They said, get a job with a pension. What sort of person starts thinking about a pension when they're seventeen? Nevertheless, I did see some point in making a decent go of it with the exams, which meant rather less time seeing Jean. Mostly just Saturdays, with an occasional evening date now and then.

One evening in the spring, we were walking along the beach, hand in hand, when she said. "Mam wants to meet you. I've told her all about you, and she wants you to come to tea on Saturday." This sounded like a serious step forwards in our relationship. Official recognition. I wondered if I was ready for such a move, but the summons could not be ignored. So I went, nervously.

I needn't have worried. Her Mam was all sweetness and light, and I suspect more nervous than I was. She had obviously gone to a lot of trouble to get things ready. The front step had received an extra scrubbing – I'm sure you could see your face in it. And the inside of the house was absolutely spotless. Tea was laid out in the front room, which, I was quite aware, was a real honour. As was the usual custom, the front parlour was reserved for special guests, such as the Minister from their Chapel. Crab sandwiches, buttered scones, Welsh cakes, everything was delightful. And underneath it all, I could clearly detect the taste of candles, mustard and linseed oil. Her Dad didn't say much, but I thought he approved of me. Afterwards, as I kissed Jean on the doorstep, she said "Thank you for coming. I think it all went well, don't you?" She kissed me again and I walked home.

Saturday evening tea at the Thomas's then became a regular feature. But after that first occasion, it was the back room, not the front parlour. This I regarded as another signal that our relationship was accepted. Perhaps I should describe their house. It was about half a mile from ours, and was similar: a typical terraced house, basically two up, two down. So there were just the two rooms downstairs: the back room, which was the everyday, all-purpose room where they had their meals and then sat around watching the telly. The kitchen was in a back extension. The front room was, as I said, reserved for special guests. Upstairs was similar, with

Mr and Mrs Thomas' bedroom at the front and Jean's at the back, although of course I never went in there until much later on. The bathroom was in the extension, over the kitchen. Originally, I think, the front room was the shop (presumably they didn't have a parlour in those days), but it must have flourished because they were able to take over the next door house as the shop. Next door's front room became the shop itself, and the back room was used as a store room plus 'office'. That's rather a grand word for what was little more than a filing cabinet, a telephone, and a typewriter. The computer didn't arrive until much later. The rooms above the shop were mainly full of empty cardboard boxes and other similar junk, all of which was supposed to have the potential to be useful someday.

Ah, the shop! I was shown round on my second visit, and it was just as entrancing as I had expected it to be. In the middle of the shop window, a pyramid of tins of paint, white gloss paint, surrounded by a miscellaneous array of containers of various sorts, ranging from creosote and linseed oil to tins of baked beans and soup. As you pushed open the door, a bell tinkled to announce your entry. You were faced by an old mahogany counter, with weighing scales and a till – the old mechanical sort, which rang when you pressed the key to open the till, after you had entered the amounts for each purchase. Behind the counter, floor to ceiling, shelves – jars of loose sweets, bags of flour and sugar, boxes of candles, salt and pepper, pots of glue, clothes pegs, fishing line, clothes lines, talcum powder, shampoo, soap, scent, dried eggs... I could go on. The list seems almost endless. In a corner, there was an old wooden step ladder so you could reach the highest shelves. Later on, Jean and I helped out in the shop from time to time. That was magic. Just being in the shop and experiencing the multitudes of aromas following one another – one moment liquorice, then scent, then creosote; they whirled around until my senses were quite dazed. Customers only came in occasionally, so we could spend a lot of time in the back room, until the bell rang to say a customer had come in. Then Jean would hastily re-arrange her clothing, pat her hair back into shape and disappear to serve them.

Returning to my story, as spring turned into summer, the exams loomed larger and larger. I hardly saw Jean at all. Most weeks, it was just Saturday evening tea at their house. Then June was over, the exams were done, and suddenly I had a lot of free time again. We started spending days on the beach again, just as we had done the previous summer. But now we were not content with just doing the same thing all the time. We spread our net wider, and visited other parts of the Gower peninsula. We went up Cefn Bryn and marvelled at Arthur's Stone. How did they get such a huge stone there, and lift it onto the other stones? We explored the North coast – much less well known than the South, where all the beaches are. Penclawdd, where the cockle women used to drive donkeys out onto the mud flats at low tide to collect cockles to sell in Swansea market. They still gather cockles there, although now with tractors, and you can still buy them in Swansea market, along with laver bread. From Llanmadoc we walked out to Whitford Point, where the water still ebbing from the estuary had a turbulent contest with the tide starting to come back in. We walked for miles, along beside the salt marsh, through the dunes, past the Victorian cast-iron lighthouse, along the sweep of the beach, and we saw no-one at all. Gower had so much to offer that we rarely went anywhere else. But once, for old times' sake, we took the steamer to Ilfracombe. It was amusing to see all the 'young people' trying to chat each other up. It made us feel like a staid old couple.

But it wasn't to last. All that free time had to come to an end. In August, I got my exam results, which were as good as I had expected (although perhaps not as good as my parents had hoped). So Dad suggested that, as I had decided not to go to University, it was about time I got a job and started to help out with the housekeeping money. I wasn't keen – I was enjoying my free time too much – but I realised that it was unavoidable. So I got a job in an office in central Swansea. My main task seemed to be making tea – did I need good A level grades for that? – but they convinced me that it would soon lead on to better things. At least I was getting paid.

We still had some days on the beach, at weekends, although it was now autumn, and the winds were cool. But there were some fine days, and the sea kept its warmth better than the land, so the contrast with the cooler air made the water seem warmer than it did in the hot days of summer. Brandy Cove was still our favourite destination, when the weather was good enough. Even on one memorable occasion, when it was not. That was an interesting experience, swimming in the rain, and afterwards, lying together on the wet sand with the rain lashing down on us. The beach was, of course, completely deserted, so it was tempting to suggest that we should strip off altogether and make love there and then. In the rain. But we didn't, although I would have liked to. I really wanted us to live together properly, including spending the night together. But, although I now had a job, it wasn't that well paid, and we had nowhere near enough money to able to get married and set up house together. Jean had got herself a job in a shop, but that was paid even less well than mine. I even suggested, on one occasion when her parents were away for a weekend, that I should spend the night at her house, but she said it just wouldn't feel right. Her parents were quite strict about that sort of thing, and she said she wouldn't able to look them in the face afterwards.

This went on for over a year. Happy, carefree days. I wished they could go on for ever – apart from the desire to take things further. Then, one evening, we were sitting in their front parlour, while her parents sat discreetly in the back room, watching television. The parlour had now been pressed into service as an alternative sitting-room, to allow us some privacy. I realised that this radical break from their usual custom was a major concession by Mrs Thomas. Suddenly,

Jean broke free from my embrace and said "Why don't we do things properly and get married now?"

"But we can't. You know as well as I do that we haven't got that sort of money. I'm getting a bit more now, but not that much. Even if we add in your wages, we couldn't afford to rent a house, or even a flat, let alone buy one. If we wait a year or two, things might change. They're putting me on their management training scheme next week, so things are looking up."

"A trainee manager?" Jean was delighted. "That's great news. You'll be earning real money soon. But we don't have to wait. We don't need to get a place of our own straight away. We could live here. There's plenty of room for us. My room is quite big enough for two."

"Are you proposing to me?"

She laughed. "I know it's not Leap Year, and it's not usually the girl's place, but if I wait for you I could wait forever!"

So the decision was taken. We went into the back room straight away to tell her parents. Mrs Thomas was delighted. She gave Jean a big hug, then hesitated and turned to me and gave me a hug as well. "Oh, Jeff, I'm sure you'll make Jean very happy."

Jean laughed. "He has already, Mam!"

I think Mr Thomas was pleased too, although he didn't say much. He just shook my hand, and said "Welcome to the family, son."

Jean's Mam started planning the wedding straight away. It wasn't a big affair – at least the reception wasn't. Hundreds of her relatives came to the Chapel of course (it seemed like hundreds, but it couldn't have been more than forty really), but we managed to avoid having them all to the reception. For the selected guests, her Mam had organised caterers to provide a grand spread in the back room of the shop. It must have taken Mr Thomas hours to shift all the stock upstairs. I made a short speech, with a great effort and a lot of nervousness, and managed, I think, to thank all the right people, and her Dad made a long rambling speech about how he wasn't losing a daughter but gaining a son.

After the guests had gone, he took me on one side and said "I meant that, you know, about gaining a son. I've always wanted a son to take over the shop, but it didn't turn out that way. Not that I'm not fond of Jean, of course, but a son is different. I've been running this shop for nearly fifty years, and it's about time I retired. I'm looking forward to putting my feet up, with my pipe and slippers, and spending more time with my pigeons. And down at the bowls club. So I want you and Jean to take over the shop."

I was thrilled by this. In reality, I had been looking forward to this day ever since Jean had first described the shop to me, on the steamer all that time ago. Well nearly three years ago anyway. The thought of spending so much time surrounded by all those exciting smells. But could I do it? After all, I did have a full-time job. Her Dad had anticipated that issue. "Of course, you could carry on with your job," he said. "In fact, I think you would need to, to get enough money to live on. The shop doesn't provide that much income these days. Jean would have to give up her job, of course, so she could look after the shop during the day. Her job doesn't pay much anyway. And you could help out in the evening and at weekends." Despite her parents being strict Chapel folk, they had succumbed to the march of time, and the shop was now opening on Sundays. After they had been to Chapel of course.

So it was arranged. Her Dad did look in on the shop from time to time, at least to start with. But that faded slowly, as he spent more time at the bowls club, or just sitting in front of the fire with his newspaper. But he didn't enjoy his retirement for very long. Early one morning, about two years after the wedding, Mrs Thomas burst into our bedroom, crying "Jean, please help me. I can't wake your Dad." We both hastily put on our dressing gowns and followed her to their room. Mr Thomas was lying in his bed, on his back, apparently sleeping peacefully. I took his wrist to try to find a pulse. I didn't really know how to do it, but I'd seen them do this on the telly. The moment I touched him, I knew what had happened. He was so cold. We called an ambulance of course, but as soon as they came in, they said that he had gone.

We gave him a good send off. The neighbours all came out in the street to watch the hearse take him away. Jean and I, and Mrs Thomas, followed in another car, and then came a long procession of cars carrying their relations. This time, they did all come back to the house after the funeral. You could hardly move for relations. Jean was a star, looking after me and her mother. I felt quite out of my depth – all these people that I didn't know, but Jean kept whispering in my ear to explain who they all were. My confusion was confounded by many of them speaking Welsh to each other. Fortunately not to me, as I wouldn't have understood a word, despite years of being taught it at school.

After the funeral was over, Mrs Thomas went, quietly, to bed. She hadn't cried as much as I'd expected, but the tears were never far from the surface. She was never the same after that. She seemed sort of lost, and kept expecting him to appear suddenly from nowhere.

But I'm getting ahead of myself again. Coming back to the day of the funeral, after Mrs Thomas had gone to bed, Jean and I were sitting by ourselves in the back room. "That's the end of an era", I said.

"Yes, it's sad, fifty years working his socks off, and then so little time to enjoy his rest."

"That's true, of course, but I don't just mean that. We need to think about the shop now. We can't go on like this."

"Why not? We're managing quite well so far. He's helped out a bit, of course, but it's been us doing almost all the work. This won't make that much difference."

"Yes," I said "but think about it. The shop is bringing in almost nothing. If it wasn't for my job, we wouldn't be able to survive. Nobody wants the sorts of things we stock. They all go down to the supermarket instead. Candles, for example. Who wants them?"

"Lots of people want candles."

"They want scented candles, hand-crafted decorative candles. Not these plain white things. Most people have a packet stuffed away in a drawer somewhere, like we do, in case of a power cut, but they just gather dust. They never use them. So they never buy any more. Then there's turpentine. Fishing line. Starch. Clothes pegs. We don't sell enough of any of them to make money out of them."

"I sold some clothes pegs yesterday."

"Great. That brings in a few pennies."

"And a packet of pins."

"Big deal."

"You're not suggesting we should give up the shop? That would break Mam's heart – so soon after Dad ..."

"No, I don't think we need to do that. But just look at the streets around. All the old families are moving out, or dying. We can't survive just catering for them."

"But it's a sort of focal point for the community. Take Mrs Jenkins for example. She comes in most days."

"Does she ever actually buy anything?"

"Er, no, not often. But she does enjoy having a chat."

"We can't afford to run the shop just to have chats with our neighbours. Besides, to put it bluntly, she must be nearly ninety, and she won't be chatting for much longer. We have to look to the future – our future, and perhaps our children when we start a family. New people are coming in, and they don't want all this sort of stuff."

"What do they want then?"

"I've been looking around, and I think there's scope for a different sort of shop. Herbal teas, dried fruit, special cheeses – goats cheese, that sort of thing. Olive oil. Spices – not just salt and pepper, but everything. Honey – not the supermarket blended stuff, but special ones. "

"I see what you mean – a sort of health food shop?"

"Yes, partly. But also local produce, and hand-made stuff. We could have those scented candles you want."

After some more research, the decision was taken. We even managed to convince Mrs Thomas that this was a change for the better.

The shop is now quite different. And when I come home from work, and I take Jean in my arms and kiss her, her lips have quite a different taste.

The stranger

Isobel was bored. And lonely. On a Friday night too. Now that Diane had paired up with Martin, all her friends had partners, and since she split up with Chris (and the less said about him the better!), there was no-one left for her to go out with. This was of course before the era of mobile phones and social media, so her options were limited. She felt that she was doomed to spend a Friday evening watching rubbish television with her parents – what a prospect!

Downstairs, the phone rang. After a pause, her Mum called upstairs: "Izzy! It's for you."

"I wish she wouldn't call me that" she grumbled as she ran down the stairs. "Isobel is a perfectly good name, and Izzy makes me feel about six!"

"Diane here. Fancy coming out to the White Horse tonight?"

"What about Martin?"

"Martin is coming too, of course."

"No way! I'm not going to spend the evening playing gooseberry, watching you two all over each other."

"Hang on, I should have explained. Martin met this really nice guy the other day. He's new around here so he doesn't know anyone, or places to go or anything, so I thought it would be really nice for the four of us to get together."

"So you're a dating agency now are you?"

"No, of course not, I'm not trying to find you a man. Or, well, I suppose the thought had crossed my mind. But really you would be doing us a favour. Martin really likes this guy, and wants to invite him out, but we need someone to make a foursome. His name's Roland, and he's really dishy. And what else would you be doing this evening- watching rubbish television with your Mum and Dad I suppose. So, how about it?"

"Roland," She thought. "Strangely old-fashioned name."

"OK," she said. "I'll see you there."

Half an hour later, Isobel pushed open the door of the pub and looked around the crowded interior. As her eyes got accustomed to the dimly-lit room, she at last spotted the three of them at a table at the far side of the bar. She made her way over. As she approached, Roland rose and Diane introduced her. Roland helped her off with her coat, and pulled a chair out for her to sit down. She was touched by the old-fashioned courtesy; went with the old-fashioned name, she said to herself.

Looking back over the evening later on, as she lay in bed, she couldn't believe how well it had gone. Roland was so easy to talk to – although she realized that while she had told him all about herself, she had found out nothing about him – not his age, nor what he did for a living. And certainly not whether he was married or not. After the pub, they had gone on to a club and danced until the early hours of the morning. Real old-fashioned dancing too, waltzes and so on.

"I don't know how to dance that sort of thing" she had objected.

"Don't worry" he said. "I'll show you".

And she just surrendered herself into his arms while he virtually carried her around the floor. So nice to feel his strong arms around her, and to rest her head on his shoulder. Really warm and comfortable, with her body pressed up against his. And then, in the taxi going home, he hadn't even taken her hand. When they got to her house, he escorted her to the door, and said good-night. Just that. Not even a kiss. Perhaps he didn't fancy her. Or maybe that was just another of his strange old-fashioned ways. She wondered if she would see him again.

He did ring the next day, but only to thank her for a lovely evening. She had to wait a week for another phone call, wondering all the time why she felt so anxious. She had only just met this guy. Sure, they'd had a nice evening together, but that was all there was to it. He'd given no indication that he fancied her at all. He was nice to talk to, and very polite – almost too much so. She wasn't used to that sort of behaviour, so unlike the other boys she'd been out with. "Maybe it's that difference that's attractive?" she thought. "And I can't really think of him as a 'boy' – he's more like a man. I wonder how old he is?"

When the phone call came, she nearly fell down the stairs in her haste to hear from him again.

"Hello, Isobel. Roland here. Are you well? I hope this is a good time to ring."

"Hello, Roland. Nice to hear from you. Yes, it's fine."

"I was just ringing to ask if you would like to come to the cinema with me tonight."

"Oh yes," she said, trying desperately not to sound too enthusiastic.

"Good. I'll pick you up about 7.30."

As she got ready to go out, she pictured how it would be, snogging in the back row – that was a suitably old-fashioned thing to do, she thought. But it wasn't like that. They just watched the film – rather a boring one she thought, all in French with sub-titles. No snogging, not even holding hands. She did try leaning against him, to encourage him a bit, but there was no response. Over coffee afterwards, he tried to talk about the film – the subtlety of the photography, why it was in black and white, the effects that the director had tried to achieve, and so on. She found it difficult to think of intelligent things to say. As they walked home, she noticed that he always walked between her and the road. Every time they crossed the street, he changed sides. She asked him about it.

He laughed. "It's how I was brought up. It's so the lady doesn't get splashed by the mud from the carriages."

More old-fashioned courtesy, she thought. And, as if to back it up, again there was not even a kiss on the doorstep.

She heard nothing from him for two weeks. She was getting desperate when another phone call came, this time asking her to go the theatre with him. That was a new experience for her. She'd never been to the theatre before, unless you count Christmas pantomime. She didn't think much of the play though. Roland explained that the title of the play meant that Nora's life was like living in a doll's house – it was a sort of metaphor, he said. But Isobel couldn't understand why Nora hadn't left her husband a lot earlier.

"I would never let a man treat me like that," she said. Roland tried to explain about a woman's position in the latter part of the nineteenth century, but Isobel was unconvinced. "How could they behave like that?"

Then another two weeks, a concert this time, another new experience. Beethoven, Schubert.

She said to Roland afterwards "There were lots of nice tunes in them, but why did they keep messing around with them? And what was the point of all the bits in between? It didn't seem to be getting anywhere."

She thought Roland looked disappointed that she hadn't enjoyed the concert, so she added quickly "Don't get me wrong. I did enjoy it. It's lovely going to concerts and plays with you."

"At least I'm getting an education," she thought. "Going to all these highbrow things. I'd never have thought of going to anything like that before I met Roland. And it's so nice, being with him – even if nothing happens between us."

So it went on, one date after another. She started to try to encourage him by taking his hand from time to time. He didn't actually draw back but there was no real positive reaction. Then she went further, and kissed him full on the mouth on the doorstep when they got home. Again, no response. She regretted this straightaway.

"Perhaps I've offended him now" she thought. "Maybe he's gay? I bet he drops me now." But he didn't, and she did gradually sense that he was warming to her. She did now get a peck on the cheek when they said good-night, and he would actually take her hand occasionally as they walked down the street. It was such a contrast with the other guys she'd been out with, she thought, when even on the first date it ended up a bit like kissing an octopus – one hand stroking her hair, one hand trying to undo her blouse, one hand trying to get inside her knickers, and the others doing she didn't quite know what. She could cope with fending them off, but how should she react to someone who wasn't trying to do anything except talk to her?

"It's strange," she thought. "With all the others, I had to work so hard to stop them doing things, yet with Roland, who doesn't even try, I spend my time imagining what it would be like if he did. He could do what he liked with me and I wouldn't stop him. I've even tried to encourage him, but he hasn't made a move at all."

The climax of the series of dates came with him asking her to go the opera with him.

"Opera?" she said. "Isn't that awfully posh? I haven't got anything to wear for something like that."

He laughed. "It's not all champagne and cucumber sandwiches these days! And you don't need to wear anything special. Some people do dress up for it of course, but you'll find most of them are wearing quite ordinary clothes."

But she thought this was an opportunity to show off a bit. So she bought herself a new dress. She deliberately chose one as provocative as she dared, to try to draw him out. "If that doesn't do it, I don't know what will."

Her mother looked askance at the degree of cleavage that it showed. "Oh, Izzy! You're not going to wear that, are you? It's almost indecent."

Isobel laughed. "Oh, mother, don't be so old fashioned. There'll be lots of people there wearing dresses much more revealing than this." But she did feel rather nervous about it, so at the last minute she added a shawl.

They had a lovely evening. Despite what he had said, Roland had turned up in a dinner jacket and black bow tie, looking extremely elegant. She felt quite proud and excited, walking into the opera on the arm of such a handsome man. She didn't understand much of what the opera was about – even Roland was a bit unsure trying to explain the symbolism of *The Magic Flute* – but that didn't matter. The music was lovely, and she was just so happy sitting next to Roland, holding his hand and leaning on his shoulder. And when they got home, Roland said "I'm so glad you didn't take any notice of what I said about not wearing anything special. Your new dress is stunning. You were the most beautiful woman there tonight." And then he kissed her, properly.

After he had left, she went upstairs to bed, ecstatically happy. She took off her dress, carefully smoothed it out, and hung it in the wardrobe. Before closing the wardrobe door, she kissed the dress. "Thank you," she whispered.

Then one day, a few weeks later, he really surprised her. Her parents were out for the evening, so she had invited him to her house for a quiet evening watching television. They were sitting side by side on the sofa, holding hands, when he suddenly said "Isobel is a lovely name, and you are a really lovely person. I so enjoy being with you, and by now you must have realised that I absolutely adore you."

He went down on one knee in front of her. "Would you do me the great honour of becoming my wife?" And he produced from his pocket a small box which he opened to show a beautiful engagement ring. She was astonished, and delighted. This was the first offer of marriage that she had received, and it had come so unexpectedly after so little physical contact. But what should she say? After all she hadn't known him that long, and she realised that she knew very little about him. Her parents hadn't even met him yet. Surely if he was that old-fashioned he should have asked her father first. But she knew what she wanted to say. All the anxieties she had felt waiting for his next phone call must mean that she was in love with him.

"Yes" she said "Oh, yes". And she bent over and kissed him, long and hard. He slipped the ring onto her finger, and she gazed at it, and at him, alternately. "It's such a lovely ring. Thank you."

"But" he said "we will have to keep our engagement a secret, for a while anyway. After all, I haven't even met your parents yet, and there are a lot of things we have to sort out before we can get married."

Although the engagement remained a secret, their dates became more demonstrative after that, with lots of kissing and she even thought that now they were engaged he might want to go further than kissing. But he didn't. And when he had gone, she would lie in her bed at night and dream about him. She imagined him unbuttoning her blouse and fondling her breasts – that would be nice. And then what would it be like when they were married? She wanted to feel his weight on top of her, to feel him inside her. Several of her friends had had sex with their boyfriends and had told her all about it. At least they claimed to have done it, but she thought they might be making it up to impress the others. They seemed to be a bit vague about some of the details, but they all said how marvellous it was. And then to wake in the morning with her head on his shoulder and him gazing down at her, stroking her hair gently. But then, when she did wake up in the morning, she realised that it was still just a dream; their marriage was a long way off, and somehow didn't seem to get any nearer. Every time she raised the subject, even just suggesting that they should come out into the open, he would make some excuse or other.

Their secret engagement had lasted three months, and her pleadings had become more and more insistent. Then one day he said "I've got to go away for a week, over to Paris. It's a sort of business trip. Why don't you come with me?"

"Paris!" she said, with elation. "I've never been abroad at all. That sounds really exciting! When are we going?"

"This evening. It's all booked."

"What, just like that? But my parents will never agree. I've not even got time to ask them."

"Don't tell them. Just come. You can leave them a note to say where you've gone and when you'll be back. You're old enough to do things by yourself. I hope you've got a passport?"

"Yes, I got one a few years ago. Dad said I ought to get one, just in case."

Her feelings were torn in two. She'd never even been on holiday without her parents, apart from a weekend in Scarborough with the girls. They'd had a great time there, but her parents had asked all sorts of questions. On the other hand, a week in Paris with Roland. What a dream! The Eiffel Tower, Notre-Dame, Montmartre, the Louvre. Romantic dinners in candlelit restaurants. She imagined a small hotel on the Left Bank. She had read a lot about Paris, in magazines, so she was able to picture all these places. And those nights alone with Roland. She couldn't miss an opportunity like this.

"Yes, I'll do it."

"Wow, that's great! Make sure you pack your best frocks – especially that one you wore to the opera; we'll be going to some posh places, so you'll have plenty of opportunity to wear them. I'll pick you up about eleven. We'll drive through the night and cross the Channel early in the morning. Your parents will be in bed by eleven?"

"Yes, they always go to bed early, and sleep really soundly. I'll be able to slip out without waking them."

She spent the evening in feverish anticipation, packing and re-packing all the things she thought she would need. As expected, her parents went to bed soon after ten, and by the time Roland came and knocked softly at the door, the house was all quiet. She let him in, and he looked her up and down. "You look great" he said, taking her in his arms. Then he stood back and had another look. "What about some jewellery? Have you got any? A necklace perhaps? It has to be good though; imitation pearls would look terrible in the sort of places we're going to."

She thought for a moment. There was that pearl necklace of Gran's that she had always loved. She'd never worn it though, and nor had her mother, who said it was too valuable for the sort of places they went to. Her mother kept it in a drawer in her dressing table. But if she was very careful she would be able to get it without waking her parents.

"OK" she said, and tip-toed carefully up the stairs. She pushed open her parents' bedroom door, slowly, and hesitated. Her father was snoring gently, and her mother was breathing deeply. Both fast asleep. She eased open the drawer where she knew the necklace was kept. She had a sudden panic when she couldn't see the box. Then she felt around the drawer, and found it underneath some other bits and pieces. She drew it out and went back to the door. Then she remembered she hadn't closed the drawer. She had to go back and do it.

When she got back downstairs, she showed Roland the necklace. He looked at it carefully. "Yes, those are real pearls. It will look great on you, but we've not got time to try it out. Have you remembered your engagement ring? You'll be able to wear it there. We won't meet anyone you know."

"I hadn't thought of that". She went back upstairs to get it, and put it on her finger. She'd tried it out many times, in her own room, but it gave her a funny feeling to be wearing it properly at last. Downstairs again, she showed it to Roland. He kissed her, and said "Right, let's go". He picked up a holdall that she hadn't noticed before.

"What's the bag for?" she asked.

"Oh, that," he said. "Just some things of mine. I was so excited I wasn't thinking straight when I came, and brought it in from the car by mistake. Have you left a note for your parents?"

She showed him the note that she had written. "OK, he said. Leave it on the kitchen table." As she did so, the parrot, in its cage in the corner of the living room, let out a squawk. "Izzy! Izzy!" it said. Isobel looked at it.

"And you can mind your own business as well," she said, and put a cover over the cage.

They closed the front door behind them, and as they walked to the car, a few yards along the street, she clung to his arm, quivering with excitement and anticipation. She couldn't see his car anywhere. Then he stopped beside a car that she didn't recognise – a large and very expensive-looking car. He noticed her surprise.

"A special occasion" he explained, as he dumped the holdall on the back seat, along with her suitcase. "And we'll be doing a lot of driving. So I've borrowed this one from a friend."

As they were driving, she thought about Paris, and that small hotel on the Left Bank. And that candlelit restaurant, with one, perhaps two, bottles of wine. And then stumbling, giggling, up the stairs to their room, trying not to wake the other guests. Standing by the window, with a view of the lights of Paris, Notre-Dame floodlit. And his fingers, deft and gentle, slowly undressing her. Then making love on the bed, her first time. He would know it was her first time, and he would be so gentle with her. Going to sleep in his arms. Waking in the morning with him beside her. Going down to breakfast, wondering if the other guests could tell. She could barely contain her excitement.

After they had been driving about half an hour, she noticed that they had left the main road and were heading towards the coast. "Bit of a detour." he said. "We've got plenty of time, and there's a rather special place that I want to show you."

The road climbed up steeply, around sharp bends with just a crash barrier separating them from the cliff edge. She peered out of the window. "I hope those barriers are strong," she said. "Is it a long way down there?"

He laughed. "They're strong all right. They need to be. They're right on the edge of the cliff and it must be two hundred feet down to the sea. Not much chance for anyone who goes over the edge."

She shuddered at the thought of a wrecked car lying at the foot of the cliff, being battered by the waves, and she huddled up to Roland. He put his arm round her, expertly guiding the car with one hand.

"You're safe enough with me," he said.

He pulled into a deserted car park and stopped the car. He got out and came round to open the door for her. A full moon was shining brightly, and she could see, beyond the car park, some open land with close-cropped grass and gorse bushes covered with orange-yellow flowers. She kicked off her shoes and stood barefoot on the grass, moist with early dew. He took her hand and led her to a spot where they could see the sea, far below. As she gazed at the view, he stood behind her and put his arms round her. She leaned back against him. "It is a beautiful spot" she whispered. It was so quiet and peaceful that it seemed wrong to speak out loud. "What's it called?"

"This is Castle Head".

That sounds familiar, she thought. Why have I heard of Castle Head? Then, just as she had imagined so many times, he was unbuttoning her blouse, and had placed his hands on her breasts. And it was just as nice as she had imagined. She could feel his penis swelling up and pressing against her.

Suddenly she realised why Castle Head sounded so familiar. "Wasn't this where they found the body of the murdered girl?"

He continued fondling her breasts. "That's right," he said. "Mary Datchet. They found her body at the bottom of the cliff. Usually the tide takes them away and they're found miles down the coast, or not at all. But she hit a shelf of rock before reaching the sea, so they found her there."

She shuddered. "Usually?" she thought. "Does it happen often?" Then she said "I'm not sure I like this place after all. Let's go somewhere else."

"No, let's stay here. This is my favourite place. It's very special to me."

"Favourite place?" she thought. "Does he bring lots of girls here?"

She became aware that his hands had left her breasts and were starting to pull up her skirt. She was starting to feel rather uncomfortable about the situation, especially after hearing about Mary Datchet.

She tried to stop him. "No, not here, not now. Let's wait till we get to Paris." She was still thinking about the small hotel on the Left Bank. This wasn't how she wanted it.

But he was starting to become insistent, roughly pulling down her knickers.

"I need to get away and think about this" she thought. Then she had an idea.

"OK," she said. "I'll do it. But let's make ourselves comfortable first. I'll get a rug from the car."

Before he had a chance to object, or to offer to fetch it himself, she had broken free and was running back to the car, leaving her knickers on the grass. She opened the car door and climbed in. She saw he had left the keys in the ignition, and she locked the doors from inside. He came over, holding his trousers up with one hand, and tried the door handle with his free hand. With relief she saw that the door wouldn't budge. He put his face to the glass and shouted "Izzy! Come back! I want to make love to you. Izzy, please!"

That did it. What right did he have to call her Izzy? She didn't like it when her mother called her Izzy, but when he did it as well, that was the last straw. She started the car engine.

That made him really angry – she hadn't seen him look like that before. Now she was really frightened. As he hammered at the window with his fists, the car started to move forwards. He flung himself across the bonnet to try to stop her. She couldn't see properly where she was going, but she didn't dare to stop. She drove out of the car park and down the road they had come up. He was still clinging to the bonnet.

She saw the first bend just in time, and swung the steering wheel over sharply to avoid crashing into the barrier. With a squeal of protest from the tyres, the car just made it round the bend, leaving some paint behind on the barrier. She was suddenly aware that she could now see where she was going. Roland had lost his grip on the bonnet, slid off, and disappeared. She stopped the car and looked back. There was no sign of him.

"Oh God" she said. "I didn't mean to hurt him. I must go back and see if he needs help."

She walked back to the bend in the road. No sign of him anywhere. She looked over the barrier. Far below, the waves were pounding against the base of the cliff. The barrier, where he had slid off the car, was, as Roland had said, right on the edge of the cliff. He must have gone straight over into the sea. She felt faint, but somehow managed to get back to the car and sit down. "I've killed him. What do I do now? I can't call for help. They would want to know what I was doing here. And my mother would give me hell about the pearls."

Reluctantly, she started the car again and drove slowly home, thinking all the time what she could do.

When she got home, her first thought was to put the pearls back. Perhaps he had put them in the holdall? She took it from the back seat of the car and opened it. Yes, there were the pearls. She took them out, and then stopped. She recognised some of the other things in the holdall. That vase was familiar. Just like the one on the mantelpiece that mother said was so valuable. And that clock. It was some sort of antique that had originally belonged to her great grandfather. She realised that while she was upstairs, Roland must have been removing valuable things that belonged to her parents. "So he's a thief? I've really been taken in by him – but that doesn't justify killing him. Have I killed him?" She still couldn't think clearly about what was going to happen next.

She took the holdall into the house and put everything back into its proper place. She went over to the parrot's cage and removed the cover. She looked at the parrot. It stared back at her and seemed to be thinking "I know what you've been doing and where you've been." She imagined that the parrot might tell on her.

"Don't say a word," she whispered "And I'll buy you a lovely new cage."

Then she went upstairs to return the pearls to the drawer in her mother's dressing table, taking great care to avoid waking her parents. She paused for a moment and looked at them. They were both still fast asleep. Then she went back to the car and took her suitcase from the back seat and carried it up to her bedroom. "No time to unpack it now," she thought. "But I don't want Mum to find it. That would really cause problems. I know, I'll push it under the bed, and then I can unpack it later."

She went back downstairs, as quietly as she could.

"Now," she thought. "What shall I do with the car? I can't leave it here. That would be too obvious. Someone would recognise it. I'll have to dump it somewhere. But not too far away. I'll have to walk back. I know. I'll leave it in the lay-by on the main road. That's only half a mile away, and it'll be ages before anyone notices it."

So she drove slowly round to the lay-by and parked the car. "I wonder what I should tell my friends? I guess I'll just tell them he's dumped me and gone away. They'll believe that. Now, is there anything else? Oh yes, my handbag. It must be in the boot."

She opened the boot, and saw her handbag. As she picked it up, she noticed another handbag behind it. "Strange," she thought. "Why would he have another handbag in the car? I wonder whose it is." She picked it up. "Should I look in it? Not very nice to rummage through someone else's handbag."

Curiosity got the better of her, and she opened it. Inside, she saw a driving licence. "That'll tell me."

She read the name, and had to cling to the car to stop herself falling to the ground. The name on the driving licence was Mary Datchet.

"Oh, God! Poor Mary!" She thought of Mary Datchet's body, lying broken on the rocks under the cliff at Castle Head.

She looked in the boot again. Behind Mary's handbag, there was a row of five others.

Sylvie

I've known Sylvie all my life. We grew up together – she wasn't exactly the girl next door, but she did live in the same street. What's more, we were born on the same day. When I was a child, I thought that was an amazing coincidence. I now know more about chance and probability, and it's not as unbelievable as most people would think, that someone you meet at random would have the same birthday as you. A chance of 1 in 365 in fact. Strange thing, chance. As a mathematics teacher, I find it fascinating. If you ask a slightly different question – what is the chance that in a class of 30 children there will be two with the same birthday – it comes out much higher than that – about 70% in fact. Our school friends didn't have much idea of the laws of chance, and were amazed by us having the same birthday. They used to refer to us as 'the twins'. But I digress. Of course, as we had the same birthday, we started school together. So that's how we met, or at least that's how our mothers met, taking us to school. Once our mothers had become friends, then we were in and out of each other's houses the whole time.

Later on, when we were old enough to go out to play together on our own, we would spend hours together. Our street was, at that time, on the edge of the town. The developer who built these houses had obviously had ideas of extending further, as the street came to a sudden stop with a rough fence across, separating us from a derelict piece of land with scrubby trees trying to grow, and old washing machines and mattresses littering the ground between them. Beyond that, the woods proper. This was, for us boys, a real adventure playground – not the sanitised version you get nowadays. We would climb the trees, and hang ropes from them to make swings. One of the ropes hung next to a stream, so you could swing right across it. You had to let go at exactly the right time: too soon, and you landed in the water; too late and you ended up swinging in mid-air over the stream, with the same result, as then the only way down was to jump into the water.

A fallen tree was turned into a sailing ship, with masts and ropes (but no sails), and we were pirates on that, casting off, and tying up ropes, sinking other (imaginary) ships and capturing loot of various descriptions. Several houses in the street found themselves suddenly without clothes lines at that time. Sylvie was a bit of a tomboy in those days, and we tolerated her participating in these activities. That is, until she started to develop an interest in dolls and frilly clothes, which didn't fit in. Even then we could see her looking out of the window – I imagine, in retrospect, wistfully – as we went noisily down the street to sink some more ships.

Our paths diverged further when we went to different secondary schools – at that time, the schools in our town were single-sex – so we acquired new, different, friends, and had different interests. Although we only rarely saw each other, we never lost contact. Our mothers were still close friends, so I heard all the news about their plans and activities. My mother seemed to think it would motivate me if she told me how well Sylvie was doing at school, and how hard she was working. I guess I needed some motivation as well. School work always seemed so boring compared to all the other things I could be doing.

Occasionally I would encounter her on the way home from school, and she would tell me about the exciting things she had done on her holidays, and where she was going next year. All those foreign countries made our annual trip to the seaside seem very mundane. I also found out that she wasn't actually doing any better than me at school. However, we were both reasonably bright kids, so we did well enough in our exams to be able to think about going to University. It was a pleasant surprise to find that she wanted to go to the same University as I did. At least there would be one person there that I knew. We both got the grades that we needed. So we were still together, in a sense, although on different courses – she studied English while I did Maths.

But it didn't work out quite as I'd expected. Such a big place, so many students, we never encountered one another. I quickly made friends with several of the Maths students, and we tended to do things together. I guess she did the same with students on the English course. So, we never saw one another at all. Until, one Friday evening in December, towards the end of our first term, when I was standing at the bar in the Students' Union, trying to buy myself a beer and wondering where all the others had got to. I saw Sylvie come in through the door. She hesitated, looking around, presumably also wondering where all her friends were. I waved to her. "Hi, Sylvie" I called. She waved back and came over. I bought her a drink and we sat at a table in the corner, comparing our experiences, the societies we had joined, our social lives, and even a bit about the courses we were doing. She seemed to be having a great time; she wasn't homesick at all. Not like some, who were quite miserable by this stage. Suddenly we realised that the evening was over; the bar had closed and everyone was going home. "I must fly," she said "or I'll be locked out." And that was it. A great evening, but no more to it than that. It was nice to have seen her again. As I walked back to the student residences, I wondered when we would next bump into each other.

Next day, however, when I turned up for the first lecture in the morning, John, one of my Maths student friends, said. "You're a bit of a dark horse! Who was that smashing bird you were so engrossed with in the bar last night?"

That amazed me. I'd never thought of Sylvie in that way at all. I realised I'd known her so long that I had never even looked at her properly.

"Oh, that's Sylvie. We're just childhood friends. She lived in the same street as me. That's all there is to it. We were just reminiscing."

John laughed. "Just good friends eh? Didn't look quite like that to me. I'd like to be 'good friends' with her any day!"

I thought all day about what John hàd said. Maybe it wouldn't be such a bad idea to ask her out for a proper date. It was certainly nice being with her, and it would at least be good for my street cred. So I decided to try it. But how to contact her? I hadn't found out where she was living, and sending a note through the internal mail seemed a bit pompous. So in the end, I just hung around outside the door of the lecture room where she was due to have a class, walking up and down to make it look like I was just passing, so she would think it was only another chance encounter. I saw her coming down the corridor. Now, looking at her in a new way, I realised that John was right; she was stunning. I was alarmed by this, and thought of turning round and walking away, but she had seen me.

"Hello, again." she said. "That was a nice evening we had yesterday."

What a perfect opportunity, I thought. "Yes, wasn't it? Perhaps we should do it again?"

So it was arranged. Another nice evening in the bar, sitting and remembering events from our childhood.

Then came the Christmas holidays. You might think that would have been the ideal chance to consolidate our relationship, but it didn't turn out like that at all. When we were back home, we fell back into our previous habits. We each had our own friends and we were too busy catching up on all their news to think of spending any time with one another. And Christmas was such a busy time in our own families. I hardly saw her at all that Christmas.

But when we were back at University, for the spring term, it was different. During the first week, I happened to see her in the corridor, and suggested another meeting in the bar. Soon, it was a regular weekly occasion. Every Friday, we would spend the evening in the bar, just talking.

Looking back on it now, I find it difficult, even impossible, to identify the point at which our relationship became more than just being good friends. Yes, I remember the first time we kissed, but that wasn't it. It was before that. The kiss just confirmed something that had already happened. Our relationship just seemed to merge imperceptibly from one state into the other, but there must have been a line that we crossed, somewhere. Perhaps there was an almost accidental touching of hands? Or maybe it was, as romantic fiction might have it, in 'some meeting of eyes when an invisible magnetic force flowed between us'?

By the time we were in the second year at University, we had moved out of University accommodation, and we were both sharing flats with other students. We then started sleeping together occasionally, usually in her flat. That was rather unnerving, emerging in the morning to face the quizzical looks and innuendoes from the other girls. Sometimes she stayed the night in my flat, and she got the same treatment, but she didn't seem to mind at all. I was more embarrassed than she was.

We were married soon after leaving University. She took it very seriously, getting married. Especially the exchange of rings. Superficially, they appeared quite ordinary plain gold rings, but she had them engraved on the inside. Jim and Sylvie, although you needed a magnifying glass to read it.

After the wedding, she said "These rings that we've exchanged, they're very important. They're a token of our love. I want you to promise that you will always wear your ring."

"Of course I will."

"Promise? Solemnly?"

"Yes, I promise."

"When you're away, even at the other end of the world, if you touch the ring, I will know that you are thinking of me."

I'm sorry to say that I laughed at that. "That's a bit over the top, isn't it? I think you're letting romantic ideas run away with you."

"Well, perhaps so. Maybe not to be taken too literally. But you must look after it, and guard it with your life. I mean that. If you lose it, or even if you let it be stolen, I'll take that to mean that you don't love me anymore. Promise?"

"I promise."

"And the same applies to my ring. I'll always wear it, and I'll always keep it, whatever happens. I promise."

I didn't see the point, at the time. I thought that if we stopped loving one another – an inconceivable prospect then, and still – we would know about it in all sorts of ways, long before we lost, or stopped wearing, our rings. But it was to be a central factor in the story I am about to relate.

We had been married about five years, and were living in a small ground floor flat in a central district of the town. I had got a job at an inner-city school, teaching maths to a load of kids who had, for the most part, little interest and still less aptitude for the subject. There were a few of them who were different in that respect, and that helped to keep my interest in the job. Sylvie found that her English degree wasn't much help in getting a job, apart from teaching, which she didn't fancy at all. But we needed more money than my salary brought in, so she got herself a job in an office. It wasn't at all exciting, but it paid well so she stuck with it.

For most of that time, we were very happy together. But my job was very demanding, and in order to keep up with things I started to work late – occasionally at first, and then more and more often. Eventually, I was working late at school almost every day, and I arrived home tired and irritable. The last thing I wanted to do was to talk about what I had been doing all day, or indeed talk about anything else. So, we ate the meal Sylvie had prepared, in silence. I barely noticed what I was eating. Then, generally, I flopped on the sofa, in front of the telly, and went to sleep, waking up several hours later to find Sylvie was already asleep in bed.

At weekends, things should have been different. But they weren't as different as they should have been. Even then, we never found time to talk much. Or perhaps we had just run out of things to talk about. And when we went to bed, Sylvie seemed to have lost interest in sex. She allowed me to make love to her, but it was clear that she didn't enjoy it any longer. Nor did I either – at least not like I used to when we were first married.

Things got even worse when I started going away to meetings and on courses. The pressure on teachers had increased so much that it was generally felt that you had to do this just to keep your job, let alone get promotion. I wanted to progress, and not get stuck in a junior post. I knew I was capable of a Head of Department post, and I dreamed of becoming Head of a school in due course. So I was away quite often during the school holidays, leaving Sylvie on her own in the flat. All this time, I was so wrapped up in my work that I never really noticed how discontented Sylvie was becoming. Until one day, when I had just returned from a conference, she said "I expect you've had a nice time, doing I don't know what. How about asking me what I've been doing?"

"OK, what have you been doing?"

"Oh, I've had a lovely time. I cleaned the flat, I did the washing, and the shopping. I've got in some food for us to eat. I wandered around the town a bit. Great. Really exciting."

I didn't like the tone of her voice, and I was nervous about what was coming next.

She continued. "We need to have a serious talk."

"About what?"

"Everything. Us, in particular. We never talk about anything these days. Not like before we were married. Where is this marriage taking us? Are we going to be stuck in this poky little flat for ever? And, we've never talked about when we should start a family. Or even if we will."

"I didn't think you wanted children? At least, not yet anyway."

"You've just assumed that. We've never actually discussed it. But it's more than that. You never take any notice of me, except occasionally when we're in bed. It seems that's all I mean to you now – someone to have sex with when you feel like it. I don't think you love me anymore."

I mumbled something about still loving her, but it didn't sound very convincing.

"Is that all you've got to say?" she demanded. "Maybe we should stop pretending and not live together any more."

I was quite taken aback by this, and I didn't know what to say. The prospect of Sylvie not being part of my life was frightening, but I was never any good at this sort of self-analysis; I just sat there, immobilized, like the proverbial rabbit in the headlights of an oncoming car.

"Oh, you're hopeless," she said, and stomped off to bed.

I was alarmed by this development. The following day, I stopped off on my way home from work and bought her a bunch of flowers. She looked at them rather scornfully – it was rather a pathetic display admittedly. But at least she didn't throw them straight in the bin. I made a point of asking her how her day had been, and offered to help with preparing the evening meal.

She laughed at that. "You're no use in the kitchen. You'd only get in the way. Besides, it's mostly done already. You can set the table though."

I was encouraged by her laugh. The strategy seemed to be working – the tension had already relaxed. I went over to where she was standing at the sink, put my arms round her and nuzzled the back of her neck. That seemed to be a good plan too. She stopped what she was doing and leant back against me. Then she said "That's enough of that. Save it for later. Now let me get on with the supper."

That night, for the first time for ages, we made love properly, just like the old days. All the issues of the previous day seemed to melt away.

For the next month or two, I made a real effort to mend my ways. I managed to get through my work more quickly so I wasn't so late coming home. I went away less often. I brought her flowers, or chocolates, or some other small gift, at least once a week. I always made a point of asking her how her day had been. And I tried to bring less work home so we could spend the evening together, reminiscing about our childhood and our days at University. Those were happy days. But it was an illusion. The issues, and her discontent, hadn't disappeared altogether, but were still lurking in the shadows. And my good intentions gradually disappeared as I slipped back into my old ways.

It all really came to a head one Saturday evening in February. It had been raining hard for hours, and when I looked out of the window I could see that a drain must be blocked. Water was starting to build up by the back door. Something had to be done, or we would get flooded. So I got out my wellingtons, and put on a waterproof jacket to go out and clear the drain. Then I remembered my watch. I would probably have to reach right down inside the blocked drain, and I didn't want to ruin my watch. So I took it off and put it on a shelf by the door. Then I saw the ring. That would get in a dreadful state as well. Or, and I shuddered at the thought, it might get caught on something and come off. I would never be able to get it back if it ended up at the bottom of the drain. So I took it off and put it on the shelf next to the watch. Clearing the drain was a terrible job. I had to reach down the drain, up to my elbow, to remove the accumulated leaves and other debris. On my hands and knees, in the pouring rain. But it worked, and I saw with satisfaction the water gurgling down the drain, and the level outside the back door starting to go down.

I took off my boots, and went back into the flat, cold, soaking wet and filthy. My hands and arms needed a thorough scrub, and my face as well. My hands were so cold, the hot water was really painful. I went back to the shelf by the door, and put my watch on again. Then I looked for the ring. Panic. It wasn't there. I was sure I had left it beside the watch, but it wasn't there. I must have put it somewhere else. I searched everywhere, but there was no sign of it.

Sylvie was standing in the kitchen. "Have you lost something?" There was something in her voice that I didn't like. I thought of prevaricating, but decided it was no use. I would have to own up. "I can't find my ring. I took it off to clear the drain but it's not where I put it."

She looked hard at me, unclenched her fist and slammed the ring down on the table. "You promised never to take it off."

"I had to, just while I was clearing the drain."

"But you promised! This is the last straw." She was close to tears now. "All those times you said you were working late, all those times spent away from home, I don't know what you were up to. Other women, I expect. And now, this. You know what we said. You don't love me anymore."

She fled into our bedroom and slammed the door. I could hear her sobbing, even through the closed door. Perhaps I should have gone to her then, and apologised, but I was cross too, at the injustice of her anger. I was still wet through and cold from clearing the drain, and this was all the thanks I got. So I left her to cry herself to sleep.

Later on, when I went to bed, I found my pyjamas outside the door with a note attached. "You can sleep on the sofa tonight."

Breakfast next morning was an icy wilderness. Nothing was said apart from "Marmalade." When I was ready to leave for work, I went to kiss her, but she flinched and turned her head away. I slept on the sofa every night for the next two, terrible, weeks. I found myself staying later and later at school, finding some sort of work that needed doing, just to postpone my return to a refrigerator of a flat – a home no longer. I even started calling in at the pub on the way home, which made matters worse, if that were possible.

One Friday evening, two weeks later, I had been working especially late at school – attempting first to decipher the writing of a group of students, and subsequently to try to understand what on earth they were thinking of in producing such rubbish – and I was walking back to the flat, looking forward to some relaxation in what remained of the evening, when I was accosted by a youth. I couldn't see his face, which was shrouded by a large hood, but from the sound of his voice I took him to be young. He asked me if I had the time, and while I was looking at my watch, he pulled out a long and rather wicked-looking knife.

"Give me your money" he demanded. I hesitated, but the knife did look very nasty, and he was waving it in my face in a decidedly intimidating manner. Wisdom prevailed over valour, and I reached into my pocket and drew out a wad of notes. A small wad, it should be said – I didn't usually carry much money around with me.

"And your wallet" he said, or rather shouted. He was now prodding me in the stomach with the knife. Money was one thing, easily replaced (although not so easily on a teacher's salary), but my wallet had all sorts of things in it, and it would be a pain stopping all my cards, getting a new driving licence and so on. But there was no choice really.

"And your watch."

I was sentimentally attached to that watch. It had been an 18th birthday present from my parents, who had both since died, and it was one of the few mementoes that I still had. He prodded me again with the knife, this time rather lower than my stomach, which was even more unnerving. With a sigh, I unstrapped the watch from my wrist and handed it over. That must be it, I thought.

He looked me up and down. Then he demanded my ring. "I can't" I pleaded. "My wife would never forgive me if I parted with that ring. It's a sort of token of my love for her. I promised her I would never part with it, whatever happened."

"Hand it over" he re-iterated. Again I refused, nervously. Now I'm for it, I thought. Will he kill me for the ring? I imagined my body being found in the morning, another mugging victim. Or will he just slash my face? Can I cope with being disfigured for life?

Much to my relief, after waving the knife around threateningly for a while longer, he then just put it away and ran off.

I was quite shaken up by this experience, and I just sat, trembling, on a nearby bench for half an hour or so, until I had recovered enough control over my legs to be able to finish the walk home.

When I got home, I was surprised to find Sylvie in her dressing gown as though ready for bed. "It's not that late is it? Bed-time already?"

She ignored the question. "Where have you been until this time? Call in at the pub again on the way home, did you?"

At least she was talking to me, in a sort of way. That was something.

"I haven't been to the pub. I was mugged on the way home. He took my watch and my money, and my wallet."

"Have you been to the police?"

"No, what could they do? I wouldn't be able to identify him, he had a hood on so I couldn't see his face."

"What was he like? You must be able to describe something about him?"

"Huge guy he was – at least 6 foot six. Swarthy, really ugly looking face."

"I thought you said he had a hood on and you couldn't see his face"

"Well, not properly. But enough to tell that he wasn't the sort of person I could take on. And I think he had a gun as well as a knife."

I was aware that I was elaborating the details somewhat, but all the way home the incident had been running and re-running through my head, so I was no longer completely sure of the boundary between fact and fiction. "It's really shaken me up. I don't think I feel like any supper."

"That's good" she said, and threw her arms around me: "You poor thing. But I know just what will cheer you up." She started unbuttoning my shirt. Soon we were making love, passionately, on the rug in front of the fire. I don't remember going upstairs to bed afterwards, but that was where I was when I woke up in the morning. We were still naked, in each other's arms. She smiled at me happily, nuzzled my neck and started caressing me all over. I was puzzled, and amazed, by the sudden change in her behaviour.

"I love you so much" she said.

"I love you too", I replied.

"I know you do", she said, and there seemed to be some sort of extra meaning in her voice, which puzzled me even more. Soon we were making love again. When I woke up for a second time, she wasn't there, but I could hear her singing in the kitchen. I lay there, wondering again at this sudden change of mood.

She called out. "Ready for breakfast now, my love? Don't move, I'll bring it to you." Breakfast in bed – we never did that, except on very special occasions. What was going on? As I lay there, I could smell bacon frying, and the aroma of newly ground coffee.

She came to the bedroom, still singing, and pushed the door open. She put the tray on a bedside table while she arranged the pillows and propped me up.

"A bit like being an invalid" I thought.

Then she put the tray on my lap. I stared at the tray, open-mouthed. Bacon, sausages, fried bread, toast, orange juice, and coffee. What a breakfast. We hardly ever had a cooked breakfast even at weekends. But that wasn't all. There, on the tray, beside the mug of coffee, was my watch. My wallet. And a, rather small, wad of notes.

"Huge guy, was he?" she said. "Swarthy, ugly face? With a gun as well as a knife? It's a good job you didn't hand over the ring, or I would have used that knife."

The beggar girl

Ralph Chisholm was rich. Very rich. Not only did he have an extremely well-paid job in a bank, but he had also inherited a very large sum from his grandfather, with the prospect of more to come when his parents died. Of course, some rich people live very modestly, and regard supporting charitable causes as a duty that goes with having lots of money. Not so Ralph. He liked to flaunt his money. He had a big house in the posh part of Cheshire, with a high wall around it, and electronic gates that slid open automatically when he drove up in his car. One of his cars, I should say. It was always a difficult decision, which to take. Should it be the Bentley today, or the Porsche? If it was an important meeting in town, he would take the Bentley. But for pleasure rides, he preferred the Porsche. And he liked showing off his valuable possessions – especially his wife Lynda. She was stunningly beautiful when decked out in expensive clothes and costly jewellery for a Charity Ball. Yes, he did support charities, when they provided him with a chance of showing everyone how well off he was. Every year, he attended the village fete. He didn't do anything as useful as running a stall – that would be beneath him, by a long way – but he enjoyed exhibiting his wealth and power by distributing a very small part of his fortune in buying, at each stall, things that were of no use to him. He threw them all away when he got home. Nor did he chat with any of the stallholders. That would be beneath him as well. Not that these stallholders were village peasants of any sort. In general they were just as rich as he was – you had to be rich just to live in that part of Cheshire. He did occasionally pause to pat a child on the head, but only if a photographer from the local paper was nearby.

Ralph thought about his possessions quite often. Lynda in particular. She was certainly an asset on big occasions. He revelled in the admiring looks she got, especially as he knew those looks also meant that they were jealous of him. But it was all becoming a bit of a charade, which irked him. When they got home, and she took off all the make-up, he could see definite wrinkles. All those expensive beauty treatments he'd paid for didn't seem to be having the desired effect. And when she took off her clothes, her boobs were sagging, and the spare tyre was increasingly obvious. "Hmm", he thought "she's past her 'Use by' date". He was amused by the aptness of the expression. And indeed, age, and having two children, had left their marks on her body so that, in the flesh, she was no longer the beauty she had been when they first met.

One morning, he was in Manchester, at a very tedious meeting. The bank had been rather cavalier in lending money for people to buy homes. Now, with unemployment rising, some of these people had lost their jobs, or been put on short time. That, coupled with the recent rise in interest rates, meant they could no longer afford the repayments. Too many people were defaulting on their mortgages, and it was costing the bank money. This meeting was to consider possible ways of dealing with the situation. Ralph had no patience with it. Why discuss it at all? If these people can't pay, then they lose their house. End of. What happens to the families? Who cares? That's their problem. If they can't afford to pay, they shouldn't have borrowed the money to start with. Put them on the street to beg. In the old days, there would have been the workhouse. Now that's an idea. That would focus their minds a bit. He started doodling pictures of workhouses on his notepad. Then he got fed up with that as well. He yawned and stretched his legs. Is this meeting going on forever? They haven't even provided any biscuits with the coffee – another economy measure he supposed. He started drawing pictures of biscuits and cakes. "Missed my vocation," he thought. "Those look quite realistic. But I don't suppose there's any money to be made out of it." The meeting was becoming more and more tedious. "'Brain-storming', they called it. More like 'brain-freezing'. I've got to get out of here. A pint would go down nicely." He pulled his mobile from his jacket pocket and pretended to read a message. Then, mumbling an apology, he fled from the room.

The Feathers was only a short walk away. He had been in there several times before, but he didn't think they knew him. He liked the Feathers. It was usually quite busy, at any time of the day. Not that he wanted to talk to any of the people in there, not his class at all, but with a lot of people in, the barman would be busy and not have time to be inquisitive, He did not want to have to explain who he was. On this occasion, before he got there, he was accosted by a young girl in dirty, ragged clothes, wearing a coat that was several sizes too big for her, who was sitting on the pavement leaning against the wall.

"Spare some change for a cup of tea? The cup that cheers," she said, hopefully, gesturing to a cap on the ground in front of her.

Ralph kicked the cap out of his way and marched on towards the pub. Then he stopped. "She had a really pretty face," he thought. "Perhaps I can have some fun out of her. And what was that about 'the cup that cheers'? Where did she get that from?" He went back.

"I can do better than a cup of tea. Come to the pub with me, and I'll buy you a drink."

After some hesitation, she agreed.

When he entered the pub, with the girl behind him, the barman took one look at her and said "You! Out of here. You know you're not allowed in here."

"It's alright," said Ralph. "She's with me."

"Well, in that case... But she can't come in the bar. The other customers wouldn't like it. But we've got a nice private room upstairs. You can use that." And he winked suggestively at Ralph.

"That sounds fine."

"It'll cost you mind. But the bed's all made up ready." And he winked at Ralph again. The familiarity of the gesture annoyed Ralph.

The girl said "I'd like something to eat as well. I'm starving. Steak pie and chips would be nice."

Ralph suggested to the barman that they put it on a tab. "We'll want some more drinks later."

"That's OK for the food and drinks," said the barman "But you must pay for the room now."

Ralph took out his wallet, watched carefully by the girl and the barman, and paid for the room. The barman said "We'll bring the steak pie up in a few minutes."

When they got upstairs, the girl took off her coat and threw it over a chair. "Well, what now?"

Ralph, carefully put his jacket on the back of the other chair and said. "I think you could do with a good wash first,"

That was very effective. "You scrub up quite well, my dear," said Ralph.

"I'm not 'your dear'. I've got a name."

"OK, what is it?"

"Call me Dolores, like they do in the stories."

Ralph was thrown by this. It sounded vaguely familiar, but from where?

"Dolores? I bet that's not your real name."

"No, it's not. My real name is Rose, if you must know, but Dolores smells as sweet."

Ralph felt uncomfortable again, that expression, which seemed odd coming from a girl like that, also rang a bell somewhere. Was it a quotation of some sort?

When the steak pie arrived, Ralph sent the waiter back for a bottle of champagne. Dolores sat at the table with the plate of pie and chips in front of her. "Upon this meat shall I, Dolores, feed," she said and started.

Ralph thought that must be another quotation from somewhere. Why was she talking in quotations all the time? Perhaps I should have a go. He made a feeble attempt.

"Is the pie good? Is it, er, the food of love?"

"Ha!" she said triumphantly. "Too easy. Twelfth Night. Point to me."

"Twelfth Night? Is it?"

"Course. Opening speech. Another point to me."

"Why?"

"Using a quotation you can't identify. Rule two."

"So it's a sort of game? Who's keeping score? "

"I am. And I'm well ahead already. I'm going to win," she sang.

"What's the prize for the winner?"

"Ah, you just wait and see," she said, darkly. "But let me give you a tip. You have to disguise the quotations, so they're not too obvious. I could hear the quotation marks in what you just said. And it doesn't have to be an exact quotation; just good enough to recognize. 'The cup that cheers' wasn't exact – it should be 'the cups that cheer'. Anyway, your quotation is about a different sort of food. We could do with some of that. At least they've got a radio in here."

She crossed over to the bedside table and switched the radio on. She fiddled with it for a while, until some dance music came on.

"That's the stuff!" She stood in the middle of the room, arms above her head, swaying her hips gracefully and seductively in time to the music. Ralph watched her, with admiration, from where he was sitting on the bed. She really had a lovely body, and knew how to use it.

"Come on," she said. "Come and dance with me!"

"But take your shoes off," she added, "I don't want those heavy things treading on my toes."

The music changed to a faster tune. She clapped her hands and started whirling round faster and faster. Ralph reluctantly got to his feet and started shuffling around. He had to admit that he had never been much of a dancer.

Suddenly she broke off. "I'm forgetting about my pie!"

She went back to the table and started eating again. "But you're not eating? Aren't you hungry?"

"Not my sort of food."

"Here, try a chip." She picked up a chip in her fingers, dipped it in the gravy and put it into Ralph's mouth. "There, isn't that nice?"

Ralph had to agree that, as chips go, it wasn't bad. Dolores finished her pie, and just had chips left on her plate. She took it, and sat on his knee, feeding him chips.

There was a discreet knock at the door, and a cough.

"Come in," said Ralph. Dolores stayed sitting on his lap, and smiled up at the waiter, as he entered, with a bottle of champagne in an ice bucket and two glasses. He put them on a table and withdrew, although not without a wink at Ralph as he went.

"Ooh, bubbly!" said Dolores. "It's been so long since I've had champagne."

They sat side by side on the bed, drinking champagne, with Dolores' head on his shoulder. He put his arm round her.

"There," she said. "That's nice and comfy."

"Tell me about yourself," he said. "How did you come to be on the streets begging? You haven't always been a beggar. I can tell that from the way you talk. And how did you come to know so many quotations?"

"What you don't know can't hurt you. The truth is never simple. And you lose another point."

"What for this time?"

"Not using a quotation. Rule eighteen."

"You've just made that up."

"No, I haven't, it's the oldest rule in the book."

"Then it ought to be number one."

She laughed. "OK, a draw there, if you can identify it."

He couldn't. Actually, he hadn't realised it was a quotation – it just seemed the natural thing to say.

"I'll give you a clue – Lewis Carroll."

"That's a pretty good clue. Must be one of the Alice books."

"Which one?"

"Er, Alice Through the Looking Glass." he hazarded a guess.

"Wrong!" she crowed. "Lose a point, and another for the wrong title."

"What's wrong with it?"

"It's just 'Through the Looking Glass'. No Alice in the title."

"So it must be Alice in Wonderland?"

"Lose another point. It's 'Alice's Adventures in Wonderland'. Trial scene, last chapter. I'm racing ahead now."

"That's not fair. I didn't know that rule."

"OK, I'll let you off this time. I suppose it is a bit picky. And each time we come up to a rule you don't know about, you can have one free go. That's easier than explaining all the rules now."

"That's a point to me! You didn't use a quotation!"

"OK," she laughed. "You're getting the hang of it. That shouldn't count really, as I was just explaining the rules, but I'll give you a point. Also, odd remarks don't count. Nor does it count if you interrupt me before I've finished."

"What rule is that?"

"It isn't actually a rule, but it's just not the done thing. Not sporting."

She got up and started dancing again. Then, without stopping, she slowly shed her clothes, her filthy, ragged and torn clothes. The transformation was remarkable. Not a beggar any longer, but an extremely pretty young girl. He admired her firm breasts, her slim waist, and her brown legs. What a contrast to how Lynda looked without her fine clothes. More like how Lynda was when he first knew her. If this continues to go well, he thought, we could make it a regular thing. He realised that he was enjoying himself, in a quite different way from all his other pleasures. I could even buy her a flat, he thought, so we could meet whenever we liked. I could easily afford that, and give her enough money to look after herself properly.

Without stopping her dance, Dolores came over to the bed and took hold of Ralph's hands. She dragged him to his feet to join in the dance. Still without stopping the dance, she helped him to remove first his shirt, then his trousers, until he was as naked as she was. He was rather self-conscious about this. He had never been naked in front of a woman before, not even Lynda. Except for a moment or two now and then, but never actually stood completely naked in front of a woman. He was a bit ashamed of his appearance as well. His flabby paunch and chest were an unpleasant contrast to Dolores' trim figure. And his enlarged penis seemed totally grotesque, flopping up and down as he tried to dance. He recalled with embarrassment the communal showers at school, after a rugby match, and the ribald comments of the boys as they compared the sizes of their cocks.

"Ooh," said Dolores. "You're blushing! You silly old thing."

"Not too old for this," he thought, as Dolores put her arms round him and pressed him to her. For a while they danced like that together, slowly, until they bumped into the bed and fell on it, locked together.

When they had finished making love, he rolled over onto his back. "That was marvellous," he whispered in her ear. "You are a lovely creature."

She smiled, and pressed his head to her breast, murmuring "Lovely is the rose." He drifted off to sleep, dreaming about the love nest he was planning to set up for them.

When he woke up, several hours later, he couldn't remember where he was at first. Then he remembered everything. He reached out an arm to touch Dolores. She wasn't there.

"She must have got up already," he thought. "I wonder what time it is."

He reached out for his watch on the bedside table. It wasn't there. "That's funny. I'm sure I put it there before, er, before we started dancing. I'd better get up anyway." He remembered that he had left the meeting to answer a phone call, hours ago. "I'd better get back to work. They'll be wondering where I've got to."

He got out of bed and looked for his clothes. "Where did I put them? They must have been scattered all over the floor. Perhaps Dolores has tidied them up. Where would she have put them?" Then he noticed her ragged dress and dirty underclothes in a pile on the floor.

"That's odd. How can she have gone out without her clothes? Even down the corridor to the bathroom, she can't have done that completely naked? Her coat is still on that chair where she flung it earlier. And my jacket – I remember putting that on the other chair when we came in."

Then he saw, lying on Dolores' coat, a note on a scrap of paper. He read it. "To the victor belong the spoils (WL Marcy)".

Dolores had gone! And she had gone wearing his clothes, and had taken all his things as well – his watch, his wallet, everything. That watch alone must be worth more than she would normally get in a month. Maybe more. He kicked at the pile of clothes on the floor. "What about my shoes? She can't have worn those? They would be much too big for her."

He sat on the bed, still naked. "What on earth do I do now? If this was a decent hotel, I could ring room service and get them to organise some clothes for me, but it's not that sort of hotel. I could ring one of my friends – Jack would do, he can be very discreet. No phone in here of course, but I can use my mobile. Where is it? Oh shit, it's in my jacket pocket, and of course she's taken that. "

He sat there for a while, unable to face the inevitable truth. Then, reluctantly, he got up, put on the dirty coat, wrapped it round him, and went downstairs, barefoot.

As soon as he entered the bar, there where whistles and jeers from all the men, and some women, clustered round the bar. The barman said "Good evening, sir. I trust you were completely *satisfied* with everything upstairs?" Ralph tried to ignore the innuendo, and said to the barman, in a low voice, "Have you seen the girl who came in with me? The one dressed as a beggar?"

The attempt at confidentiality was futile. It just made everyone try to get closer to hear the conversation.

"Girl was it? I thought it was a man."

"What? Did she look like a man? Why would I be upstairs with a man?"

"I don't know, sir. We get all sorts in here, and it's not my place to enquire into customers' sexual preferences. All I know is that he... she... came down dressed as a man. Very smart she looked too. Except the jacket sleeves were rather too long, and Monica over there had to lend her a couple of safety pins to pin up her trouser bottoms, which were dragging on the ground. Otherwise, as I say, very smart indeed."

Ralph swore. "Hell's teeth, she's taken all my things – all my clothes, watch, wallet, everything. All that was left was her old coat. I think she's even taken my shoes."

"Yes," said the barman. "Now you mention it, she was carrying a pair of shoes."

"Shit," said Ralph. "She must be planning to sell them. Or give them to one of her beggar friends. Look, I need to ring someone to come and rescue me. Can I use your phone?"

All the customers round the bar were now laughing hysterically, and others in the pub came over to find out what the joke was. Ralph usually liked being the centre of attention, but he was definitely not used to being a figure of fun.

"Of course, sir," said the barman. The tone of ironic politeness added to Ralph's discomfort. He was just about to ring Jack when he noticed the time on the clock behind the bar.

"Oh, shit. Jack will have gone home by now, and he lives miles out – Buxton or somewhere. He won't want to come back for me." He paused, and tried to think who else he could ring. No good. It would just have to be Lynda. That would mean a lot of awkward questions – and recriminations. He wasn't looking forward to it at all, but it had to be done.

He dialled the number.

"Hello, Lynda Chisholm here."

"Lynda, it's me."

"Ralph! Where have you been? Everyone's been worried about you. They rang up from the bank and said you'd disappeared."

"I need your help. Can you come and get me, please?"

"Why? What's happened? You haven't been arrested have you? Are you at the police station?"

"No, nothing like that. But I need you to come and get me. And bring some clothes."

"Clothes? What's wrong with the ones you've got?"

143

"I haven't got any clothes, that's why I need you to bring some."

By now, the whole pub was crowded round him listening to the conversation, cheering and laughing. He could hardly hear her for the noise.

"Where are you? It sounds like you're in a pub or something."

"I am," he replied. "In the Feathers."

"Let's get this straight. You're standing in a bar, talking to me, without any clothes on?" She was spluttering, trying to sound cross while laughing at the same time. "Have you been playing strip poker or something?"

That sounded to Ralph like a good line, so he went along with it. "She took my watch and wallet as well. So I haven't any money. And my phone – that's why I'm using the pub phone." As soon as he'd said this, he regretted that "she".

"She?" Lynda said. "So you've been playing strip poker in a pub with some floozy, you've lost all your clothes, and now you're standing naked in the bar, surrounded by people, and asking me to come and get you?"

"Yes, please," he said, meekly.

"About half an hour; maybe more," Lynda said, and put the phone down.

Ralph turned to the barman. "I can't pay you for the call – or the tab either. I'll settle up when my wife gets here."

Everyone in the crowd cheered again, looking forward to the fun when his wife arrived.

"That's all right, sir. Your, er, friend paid the bill before she left. And she bought a round of drinks. And a very generous tip as well. The tip will cover the call. And you can have a drink on the house as well, while you're waiting," said the barman, and added, emphatically "Waiting for your wife."

Ralph at first thought that was a kind gesture, until he realised that he was the pub entertainment for the time being. While this was going on, a lot of customers who would otherwise be hurrying home were going to stay on for the fun, and buy more drinks while they waited. And indeed they did. Not just drinks for themselves, but for Ralph as well. By the time Lynda arrived, over an hour later, he thought he must have had six, or was it eight, double whiskies? Certainly enough for him to lose his inhibitions about the predicament he was in. He started joining in the merriment, even though he was the target, which of course added to the hilarity.

Lynda pushed open the pub door, and was amazed by the scene in front of her. The pub was crowded with people, laughing and shouting, and all centred around a bizarre figure leaning on the bar, obviously drunk, barefoot and covered in a strange, dirty and ragged, coat. Ralph saw her, and started to push through the crowd to get to her. They all cheered, and parted to make way for him. Unfortunately, in his relief to see her, coupled with his advanced state of inebriation, he forgot that the coat wasn't fastened in any way. He let go of the coat and opened his arms to welcome her. Lynda looked at him, up and down. "I've seen that before," she said. "But not in public. It's not very impressive. I think you'd better put it away."

Ralph looked down. "Oh, God! I'm sorry, Lynda, I'm so sorry." And he wrapped the coat round himself again.

The crowd cheered again. Someone offered to buy Lynda a drink, in the hope of prolonging the fun.

"Why not?" she said. "I could always get Ralph to drive home. He might get picked up by the police. That would be entertaining. I'll have a gin and tonic, thank you. A large one. I think I need it."

Ralph started to explain what had happened. "I'm sorry, Lynda, love. There was this beggar you see, and I felt sorry for her, and..."

"Save it," she snapped. "Don't make an exhibition of yourself. Well, you've done that already, literally as well as metaphorically. Don't drag me into it as well. I'll deal with you when we get home."

More cheers from the crowd, although mingled with a touch of disappointment. They had been looking forward to a show-down there and then.

"What do you think I should do with him?" she asked the crowd of customers.

"Make him walk home!"

"That is part of the plan," Lynda agreed. "But maybe not all the way. It's over twenty miles, and he's not used to walking. Especially not barefoot! I don't think he'd make it. That might be construed as manslaughter. Any other suggestions?"

"Make him sleep in the dog-kennel!"

"I like that idea. There is a problem though. We don't have a dog kennel. Nor a dog either."

"Show him who wears the trousers!"

Everyone laughed at that, even Ralph.

"Definitely," said Lynda. "I did some shopping on the way here." She opened her bag and produced a brightly coloured apron, with flowers all over it. "That's for doing the washing-up. OK, I know we've got a dishwasher, but he's not going to be allowed to use it." She rummaged in her bag again and drew out a yellow duster and some pink rubber gloves. "For cleaning around the house. The other stuff's at home. He'll have to learn how to use the vacuum cleaner, and the iron – but not on my clothes of course. There's something else as well." She looked in the bag again, and produced a book. "I'm not going to trust him to do much of the cooking – I want some eatable food myself – but this tells him how to boil an egg for breakfast. And I think he can get as far as boiling potatoes."

Lynda finished her drink and put the glass on the bar. "Come on, we're going home." And she led the way to the door.

Ralph hesitated. "But where are my clothes? Did you bring any?"

"No, I haven't. You can come as you are."

"What? Like this? I hope the car is somewhere near. Where did you park it?"

Over her shoulder she said "Up by Victoria Station."

Ralph protested. "But that's the other end of Deansgate! You can't expect me to walk all the way along Deansgate, dressed like this!"

"Oh yes I can," she replied coldly. "I got a taxi down, but we're going to walk back. It will be good for you."

Deansgate was crowded. Although the rush hour was nearing its end, there were still some people hurrying home from work, mingling with the evening shoppers. Everyone stopped and stared as the strange procession slowly wound its way along the street – a smartly-dressed woman, followed, as though on a lead, by a shambling, barefoot man dressed as a beggar in a ragged dirty coat. Followed in turn by some of the customers from the Feathers, who had left the pub to continue the entertainment. Some of the shoppers even joined in, out of curiosity, to find out what this parade was about. Was it a fancy-dress charity event? Or perhaps some form of performance art?

By the time they got to the car, Ralph could barely walk another step, and his feet were bleeding. He was about to get in the car when Lynda stopped him.

"I'm not having that filthy coat in my car," she said. "Take it off and dump it in the nearest bin."

"But, but I've got nothing on underneath!"

"I know," she said coldly. "I've seen that already. You should have thought of that earlier. Now dump it."

Ralph had no choice. Fortunately there was a bin only ten yards away. He went over to it, took off the coat and dropped it into the bin. Then, crouched over, and trying to cover himself with his hands, crept back to the car, accompanied by cheering and laughter from the hundreds of people who were now gathered round. Ralph's humiliation was complete, or so he thought.

But there was still the journey home. The streets in central Manchester were very congested, so they were often stationary. Ralph could see the driver of the car alongside glance round, and then swivel his head back again, to make sure his eyes weren't deceiving him. Then a comment to his passenger and they burst out laughing. That happened again and again. And Lynda seemed to be taking a very strange route, down all the busiest streets. Was she doing that deliberately? At the next traffic lights, the driver of a van alongside wound down his window and shouted something extremely rude. "What did he say?" asked Lynda. Ralph pretended that he hadn't heard it. Further along, they drew up beside a large people carrier full of children. The windows were open, and Ralph could hear clearly what the children were saying.

"Mummy, there's a naked man in that car."

"Nonsense, dear, there can't be."

"But there is, really. Why is there a naked man in that car?"

The woman who was driving looked round and said, hastily, "Children, look at the cakes in that shop. Aren't they lovely?"

But the children, unusually, weren't interested in cakes. Not at that moment. They all wanted to see the naked man.

"I can see his willy!"

"No you can't!"

"Yes I can!"

The children clambered over one another, as Ralph quickly put his hands back in his lap.

"Let me look! Let me look!"

The lights turned to green. "Children! Back in your seats and put your seat belts on. We're starting to move again."

As the cars drew away, Ralph heard a plaintive wail "I didn't see it. It's not fair! I didn't see it!"

When they reached home, Lynda swung the car into the drive and stopped. "Hang on a moment," she said. It was only a few yards to the front door, and there didn't seem to be anybody about, but you never knew when one of the neighbours might go past. Despite the gate and the wall, it was possible to see the front door from the road. Or they might be looking out of their windows. It was one thing to humiliate Ralph in front of an anonymous crowd in central Manchester, but in front of the neighbours was another matter. She would feel humiliated as well.

"Wait there," she said. "I'll fetch you a coat."

It is tempting to suggest that Ralph was a totally reformed character after his experiences. Tempting, but too easy. It wasn't quite like that. He didn't give all his money away and devote his life to helping the poor and destitute of Manchester. But his pride and arrogance were softened a lot, and this was most evident in his dealings at work with those who found they couldn't keep up their mortgage repayments. He often wondered what had happened to Dolores, and whether she had made good use of her acquired resources. He noticed that she had used his credit cards occasionally, for a short while, but she hadn't gone wild with them, so he didn't do anything about it. The Bentley had gone too; he wondered how she had found out where he had parked it. He hadn't even reported his loss to the police – he would have found all the questions much too embarrassing. He looked for her on the streets of Manchester, but he never saw her again. He tried asking some of the destitute people who were begging on the streets, but they made it quite clear, on one occasion painfully so, that such questions were not welcome.

Lynda took her final revenge in a quite different way. Every half term, she took the children to stay with her mother, and then disappeared for a few days. Ralph never asked her where she went, but he noticed that when she came back she had a mysterious smile and a spring in her step, and was often wearing a new scarf, or a brooch that he didn't recognise.

The birthmark

The Glanmor farm was appropriately named. It was indeed by the sea, or to be more accurate, its fields sloped down to the sea. The house itself, an old, stone-built building, with a slate roof, was set back, nestling in a fold of a small hill overlooking Cardigan Bay. Below the house, a row of hawthorn bushes that had once been a hedge was bent over towards the house by the winds and salt spray driven up from the sea.

Goronwy Roberts, coming down the hill from the higher ground where the sheep were eking out their summer living on the rough grass, surveyed the prospect below him. The grass grew well in the fields below the house, watered by the frequent rains sweeping in on the south-westerly winds. It looked good, but he was not happy. Costs were rising all the time, and the price he could get for his sheep was not. And as for the fleeces – it was hardly worth having them sheared. It barely covered what he had to pay to the shearers. And then, looking again at the fields of grass – the grass was growing well, but the hedges and fences needed a lot of work. "We usually get Huw Williams in to do that," he mused. "But I can't afford to pay him this year. I suppose I could get Ieuan to patch things up for the time being. He's good at doing things like that."

He was very fond of his two children – a more demonstrative man would have said he loved them, but that was not his way. Bronwen was still at school – but perhaps not for much longer. She was growing up into a very attractive young woman, but they hadn't seen much sign of boyfriends as yet. With her school work, she didn't have much time to help with the farm. But Ieuan was a different matter. He had done well enough at school, but that was over now – no indication that he wanted to go on to University or anything like that. "Lack of ambition, I suppose. Just as well not to be ambitious, if all he'll inherit will be this wreck of a farm. At least it means he's got plenty of time to do all the odd jobs that are needed. But that broken gate on Three Ash Field needs more than just patching up. It's past it. We ought to get a new one. That will cost money we don't have. And then there's the house." Looking at it, from above on the hill, he could see where there were slates missing, and the chimneys that needed re-pointing. "We ought to do something there before the winter sets in. How can we get the cash to do that?"

Now thoroughly depressed, he continued trudging down towards the farm.

Over tea, Mr Roberts said to his wife "I've been thinking about the farm Bethan, and there's a lot we need to talk about. All of us, Ieuan and Bronwen as well."

"This sounds serious Dad," said Ieuan.

"It is. I had a good look round this afternoon, and the farm's not in good shape. There are so many things that need doing. Fences and hedges for a start."

"I can do that," Ieuan broke in.

"OK, but let me go on. The house needs a lot of money spent on it – there are slates missing, the chimneys need re-pointing, the flashing is coming away – you can't do that. If we don't do it before winter, we're going to have real problems. And there's the Landrover; it must be twenty years old if it's a day, and it's clapped out. We ought to replace it. Even a second-hand one will cost more than we can afford. The money's just not coming in for us to be able to keep up with repairs, let alone improve the farm. I just don't know what we're going to do. I'm starting to think that maybe we should just sell up."

Bethan was horrified. "You can't do that! This farm's been in the family for generations, you can't just give up."

Ieuan agreed. "That would be terrible. It would be bought up by someone from England, as a holiday home. Dai Williams sold up two years ago, and look what happened. The house is empty for nine or ten months of the year. When they do come down, they don't spend any money in the local shops, you don't see them in the pub. And there's other farms have gone the same way. It's taking the life out of the place."

"Or a caravan park," Bronwen added. "Like around Abermawr. We've escaped that so far, but up there the coast is ruined by them."

"I know all that," said Goronwy. "But what can we do? We have to face it – the farm just doesn't bring in enough money. If we don't do something, it will go to rack and ruin."

Ieuan agreed. "There is one way. I could get a job in town. Then I would be able to pay you and Mam something by way of rent."

"How would that help? I can't afford to take on someone to replace you. What you would pay wouldn't cover it."

"You wouldn't need to. You don't really need anyone else to run the farm, at least not full-time. And I would be able to help out, evenings and weekends. That'll be enough time for the odd jobs I'm doing now."

"What do you think, Bethan?" asked Goronwy.

"It might help," she said, doubtfully.

Bronwen added "I can help with the farm too."

"But you've got your schoolwork to do, with exams coming up next year as well." said Bethan.

"Oh, I can cope with that. At least until the exams are a bit nearer."

So it was agreed, although Ieuan secretly thought of it as a temporary arrangement. Despite what his father thought, he *was* ambitious. He had grand ideas for improving the farm, making it into a going concern, but he didn't share these plans with them. They would need money, lots of it, and much more than he would ever get working in Abernant. He would have to leave home and get a much better paid job elsewhere – maybe in London, or perhaps abroad. Not the sort of thing he could possibly discuss with his parents.

However, for the moment, he went along with the plan. He got himself a job in Abernant, in the supermarket. He bought a second-hand bicycle so he could cycle the ten miles into town. The job didn't pay much, but the money he was able to give his mother at the end of the week did go a long way towards covering the housekeeping costs. But he soon began to find it irksome, helping out on the farm after a full day's work, especially after the effort of cycling home. He found the cycling hard work. The road went up and down rather more than he thought necessary; the hills weren't huge, but they were big enough. And there always seemed to be more uphill than down, whichever direction he was going in. At first, his pride insisted on pedalling all the way up. Later on, he gave up on that and started pushing the bike up the hills. The wind always seemed to be against him as well; he didn't understand that either. But the rain was the worst. After a few occasions arriving at work soaking wet, he started taking a spare set of clothing so he could change when he got there.

He stuck at it for a year or so. But he was getting more and more fed up with it, and his dreams of other things he could be doing started to take concrete shape. He talked to people at work, and heard stories about men who had gone to other countries – Canada, South Africa and Latin America – and how they had made their fortune there. But the country that fascinated him most was Australia. They had sheep farms there, enormous ones, and he knew about sheep. There would be plenty of opportunities there. He started to save up what was left of his wages, towards the fare to get there.

It was a fine morning in June. The sun was already showing over the hill behind the house when Mrs Roberts came downstairs to start getting breakfast ready for the family. Ieuan had to go off to work, and Bronwen had to catch the school bus. Bethan was singing quietly to herself – it was that sort of morning – as she put the kettle on the hob. She turned to set the table. Then she noticed a note on the table. Her hands trembled a bit as she picked it up.

"Dear Mam and Dad.

I've been thinking about the future, and I've decided that we can't go on like this. I'm not bringing in enough money to save the farm, and the only answer is for me to go abroad to 'seek my fortune'. I've heard a lot about the opportunities in Australia, and I've decided that is the answer. I couldn't discuss it with you – I knew you would try to stop me, and it would only have led to an argument that would upset us all more. There's nothing you could have said to stop me. I'll write when I've got there, and I'll soon be able to start sending some money home. I'm sorry to have to go like this, but it's the only way.

Ieuan."

Mrs Roberts sat down heavily and put her head in her hands. She was still sitting there, crying softly, with the breakfast half laid and the kettle singing on the hob, when Bronwen came down. "What's the matter, Mam?" Mrs Roberts passed her the note. Bronwen read it, paused, and then read it again. She bent over and put her arms round her mother's shoulders. Then she heard her father coming downstairs, whistling. She ran to intercept him, and whispered the news. Mrs Roberts got up, wiped the tears from her eyes, and fell into his arms.

"Oh, Bethan." he said. "What are we going to do? "

"I can't bear it," she said. "We've lost our only son. The hopes and dreams we had, of him taking over the farm, settling down with some nice girl. And looking after us when we're too old to work."

He tried to console her. "He's not dead. Perhaps he will make his fortune in Australia, and come back a rich man." But he didn't really believe it, and try as he could, the words sounded empty, hollow.

Mrs Roberts felt the loss keenly. The house seemed bare without Ieuan. At mealtimes, the empty chair at the table was a constant reminder of his absence. She tried putting it in a corner of the room instead of by the table, but that was worse. It seemed like rejecting him. So after a day or two like that, she put the chair back where it had always been, at the table. Nobody commented on it, but Bronwen noticed. She had always been close to Ieuan, and she missed him. But she hid it from her parents, and tried to help them to cope with the situation.

Although he didn't say much, it was Mr Roberts who felt the loss most. Not just because he had lost some help around the farm. That was bad enough. But it seemed like the end of everything he had worked for. There seemed to be no point in going on. And he just couldn't bring himself to talk to his wife, or his daughter, about how he felt. He never even mentioned Ieuan's name. Mrs Roberts wanted to talk about him all the time, and was hurt when her husband wouldn't respond. She didn't understand that it was because he was also hurting, and hurting too much to talk – in fact she drew the opposite conclusion that he didn't care.

But she was wrong. He did care, and very deeply. But instead of sharing his grief with his wife, he turned to drink. He thought this might dull the pain. And for a while, it did. Most evenings, he went down to the pub in the village. Standing at the bar in the Cross Keys, with a pint of bitter in his hand, swapping jokes and tales with his friends, he could forget his own troubles.

Bronwen started to spend more time out of the house, with a group of girls from her school. Their exams were over now, so they didn't need to bother about schoolwork any longer. That left Mrs Roberts alone in the house, to grieve by herself, re-living over and over, all the memories of the past, and wondering, desperately, what Ieuan was doing. She waited up until her husband came home, late, and smelling of drink. She couldn't bear it, and she made no secret of her feelings. "Oh, Goronwy, you've been down the pub again, spending our money. You don't care how I feel."

"Don't go on at me, woman. Can't a man have a drink after a hard day's work? I'm tired, I'm going to bed." And he stomped off up the stairs. She could hear him blundering about, falling over something and swearing, until she heard the thump as he flopped into his bed. Soon he was snoring loudly. She stayed downstairs for a while, staring into the fire, until eventually she too crept upstairs and lay in bed, crying quietly.

Ieuan did write when he got to Australia. It seemed that things weren't quite as easy as he'd expected. He hadn't anticipated all the bureaucratic difficulties, but even when those were overcome, he hadn't walked straight into the sort of job he wanted. He was still looking around, and getting by for the moment with a temporary job in a restaurant, washing dishes. Mrs Roberts thought that didn't sound any better than what he was doing when he was at home. But he was still talking about getting a better job, and then he would be able to start sending money home.

As the months passed, letters from Australia came only intermittently. Mr Roberts' drinking got worse. He started bringing bottles of whisky home. To start with, he would just have a glass when he got back from the pub; then, it would be a couple of glasses. A few weeks later, he started having a glass of whisky before he went to the pub. A month after that, he stopped going to the pub every night. Instead, some nights, he would stay at home with the bottle of whisky, sitting in a corner of the kitchen, staring morosely at his glass, which he kept re-filling until he had finished the whole bottle. In the end, he dispensed with the glass, and just drank straight from the bottle. Except, some nights, after two or three swigs of whisky, he put on his coat and went out. She thought he was going to the pub again, but he didn't come back until sometime in the early hours of the morning. One morning, she was talking to Mrs Jenkins, from the neighbouring farm, in the village shop.

"Where's your Goronwy been this last month or two? Dai hasn't seen him in the Cross Keys for ages."

Bethan made some excuse about him having a lot of work to do on the farm, but she knew that wasn't true. She realised that she now had more to worry about. Where was the money coming from? And what was he doing in these unexplained absences?

She got more and more worried. One day, she built up her courage to tackle him. "Where do you go, that keeps you out most of the night? And where's all the money coming from, that you're spending on booze? Why can't you spend some of it on the house instead?" Indeed, the house did need repairs, urgently. There were even more slates missing from the roof, and the chimney repairs had not been done. The damp patch on the bedroom ceiling showed that the rain was getting in. And the window frames hadn't been re-painted for years – there were clear signs of rot starting. The barn seemed to be about to fall down – she was frightened to go in there now.

"You mind your business and I'll mind mine!" he snarled.

She was shocked. He had never spoken to her like that before, in twenty-five years of married life. She didn't try to remonstrate further; it was obviously useless. She was getting desperate, trying to work out what was going on. The next evening, after he had gone to sleep, she got up and silently went through the pockets of his coat, which was hanging on the door downstairs. Nothing in the left hand pocket, except a rather dirty and crumpled handkerchief. In the right hand pocket, her hand met a sort of box. She pulled it out and opened it. She gently drew out a very expensive-looking necklace. It sparkled in the light. She gasped. She had never seen anything so beautiful. Not close up anyway. Only on the neck of some posh lady. Where on earth had he got this from? And what was he doing with it? She heard Goronwy stirring upstairs, and she hastily put the necklace back in its box, and slipped it into his coat pocket. She went back to bed, but couldn't sleep. She lay there all the rest of the night, wondering what it all meant.

The next morning, after Mr Roberts had gone out, there was a knock at the door.

"Hullo, Jack," she said. "Don't often see a policeman around here. Come in and have a cup of tea."

"No thanks, Bethan, Mrs Roberts I mean. This is official business."

"What's all this 'Mrs Roberts'? I've been Bethan to you for years."

"As I say, I'm here in an official capacity. Serious matters. Is your Goron..., er, Mr Roberts, in?"

"No, he's out on the farm. Can I help?"

"Perhaps you can. Can you tell me where he was on Tuesday night?"

She hesitated. It sounded as though Goronwy might be in some sort of trouble. Should she cover up for him? But her Methodist upbringing made her flinch at the prospect of telling lies to a policeman. Especially as she wasn't sure what it was about; if it was nothing like that, she would look a fool. "No, I'm afraid I can't. He went out, and hadn't come back when I went to bed. What's it all about?"

It was his turn to hesitate. "I probably shouldn't tell you this, but it will all come out soon enough. There was a burglary on Tuesday night – one of a string of burglaries we think – and we've got someone in for questioning. The talk in Abernant is that this man and Goronwy have been going around together."

"So you think Goronwy was involved in this burglary? Surely not? He would never do anything like that." But she thought about the necklace, and trembled.

When Mr Roberts came in for his tea that evening, she told him that the police had been there, asking where he was on Tuesday night.

"What did you say? I hope you told him I was safe home in bed?"

"Of course not. I told him the truth. What else do you expect me to say?"

"You bloody fool!" he shouted. "Do you want me to go to prison?" He raised his fist and hit her full in the face. She staggered back and collapsed in a heap on the floor, blood pouring from her cheek.

He stood over her for a moment, rather taken aback at what he had done, and then went out, slamming the door behind him.

An hour later Bronwen came back. Her mother was sitting at the kitchen table, crying. She had managed to stop the bleeding, but her cheek was badly swollen, and the beginnings of a nasty black eye were starting to show. She turned her face away as Bronwen came in.

"Hello, Mam, I'm back," she said. Her mother still didn't look at her.

"What's the matter, Mam?" Her mother slowly turned towards her. Bronwen gasped. "What's happened?"

"I fell over, and hit my head on the kitchen table," Bethan said.

Bronwen took her mother's face between her hands and turned it towards the light. "You don't expect me to believe that, do you? You never did this on the kitchen table. And why are you crying? It's not Dad, is it? The bastard's hit you!"

Mrs Roberts burst into tears. "He's a good man really. He's just so worried about the farm and Ieuan and everything. It all got too much for him. I'm sure it won't happen again. Make me a cup of tea, love, and I'll be all right."

But it did happen again. And again. That first occasion seemed to mark a watershed; some sort of taboo had been vanquished, so violence became part of their lives. Not every day, but frequently enough. Mostly he avoided hitting her in the face again, as he realised that the marks would lead to awkward questions, but there were plenty of other places – arms, legs, body. He got a heavy leather strap from the barn and hung it up by the door. Sometimes he would use that. But occasionally, when he was drunk, he forgot himself and hit her in the face.

She cowered every time he came in the house after work, or, especially, after he had been drinking. Some days, she was too frightened to go down to the village shop, afraid that they would notice the marks. Suffering the violence was bad enough, but having other people know about it would be much worse. Then, if she hadn't done the shopping, there would be nothing much for tea, which would provide an excuse for more violence. What frightened her most though was not the violence towards herself, but the thought that one day he would start doing the same to Bronwen. Many nights she lay awake wondering how she could stop that from happening.

One day, when she and Bronwen were alone in the house, she said "I think you ought to move out."

Bronwen didn't need to ask why. "I can't leave you alone with, with that man."

Mrs Roberts noticed that she had stopped referring to him as her father. "Yes, you can, and you must. I can stand it, but I couldn't bear it if anything happened to you. Now, you know that Gethin Davies in Abernant lost his wife a couple of months ago?"

"Yes, I heard that. Really sad, so young to die. They were a lovely couple."

"Well, I happen to know that he's thinking of looking for someone to keep house for him. He's really not coping very well by himself. A nice man, but he's absolutely hopeless in the kitchen. And the house is getting into quite a state. You'd be perfect for the job. It wouldn't be full-time of course, so you'd be able to get yourself a part-time job in town as well. I don't suppose he would be able to pay you much. Maybe just your keep."

Bronwen hesitated. "Is that a good idea, Mam? Wouldn't people talk? You know, a single girl living in with a widower?"

Her mother laughed. "People always talk! Don't worry about them. I'll put them straight. And they'll soon lose interest."

So Bronwen moved out. Gethin Davies was delighted by the arrangement. Someone to do the shopping, cook some simple meals, and keep the house reasonably clean and tidy, that was all he needed. Beyond that, her time was her own. He kept himself to himself, and she did likewise. They got on splendidly.

Mr Roberts barely seemed to notice that Bronwen wasn't there any longer. Bethan didn't see the need to tell him about the arrangement. He kept drinking, and he kept going out late at night. Although on that first occasion, the police hadn't been able to get enough evidence to charge him with anything, it wasn't to last. Early one morning, several months later, when they were still in bed, they were woken by repeated loud banging on the door.

"Police! Open up!"

Mrs Roberts went down and opened the door. It wasn't Jack Thomas this time, but a group of policemen that she didn't know. They barged in. "We're looking for Goronwy Roberts. Is he in? We have a warrant for his arrest."

"He's still in bed. What do you want him for?"

They didn't answer, but two of them went upstairs and waited while he got dressed. They came down with him and bundled him into the van outside, while the others started searching the house. Then they left, carrying two bags of things they had found, leaving Mrs Roberts standing, stunned, in the kitchen.

He was sentenced to two years in prison for that burglary, and several others that his solicitor had advised him to ask to be taken into consideration as well. During his absence,

Bethan managed to keep the farm going, in a way, thanks to a great deal of help from Dai Jenkins. Bronwen came out from town to help out as well, when she could get away. Bethan even managed to get the slates fixed on the roof, but the barn fell down, as she had expected. Fortunately, it was empty at the time.

Five years went past. Mr Roberts served eighteen months in prison. When he came out, he wasn't exactly a reformed character. He was still drinking heavily, but the night-time disappearances stopped. Bethan wasn't sure that he had ended his criminal activities – he was still getting money from somewhere – but at least he must have become more cautious in what he did. Despite all her troubles, Mrs Roberts hadn't forgotten about Ieuan. The letters from Australia came from time to time. Although they didn't say much about what he was doing, money started to arrive, so she knew that he must be doing well.

One day, after Gethin Davies had had his breakfast and gone out to work, Bronwen was just starting to clean the house when there was a knock at the door. She opened it. Outside, there was a tall stranger, sunburnt and weather-beaten, with a beard.

"I'm sorry, Mr Davies is out," she said. "Can I help you?"

He grinned. "It's not Gethin I've come to see, Bronwen, it's you."

She looked at him suspiciously. "Who are you? You're not from round here, I know that much. And how do you know my name?" But there was something familiar about his voice, although she couldn't place it.

He grinned again, then, slowly and theatrically, he rolled up his left sleeve. There, on his forearm, was the familiar coffee-coloured blotch.

She stared at it. "Ieuan? Oh Ieuan, you've come back!" She threw her arms round him and rested her head on his chest, not knowing whether to laugh or cry.

After a few moments, he freed himself and said "Aren't you going to ask me in?"

She led the way into the kitchen and over a cup of coffee and a plate of freshly made Welsh cakes, they started to talk.

"First of all," she said. "How did you find out where I was?"

"Oh, that was easy. I drove down overnight from London, so I got to Abernant at first light. I wanted to find out how the land lay, before going out to Glanmor. I've been here a few hours, which is plenty of time to catch up on the gossip – principally about the scandalous situation of Bronwen Roberts living with a widower ten years older than her."

"I'm not 'living with him', I'm living in his house," she retorted sharply. "Not the same thing at all."

"I don't think the gossips of the town see the difference."

"You don't believe that, do you?"

He laughed. "Of course not. I know you better than that, Bronwen. Come to that, I know Gethin better than that as well." He paused, and looked at her with a wry expression. "Mind you, you could do worse, if he wanted more than just his meals cooked. He's a good man, one of the best, and only ten years older than you." He was amused to see that she blushed. "Aha," he thought. "Not far off the mark there!"

She changed the subject. "Tell me all about Australia."

There was a lot to tell. After a succession of short-term, menial jobs, he had tried his hand at various things – even gold prospecting. "But I quickly realised that it was a mug's game. Even the few, very few, men who found anything, didn't make much out of it. Less than I had been getting washing dishes. But I fell on my feet eventually – got a job as a hand on a sheep farm. It's so different there, you've no idea. This farm was about the size of Wales!"

She thought this must be a bit of an exaggeration, but she let him continue,

"I got on well with the manager, and after a year or so, I found myself acting as a sort of assistant manager. I didn't have much to spend my money on – some of the guys drank most of theirs, but I wanted to build up enough money to be able to come back here and do things with Glanmor. Anyway, tell me about the farm. How are things out there? The Abernant gossips went strangely quiet when I asked them. Is something wrong?"

She didn't know what to say. How much should she tell him? In the end, she told him almost the full story – her father's drinking, his time in prison, all that would come out soon enough anyway, so he might as well hear it from her. But she didn't tell him about Goronwy's violence towards their mother. She was afraid of his reaction; she didn't want a scene to mar his homecoming.

"But you must go out there straightaway. They will be so pleased to see you. Mam has worried about you so much." She realised that most of the day had slipped away. "I won't be able to come with you today. I've got to get Gethin's tea ready, and I haven't done any of the housework that I'd planned to do. I'll come out first thing tomorrow. It's a pity, though. I'd really like to be there, to see their reaction when you turn up." She paused, as a sudden thought struck her. She laughed. "We could play a trick on them. You know that I didn't recognise you at all?"

He nodded. "Well?"

"Well, I'm sure they won't recognise you either. So don't tell them who you are. We'll make it a big surprise when I get there tomorrow. That will be marvellous, to see the expression on their faces." She bubbled with excitement, anticipating the event the next day.

So Ieuan left for the short drive out to Glanmor Farm, leaving Bronwen to get Gethin Davies' tea.

When he arrived at Glanmor Farm, he parked his car in the familiar yard and knocked at the door. Mrs Roberts opened the door. "Good evening," she said. As Bronwen had expected, she obviously hadn't recognised him.

"Good evening, Mrs Roberts. I wonder if you can help me. I'm travelling in the area, and I'm looking for somewhere to stay the night. I asked at the village pub – Cross Keys, is it? They hadn't got a room. But they said you had a spare room that you might be able to let me have. Just for one night, at the moment anyway."

"You wouldn't want to stay at that pub. Filthy place. But I'm afraid you've been sent on a fool's errand. We don't let out rooms."

Mr Roberts came up behind her. "Who is it, Bethan?"

"Gentleman wants a room for the night. I told him we don't let out rooms."

"Hang on a moment." He took her on one side, and said, in a whisper "He could have Ieuan's room. Don't you see that car, and the clothes? And that expensive watch? He must have pots of money. We could charge him well over the odds for the room." He also thought, but didn't say, that they would be able to relieve him of some of his possessions overnight, as well as the charge for the room. Over his wife's shoulder he said to the stranger "It's all right, sir. We have a room that you can have. But it's a lot of extra work for us, so it won't be cheap. Shall we say £100?" The stranger pulled a wallet from his jacket pocket and extracted two £50 notes. Mr Roberts saw the contents of the wallet, and cursed himself for not asking more.

While Mrs Roberts was getting the room ready, the stranger fetched some luggage in from the car. Mr Roberts noticed the expensive suitcase, and the camera case. "Rich pickings here indeed," he thought. He tried to find out where the stranger was from, and what he was doing in the area, but he seemed strangely reticent. He did find out that his name was John Smith, although he had a feeling that it wasn't his real name.

When Mrs Roberts came downstairs again, she said "The room's ready for you now. Would you like something to eat?"

The stranger yawned. "No thank you. I've had a long day and I'm tired out. I'll just go straight to bed, if it's all the same to you."

When Bethan and Goronwy were alone again, he took out the whisky bottle and had a few mouthfuls. "Well, Bethan, we've got a gold-mine under our roof tonight."

"What do you mean?" But in her heart she knew what he had in mind. She felt sick.

"Didn't you see how much cash he had in his wallet? And that watch, and camera. Those alone would set us up for months."

"You're not going to steal from him? A stranger under our roof? You'll be caught and go to prison again."

"Just leave the thinking to me. You do as you're told, and it'll be OK."

Upstairs, Ieuan looked round the room. It was odd, being back in his old room after all these years. Nothing seemed to have changed. Even the book on the bedside table, the one he had been reading when he went away. The bookmark was still in it. He picked it up and started reading from where he had left off, but he kept drifting away into memories of his childhood. He looked out of the window. It was almost dark by now, but he could make out the outline of the tree that he remembered climbing, with Bronwen hesitating below, saying "Isn't it dangerous? Do be careful." "Come on up," he had shouted "It's quite safe." She tried, but couldn't. Then a branch had broken, and he fell heavily to the ground. His mother rushed out, saying "Are you hurt?" He remembered his father picking him up and carrying him into the house, and Mam fussing over him, checking that there were no bones broken. With all his memories flooding round him, he lay back on the pillow. The book slipped from his hands, and he was asleep.

Mr Roberts heard the heavy regular breathing and said "We'll give it a bit more time and then we'll do it."

"We? I'm not having any part of this."

"You just do as you're told," he growled "Or you'll feel my fist again. I need someone to hold the torch." He took a few more drinks from the bottle. "Right, now bring the torch and follow me. And whatever you do, keep quiet!"

Slowly and softly he crept up the stairs, carefully missing out the one that creaked. Mrs Roberts followed, reluctantly, and trembling with fear. He opened the bedroom door. That did creak, and he paused for a moment. No change in the breathing. That was all right. He saw the jacket hanging on the door and drew out the wallet from the inside pocket. He carefully extracted the wad of notes, and put the wallet back in the jacket pocket. He moved over to the bedside table. "Shine the light over here," he whispered. "Not on his face, you fool!" He went to pick up the watch, but Bethan's hand was shaking too much to hold the torch steady. He missed his grasp on the watch and it fell back on the table.

Ieuan opened his eyes. "What was that?" he mumbled, still more than half asleep. "Where am I?" he thought. "What's going on? Who are these people in my room?" Even in his partially conscious state, he could sense that something was happening that needed to be stopped. He tried to get up and grapple with Mr Roberts. Goronwy attempted to push him back onto the bed, but Ieuan was too strong for him. Suddenly, Ieuan gasped and fell back, limp, onto the pillows.

"You can switch the light on now," Goronwy said. "He won't wake up now."

Bethan looked, horrified, at the scene. There was blood everywhere, all over the sheets, and Goronwy's shirt was dripping with it. He pulled out the knife, looked at it, and carefully wiped the blade on the bedclothes before putting it back in its sheath.

"Oh, God! I didn't know you had a knife! Is he dead?"

"Shut your mouth, woman, and help me deal with this. We've got a lot of cleaning up to do, but first we must get rid of him." And he gestured towards the lifeless form on the bed.

Mrs Roberts still stood by the door, too petrified to move.

"Hell's teeth, you're useless! At least hold the door open while I get him out."

He took hold of Ieuan's feet and dragged him off the bed. His head fell with a bang onto the floorboards. Bethan shrieked, and Goronwy swore at her again, "Hold that bloody door open!"

He pulled the body through the door and down the stairs, the head banging sickeningly on each step. "Come on," he shouted. "Open the front door and then bring the Landrover up to the door. I'm not going to drag him all the way across the bloody yard!"

Bethan was too horrified, and frightened, to do anything except obey her husband's commands unquestioningly. They drove, without speaking, across the fields and down to the edge of the cliffs. The wind had risen during the evening, and was now driving the rain against the windscreen. Goronwy dragged the body out of the Landrover, and laid it by the cliff edge. Then, with his foot, he propelled it over the edge and into the breakers that were thundering against the rocks.

When they got back to the house, he saw the car parked outside. "Damn," he said. I'll have to do something with that car. I'll put it round the back for now. I know someone who'll take it off my hands, no questions asked. The cleaning up can wait till the morning. I'm going to bed."

"How can you even think of sleeping, after what you've done? You can't think you'll get away with this!"

"Me? It's us, not me. If I go down for this, you will as well. So make sure you keep your mouth shut. Anyway, he's a stranger round here. No-one will miss him." He took another drink from the bottle and stomped off up the stairs.

Bethan sat alone in the kitchen. "Oh, that poor lad! What have we done?" Then a thought struck her. "He must have a mother somewhere. Waiting for him to come home, wondering where he is, hoping that every footstep on the path is him returning. Just like I hope and pray for Ieuan to come back." She sat there and wept until morning.

Bronwen was almost hopping with excitement as she cooked breakfast for Gethin Davies. She hadn't told him about Ieuan's visit, although she guessed that he must have heard about the strange man in the town asking questions. Gethin could tell something was up, but he didn't ask her about it. "She'll tell me when she's ready," he thought. When he had gone out to work, she got into her car to drive out to Glanmor Farm. "What a blessing to have this little car. It was so generous of Gethin to lend me the money." He had actually offered to give her the money, as he said that it was in his interest for her to have a car, so as to be able to do the shopping easily, but she had refused. "I want to be able to look the gossips straight in the eye," she had said. So, Gethin made it a loan, but said that there was no hurry paying it back. "Typical of him," she thought. "Such a nice man." She thought of what Ieuan had said the day before, and she smiled. "We really do get on well together, and I've grown quite, sort of, fond of him. And as Ieuan said, he's only ten years older than me. But I've never thought of him as more than my employer – a very friendly sort of employer – and he's not given any indication that he might think of me in any other way."

Her excitement grew stronger as she neared the farm, so she had difficulty keeping the car on the road. The wind howled, and the rain beat against the windscreen, but she could only think about what would happen when she got there and they told their parents the news. "How surprised they'll be when they find out who the 'stranger' really is!" She tried to imagine the expression on her mother's face. "And Dad too, perhaps it will be just what is needed to put him back on the proper path again. Just like he used to be." She remembered, when she was a little girl, her father taking her to see the new-born lambs – some just a few hours old, and her delight in watching them trying to get milk from their mother. She remembered listening to his rich voice telling bed-time stories, many of them ones he made up as he went. Or singing to her. He had a beautiful voice. She started humming the Welsh lullaby Suo Gan, one of her father's favourite songs, as she drove.

When Bronwen pushed open the farmhouse door, she could tell straight away that something was wrong. Her mother had obviously been crying. "He's not been hitting her again, has he? Surely not with a stranger in the house?"

Her mother looked up, and tried to smile. "Hello, Bronwen love," she said. "How nice to see you. But what brings you out here? We weren't expecting you today."

"I've come to see what you think of that man who came out here last night. How are you getting on with him?"

Her father had appeared in the doorway. "What man? No-one came here last night."

Bronwen was puzzled. "I saw him in Abernant yesterday, and I told him to come out here. He was looking for somewhere to stay the night."

"Maybe he changed his mind and went somewhere else," Mr Roberts said, casually.

"What's gone wrong?" Bronwen said to herself. "I'll just have to tell them, although it will spoil the surprise for Ieuan. I wonder where he's gone?"

"He must have come here. He wouldn't have gone anywhere else. Oh Mam", she blurted. "It was Ieuan! I didn't recognise him at first, but then I saw the birthmark on his arm, and I knew it was him."

But Mrs Roberts wasn't listening any more. She tried to grab hold of a chair for support, missed, and fell heavily to the floor with the chair on top of her.

Bronwen ran to her. "What's the matter Mam?" she cried.

Mrs Roberts just moaned. "My son, my son. Oh Ieuan, my son. What have we done?"

Bronwen turned to her father. "Dad, what's happened? What's Mam talking about?"

Mr Roberts just stood there, open-mouthed. He tried to speak but no words came out.

Bethan raised herself up and looked at her husband. "Oh, Goronwy, we've killed our only son. Oh poor Ieuan."

Bronwen was horrified. She couldn't believe it. "Dad, say something. You've killed Ieuan? That can't be true. Why would you do such a thing?"

Mr Roberts was still speechless.

"Oh God," Bronwen cried, and fled from the house.

Gethin Davies had found that he had unexpectedly been given the day off, so he was back home when Bronwen arrived. He saw at a glance that something was seriously wrong. He instinctively knew what was needed, so, without hesitation, and without asking any questions, he put his arms round her and held her close. Her whole body was heaving with sobs. "Bronwen, love" he said, and gently kissed the top of her head. Slowly her sobs subsided. They stayed like that, locked together, for a long time after she had stopped crying.

Bethan and Goronwy Roberts stood, silent, in the kitchen at Glanmor Farm. Outside, the wind was still howling, and the rain beat against the windows. But they didn't hear it. Eventually, Goronwy went over to Bethan and, for the first time in years, he put his arms around his wife. "Bethan," he said. "There's only one way out. Only one thing we can do."

She knew what he meant. She nodded. "Yes, it must be."

He led her out of the kitchen and through the driving rain to where the Landrover waited in the yard. Silently, they got in and drove off.

Next morning, the storm had passed. The leaves on the trees were waving gently in the light breeze as the sun rose over the hill into a cloudless sky. Larks were singing high overhead. Down by the sea, a group of ramblers walking the Coastal Path were enjoying the fine weather, after the drenching they had received the previous day. As they climbed up the path and reached the cliff-top, they noticed a set of wheel tracks leading directly to the edge of the cliff. Cautiously they peered over. There, on the rocks far below, washed gently by the now calm sea, they saw the shattered remains of a Landrover.

The blind husband

It had been a busy week. I had to work late every day, and I'd brought lots of work home as well. So by the time Friday came, I was ready for an evening at the Rose and Crown. In fact, I had been looking forward to it all week. Maybe Dai would have another of his famous stories to entertain us. As usual on a Friday night, the pub was crowded, but I soon saw the three familiar faces, Dai, Evan and Brian, at their usual table in a corner. I pushed my way through the crowd to join them.

"I need a drink," I said. "You ready for another?"

They all nodded. "Just a half for me," said Evan.

I went over to the bar, and eventually came back with a tray carrying three pints of bitter and one half pint.

Dai said "Evan was asking how to get rid of his wife, so he could drink pints with us, instead of halves."

Evan protested. "That's not what I said at all. I've no intention of getting rid of Blodwen. What a ridiculous idea. We're happily married, although she can be a bit of a tartar at times. I was just thinking, in abstract terms, about how a man could get rid of his wife, or vice versa, without being found out."

"I take it," I said "that you mean bumping them off, rather than just divorcing them?"

"That's right," said Brian. "We were thinking about that case that's been in the news this week."

"That was a bit extreme," I said. "Didn't she hit him over the head with a frying pan? Not very subtle. Why didn't she just divorce him?"

"No grounds," said Evan. "She was just fed up with him. He just said, and did, the same things every day, taking no real notice of her. It got on her nerves, and eventually she just snapped."

Brian added, "We were just considering whether there was any way in which she could have done it without being found out."

"I know of one case," said Dai. "The wife thought she had found a fool-proof way of doing it. I'll tell you about it if you want. You may think it's a bit far-fetched, though."

"All your stories are far-fetched," said Evan.

"Go on," said Brian. "Try us."

So Dai started. "It's about this couple, let's call them Mr and Mrs Jenkins, Huw and Mari. They were an ideal married couple. Or so everyone thought. After all, they had been married for eighteen years, and none of their friends had ever heard a cross word spoken between them. They lived in a small, stone-built, end-of-terrace cottage, with two cats for company. Although they had no children, Mrs Jenkins always said, when asked if she was disappointed to be childless, 'We've got each other. That's all we need.' And she would squeeze her husband's arm.

The cottage opened straight onto the street, with no front garden, but there was a small garden at the back where Mrs Jenkins grew flowers that she would pick to decorate the house. Every weekday morning, after cereal and toast for breakfast, Mr Jenkins walked into town where he worked in a bank. After he had gone, Mrs Jenkins went round cleaning the already spotless house. Every day, the same format. Except at weekends, when Mr Jenkins sat and read the paper for a while after breakfast, before saying "Well, honey bunch, time to grow some vegetables." Mr Jenkins had an allotment ten minutes' walk away. He often spent most of the day there, at weekends, tending his vegetables, and in between digging and hoeing, or if it was raining, sitting in the shed smoking his pipe and thinking how good life was. In the evenings, they sat quietly in front of the television, only sometimes watching what was happening, until it was time for bed. Every Friday, he would spend the evening down at the pub instead, and come back home smelling of drink. Apart from occasional outings to Barry Island or Porthcawl, where they would walk along beside the sea, eating ice-creams, or just sit in deck chairs, side by side, on the beach reading the newspaper and snoozing. And every year they spent a week at a holiday camp. That varied somewhat. Some years it was Minehead. Other years, it was Pwllheli.

But, unsuspected by Mr Jenkins, all was not right in their household. Mrs Jenkins was fed up. Fed up with the house, the days out in Porthcawl, the garden, and above all fed up with Mr Jenkins. It wasn't just the routine that was monotonous. He was. Every day, he came down to breakfast, said 'Here I am then' and kissed her on the left cheek. Always the left one, and always in exactly the same spot. She felt that there must be an invisible target there that he aimed for. One day, she even put a sticking plaster over the spot to see what would happen. He didn't even notice. He just kissed the plaster. And in the afternoon, when he came back from work, or from the allotment, again the same routine, except that now he smelt of pipe smoke. 'Hello, honey bunch. Here I am. Have a nice day?' And he kissed the same spot on her left cheek. How she wished for a bit of variety, even if it was just kissing the right cheek instead.

And then there were the Saturday nights in bed. Every Saturday night, she would lie in bed, waiting for him to come, and knowing what would happen. He would take his trousers off, as usual, and put his pyjama trousers on, as usual. Then he would take off his shirt and put on his pyjama top. In this way, he always managed to avoid being naked in front of her. She realised that she had never seen him completely naked. She had glimpses now and then, when he thought she wasn't looking, and she wondered how he managed to walk, or sit down, without all those bits getting squashed. Then he would climb into bed, as usual. But on a Saturday night, instead of a kiss on the left cheek and a 'Good-night, honey bunch', which was the procedure on other nights, he would say 'Saturday again; another week gone' and roll over on top of her. She felt his thing pressing against her, searching for the way in, she thought. 'What's the purpose of all this?' she wondered. Of course she knew about making babies and all that, but that was all in the past. She remembered the baby that she had lost, and being told then that she would never be able to have another, so all this messy business seemed totally pointless. She recalled her mother telling her that it was something men needed to do from time to time, and it was one of the duties of a wife to put up with it. 'I suppose it's fair enough. He works to bring in the money, and I clean the house, cook for him, and do this for him. But that sounds rather like those women I read about who do it for money. It doesn't sound very different does it? But it would have been nice to have had a baby, and watch him growing up. Ah, he's found the way in now.'"

Evan interrupted. "This is absurd. You're putting words in her mouth – or at least thoughts in her head. You can't possibly know what she was thinking while they were having sex."

Dai was cross at being interrupted, and at such a key point as well. "Of course I'm putting words in her mouth. That's what a narrator does. If I just told you what I'd seen with my own eyes, it wouldn't be much of a story, would it? The thoughts in their heads are an essential part of the story."

Brian agreed. "If someone was reading this story about us, Evan, are you saying they should only hear what Dai was thinking or saying?"

"No," I said. "They would hear what I was thinking, not Dai. I'm the real narrator of that story."

They all looked at me.

"Who gave you the right to be the narrator?" asked Evan. "I don't remember deciding that."

Dai said "This is getting too philosophical. And I'm losing my thread now. Can I get on with *my* story now? Where had I got to?"

"They were just about to have sex," I said.

"Oh, yes," said Dai, "Well, Huw was having sex. She was just lying there, thinking about all sorts of things. So, here goes – and I'm going to go on putting words in their mouths, whatever anyone says. If you don't like it, just keep quiet." And he glared at Evan.

"Mari looked up at the clock on the wall. There was enough light in the room to be able to see the time. 'It usually takes about thirty seconds from this point, although there was one time when it was as little as five seconds. And another time, it was nearly five minutes – I thought it would never end. I hope I got all the shopping today that we need. Sunday roast dinner tomorrow, I've got all we need for that. But what shall we have next week? Perhaps a nice casserole? I suppose I could go to the shops again on Monday. Think about that tomorrow. If I do go shopping, I could look in at Parry's as well; I could do with some new clothes. I wish he would take a bit more of the weight, I can hardly breathe. I think we need some more cat food. All this pushing and panting, it's quite horrible. I hope it's fine on Monday, I must wash the sheets. And the kitchen could do with a good clean, Maybe I'll empty out the cupboards and drawers and scrub them. And the fridge – under and behind it is quite disgusting. But there's no point in doing it now. If I can persuade Huw to get a new one I can do it then. That fridge must be at least ten years old – no, fifteen. I wonder what it would be like doing this with other men. That magazine I was reading the other day when Huw came in – I had to hide it quickly so I never got a chance to finish it – it was saying something about different positions. I can't see how that would work. I would need to be some sort of contortionist, like in the circus. If I do the washing on Monday I'll need to get some more powder for the machine. Huw always does it exactly the same. Apart from the timing. Nearly sixty seconds now, so it should be over soon. Unless this is a long one. Funny thing, he never really touches me apart from these Saturday nights. Before we were married, he had his hands all over me. Always fending him off. Apart from that one time when I let him put his hand up my jumper, just to see what it was like. Nice actually, but of course I had to stop him pretty quickly. Then, once we were married, he seemed to lose all interest in that sort of thing. Apart from these weekly bedroom things. Although being married I suppose I would have let him. Perhaps that's why he lost interest. Forbidden fruit and all that. It might have been nice, but I suppose I will never know. I think we need some more toilet paper as well. It feels like he's nearly there now – eighty seconds. Now there'll be that sort of spasm, like some sort of fit, and then he'll roll over and go to sleep.'

A few moments later, Huw Jenkins was indeed snoring by her side, while Mari lay there, still imagining what it would be like with other men. 'Respectable married women don't do that sort of thing, do they? But suppose something should happen to Huw? Would I get married again? Then I would find out what it's like. I wonder how John does it with Joan? I could ask her.' She giggled, quietly, at the thought. She remembered the girls at school talking about what they had done with their boyfriends, but she didn't believe most of what they said. Still imagining other men, and making shopping lists, she drifted off to sleep.

The one bright spot in Mari Jenkins' day was when she went round to Joan's house for tea and a chat. Sometimes Joan's husband John was there, but usually he was out. He also had an allotment, next to Huw's. When John wasn't there, Mari and Joan could talk at length about their home life, and that of all the other people in the street. It was amazing, what people got up to in such a quiet street.

It was at Joan's house that she met Ted. He was really Edward, but everybody called him Ted. He was Joan's brother, and his wife had died the previous year, so he was rather lonely. Mari really took to him. He was a perfect gentleman, kind and considerate. And he noticed things, like when she had had her hair done, or when she wore a new blouse. He always said how nice she looked. Huw never did that. He never even noticed. She found that she was able to talk to Ted about all sorts of things, in a way that she just couldn't with her husband. Conversations with Huw tended to be limited to what they should have for supper. She started to dream about what it would be like if she wasn't married. She could imagine how nice it would be to feel Ted's arms around her, and kissing her properly, not a token peck on the cheek. Of course, this was just a dream. She was a married woman after all, which meant something to her. Especially when it meant not having affairs with other men. Still there was no harm in dreaming, was there?

She started thinking about what could happen if Huw was no longer around. After all, they weren't getting any younger, and you never knew when you might be taken away. She didn't actually wish his death – that was a terrible thing, to even think of it – but just suppose it did happen. She dreamed of Ted saying just the right things to console her. Maybe she would burst into tears, and he would enfold her in his arms so she could cry on his shoulder. And, you never knew, one thing might lead to another. Eventually, after a suitable interval of course, they might get married. How good that would be. The things they would do together, the places they would go to – even foreign countries. She had never been abroad, but she had read about it in magazines, and it all looked so exciting.

One day she said to Huw, out of the blue 'I think we should get a computer.'

'What for?' He was surprised, and a bit apprehensive at this change in their routine.

'Well, all my friends have got one, and they say it's marvellous. They do their shopping on it, 'on-line' they call it. They use it to read books, and to get music. All sorts of things. And they're not very expensive now. Joan's got one, and she showed me the other day how to use it. It's quite easy really.'

'All right then, honey bunch. If that's what you want.'

And so they did. A very helpful young man came round to set it up for them and showed them how to use it.

Mrs Jenkins started to spend more and more of her time using the computer, and less time on her housework. The house was no longer quite as spotless as it used to be – but Mr Jenkins didn't notice. She even started to buy ready meals from the local shop instead of cooking them herself. Mr Jenkins didn't notice that either."

Dai paused. His glass was empty. "Whose round is it?"

"Mine" said Brian. "Same again?"

"Just a half for me," said Evan.

Brian took the empty glasses back to the bar.

"How's your allotment doing, Evan?" I asked.

Evan groaned. "This dry weather is terrible. I'm having to spend hours watering things. The lettuces have all bolted, and the latest lot of seedlings failed completely. Some of the early crops did well though. We got a good lot of early peas. And the rhubarb is going crazy. Would Margaret like some?"

"I'm sure she would. She could make some rhubarb and ginger jam, that's a good one. Tell you what, you give us some rhubarb, and we'll give you some jam."

"How about you, Dai? Would Gwen like some rhubarb?"

"She'd be over the moon. She loves rhubarb pie. So do I, come to that."

Brian came back with the drinks. As usual, he'd spilled some on the tray, but we refrained from making our usual comment about needing medical attention for his shaking hands. The joke was getting a bit stale, but I was starting to wonder whether, as a doctor, he was aware that he might have a problem. It did seem to be getting worse.

"Right," said Dai. "So Mari Jenkins had got herself a computer, and was spending a lot of time on it. Now we need to start considering what Huw Jenkins was doing all this time. He may not have noticed that the house wasn't as spotless as it used to be, and he hadn't noticed how bored and fed up Mari was. But he had noticed how attractive Eirlys Roberts was. She was a customer at the bank, and seemed to come in rather more often than was necessary. And when she came in, she always seemed to seek him out, sometimes just to withdraw a small amount of money, sometimes to make a small deposit, and quite often just to ask him some rather trivial question.

'Hello, Mrs Roberts,' he would say. 'You again? What can I do for you today?'

Then they would have a chat about the weather, about the new shop that had just opened on the High Street, and similar things. After a while, they started talking about more personal things. He found out that she was a widow, and her husband had died five years ago. Then, one day when he had popped out to get some lunch, he saw her in the cafe. She waved and beckoned him over to her table. He thought it would be churlish to ignore her, so he joined her, and they had lunch together.

The next day, she was there again. It almost seemed like she was waiting for him. But he didn't mind. It was nice to have someone to talk to, although his lunch break was quite short. These lunches together became a regular occasion. Huw didn't even think about the possibility that it might develop into something more than that. His imagination wasn't as fertile as his wife's, so there was no dreaming about putting his arms round her and kissing her. He was just having lunch with a friend.

Of course, Mari got to hear about it. The local gossips took great delight in telling her that her husband was having lunch dates with an attractive widow. Even Joan got to hear about it, and asked Mari if she knew what was going on. Mari just shrugged it off. It wasn't just that she trusted her husband. It was more that she knew Huw was incapable of having an affair. He was too predictable, too boring, to do anything so exciting, even with an attractive widow. But it did make her think about her relationship – her possible relationship – with Ted. 'I'm not like Huw; I'm not too boring to have an affair, am I?' she thought to herself. Her dreams started to become more concrete.

One day, after Huw had gone out to work, on an impulse, she rang Ted.

'I wonder if you can help me?' she said. 'There's a hanging basket I want fixed up, and I can't get Huw to do it. He's useless at things like that.'

So Ted came round with his toolbox, and fixed up the bracket for the hanging basket. Mari had already planted the basket with petunias and lobelia, trailing over the edge. He took it from her and hung it on the bracket. Then they stood back, side by side, and admired their joint handiwork. 'Thank you,' she said. 'It looks lovely.' She suddenly realised she was holding his hand. She turned and looked up into his eyes. Something in her look, combined with the loneliness he had felt since his wife died, got to him, and he bent down and kissed her. He had meant to kiss her cheek, but at the last moment she turned her head so their lips met.

'I'm sorry,' he stammered. 'I didn't mean that to happen.'

'Don't apologise. It was nice. You can do it again if you like.'

So they did. Then they went indoors and Mari made them both some coffee and they sat together on the sofa.

Ted came round quite often after that, and Mari's dreams became more and more explicit. Their cuddles on the sofa filled in a big gap in her life – but the relationship never got further than that. Mari often wondered if it would. She always wore her best frilly underwear for Ted's visits, just in case, but always in vain.

Then one day, when Mrs Jenkins was out, Huw thought he ought to try using the computer himself. He had often wondered what she was doing, spending so much time on it. 'Maybe I can do something with it as well,' he thought.

Mari had already shown him the basics. He explored it quite randomly, clicking here and there without knowing really what he was doing. Then he saw a button marked 'history'. 'That would be interesting,' he thought. 'I've always liked history. Maybe it will tell me something about the First World War. I remember Mam telling me about her Dad who was killed in France.'

He wasn't prepared for what he saw. Not the sort of history he was expecting at all, but a long list of things he didn't understand. A lot of them seemed to be rather similar, something about wives being bored and fed up. What was that all about? He clicked on one of them at random. That was extraordinary – lots of photographs, many of them quite disgusting, he thought. He quickly tried another one. This was different. It seemed to be a lot of people complaining about how bored they were with their husbands. Many of them seemed to involve someone called Mari. 'That's funny,' he thought. 'That must be my Mari. Has she been telling all these people how bored she is? She's never complained to me.'

He started reading them. The first few were just going on about how bored they were, and about the habits of their husbands that they found annoying. Including a lot of comments from Mari about himself. 'That's really unfair,' he thought. 'Nothing about how hard I work to bring in enough money to keep the house nice. And saying I do nothing to help around the house! Who cleans the drains, mows the lawn, all sorts of things. Besides, what else has she to spend her time on? And complaining about always going to Porthcawl; I thought she enjoyed our trips. I'm glad that she hasn't gone on about bedroom activities, not like some of the other women. A bit of an eye-opener though; the things some men get up to! Not that everything there is marvellous with us. She's always so unresponsive. A bit like making love to a cabbage. I wonder what it would be like with other women?' And. perhaps for the first time, he started thinking about Eirlys in that context. Not just someone to have a nice chat with over lunch, but kissing her, even making love to her. He quickly dismissed the thought. 'Married men don't do things like that. They shouldn't even think about them.'

Then he saw that the messages went on to discuss how women could get rid of their husbands. Not just divorcing them – that would be as boring as keeping them – but actually murdering them. Many of the suggestions were quite bizarre and totally impractical, but as he read on he realised that the discussion was starting to focus on one specific strategy. If you could give your husband something to make him go blind, then you could take him for a walk by the river so that he would fall in and drown, and it would look like a tragic accident, or even suicide. Nobody would ever know the truth. But how to make him go blind? There was a lot of discussion on this point. The favourite recipe involved collecting various plants from the garden or the hedgerows and boiling them up into a sort of broth. 'I suppose it's quite harmless,' he thought. 'Indulging in a bit of fantasy. Gets it out of the system. No chance that it would actually work. Do they really think that boiling up a few plants would produce something that made you blind? Could make you ill though – probably get terrible indigestion. But it's horrible that Mari could be thinking of such a thing – after eighteen years of marriage.' Then he heard Mari come in. He quickly closed down the computer and went to meet her. 'Had a nice day, honey bunch?' he said, and kissed her on the left cheek. She smiled, wanly, and went to prepare the supper."

Dai stopped. His glass was empty again. "My round," said Evan, and went up to the bar

Brian said "Have you heard about this scheme to build a load of new houses up on North Hill? Two hundred of them, I heard."

"Yes," I said. "It seems crazy to me. I suppose we have to have more houses, but why up there, when there's so much derelict land near the town centre?"

Dai agreed. "The council didn't want them, but they appealed, and the government is letting them go ahead. It's going to add to the traffic problems as well. They're not going to be working in the town; they'll mostly be commuters. And they're not going to want to walk to the station from right up there, so they'll drive to work."

"And where are they going to shop?" asked Brian. "They won't walk to the town centre for their shopping. They'll get in their cars and go to an out of town supermarket. The town centre shops will get even more run down. It'll just contribute to – what's the phrase? – the hollowing out of the town."

"There's another factor too," I said. "I bet the first thing they do is to put drains in, so all the rainwater, instead of soaking into the hillside, will pour straight down into the brook. We've just had all that flood prevention work, and now this is going to put us right back where we started. Mark my words, we'll see floods again."

Evan came back with the tray; three pints of bitter, and a half for himself.

Dai resumed his story. "Now, where was I? Oh, yes. Huw Jenkins had found out that Mari had been trawling the web looking for ways to make her husband go blind so she could push him in the river."

"It was a week later when Mari said to Huw 'You know you've been complaining about those pains in your back?'

'Yes, but it's nothing to worry about. I think I've been doing too much digging on the allotment.'

'It might be more than that, you should do something about it. I know just the thing. Joan has given me a nice recipe for a remedy that she swears by. She said that John's back trouble cleared up completely. I'll make you some.'

It tasted absolutely horrible, but she was watching him closely, so he had to drink it all.

Next day, she said 'How's your back now? Did the broth make it any better?'

It didn't seem to him to have made any difference, but he thought he had better humour her, so he said 'Well, it might be a little better.'

'Good. I'll make you some more this afternoon.'

This went on for a few more days. 'Is she trying out one of those recipes that she was reading about on the computer?' he thought. 'I'll try her out to see if that's it.'

He didn't say anything, but started deliberately bumping into things, and groping around the house. One Friday morning, at breakfast, he poured the milk over the table instead of on his cereal. She looked at him. 'Are you feeling all right?'

'I'm just having a bit of a problem with my eyes. I can't seem to see straight.'

'Perhaps you'd better take a day off work.'

'I'll be OK when I get going. But I'll call the optician and make an appointment to have my eyes tested.'

'I can do that. I'll call in when I go down the shops.'

'OK. Make it next week sometime. First thing in the morning would be fine. I can take half a day off work.'

When he got home that afternoon, she was very solicitous. 'How did you get on today? Did you manage all right with your eyes?'

'Well, it wasn't too bad. They don't seem to have got any worse.'

'That's good. I made that appointment with the opticians, but they couldn't fit you in before Tuesday. I told them it was serious but they were fully booked on Monday. Can you manage until then?'

He was puzzled by this. Surely if she was trying to poison him, she wouldn't want him to see an optician. He had really expected her to forget to make an appointment. Perhaps he was doing her an injustice, and she really thought that there was something wrong with his eyes. 'I expect it will be OK. Let's see how it goes. If it gets worse, I can go to the hospital over the weekend.'

'And how's your back? Is it any better?'

He had forgotten all about his supposed back problem. 'It seems to be a lot better now.'

'Good. The remedy seems to be working. I'll make up some more and you can have it before you go to bed.'

'Hm,' he thought. 'Now what do I make of that?'

'OK, I'll have it when I get back from the pub.'

'You're not going there this evening, are you? Do you think that's a good idea? Shouldn't you be resting?'

'I always go to the pub on Fridays. They'll be expecting me. And I can still see well enough to get there and back.'

Next morning, Saturday, when he woke up, he said to Mari, who was starting to get dressed, 'Why are you getting up in the middle of the night?'

'It's morning,' she said, 'and the sun is coming in the window. Can't you see it?'

'I can't see anything at all. It's pitch black.'

She was smiling at the apparent success of her plan. 'You've got a hangover. You drank too much last night. We'll go out for a walk after breakfast. That will clear your head.'

She helped him to get dressed and took him downstairs where she fed him with his usual cereal and toast.

'Do you feel up to a walk now?'

'OK, if you think it might help.'

She took his arm and led him slowly out of the house and down the road. Fortunately they didn't meet any of their neighbours on the way or there would have been some difficult explaining to do.

'Where are we now?'

'Down by the river. Can you hear the ducks? Be careful how you go; it's quite slippery here and the bank is steep.'

She looked around. There was no-one in sight. Now was the moment. She realised that it would take more than a shove to push him into the water, so she let go of his arm and took a few steps away.

He waved his arms about to try to find her. 'Where have you gone? Don't let go, I can't see where to go.'

But he could see well enough. As she ran towards him, he moved aside and she went straight over the edge, down the steep bank and into the water.

'Help!' she cried. 'Pull me out! I can't swim!'

'Where are you? I can't see you!'

'I'm over here! Pull me out or I'll drown.'

'But I can't see you at all.' He picked up a dead tree branch that was lying nearby and thrust it into the water. 'Grab hold of this and I'll pull you out.'

As she tried to grasp it, he moved it away from her hands and pushed her hard in the stomach.

'You fool, you're pushing me further in. Just keep it still and I'll grab hold of it.'

He kept moving it away from her hands, and pushing hard until her cries became fainter and she finally went under the water.

When he got home, he looked around the house. 'Mari has been letting this place go,' he thought. So he got out the vacuum cleaner and gave it a good going over, upstairs and down. Then he cleaned the bath and the washbasin, and dusted around the ornaments on the sideboard. When he had finished, he stood back and looked at his work with a smile of satisfaction. 'That's more like it,' he said. He made himself a cup of coffee and sat down to read the paper. But he found it difficult to concentrate. His thoughts kept drifting away; now that he was single again he could fantasise freely about Eirlys. When he had, eventually, finished the paper, he picked up the phone and dialled the police. 'I'm worried about my wife. She went out for a walk down by the river and hasn't come back. I'm afraid something has happened to her.'

Dai stopped, and drained the last of his beer.

Evan protested. "You can't just stop there! What happened next? Did he get found out? Did he get off with Eirlys?"

Dai looked at his watch. "Sorry, got to go. No time for more. Gwen and I are going away for a few days, and we've got to make an early start. I promised I wouldn't be late home. You'll have to make up the rest for yourselves." With that, he stood up and made his way over to the door.

The farmer's sons

Jack Croker leaned on a gate. It was a pleasant evening, and work for the day was over. The weather had been kind, and he looked with satisfaction at the bales of hay, wrapped in black plastic, piled up in the corner of the field, waiting to be taken down to the farm. But that could wait till tomorrow. Beyond the field, he could see some of the houses of the town, hidden away in the valley, with glimpses of the river here and there. He thought, with some pride, of how he had built the farm up from the few fields that he had inherited from his father. Leasing, to start with and then buying outright, some of the adjacent fields. And then, eventually, the Wilson's farm. That had been a good deal, he thought. He had separated off, and kept, most of the fields, and sold the house itself, with a good bit of land, separately – for nearly as much as he had paid for the whole farm. Things were different then, of course. At that time, there was no prospect of anyone being allowed to build houses there, so you could get land for a sensible price. "I wonder how much I would get now if I sold up? The land alone must be worth a small fortune." He had been lucky in finding the right buyer for the house; someone from London, with more money than sense, who had been looking for ages for a house just like that. They must have had pots of money – not only paying over the odds for the house but then spending a small fortune doing it up. He had been inside, once, and was amazed at what they had done. The kitchen, gleaming with marble worktops and stainless steel appliances of all sorts. And that enormous picture window. Rather spoilt the look of the place, but it was fantastic to sit in the living room and admire the view.

Merging the two farms had given him a good sized farm. It had been a long haul, he thought, but now I've got somewhere. A big enough unit to be able to pay workers to take some of the load. "Of course I couldn't have done it without Molly," he said to himself. "She has been a star – doing a full day's work on the farm as well as bringing up three children."

At that thought, he sighed. The children, they were something of a fly in the ointment. He remembered well when William was born, and the pleasure he had felt at having a son who would help him on the farm, and to whom he could pass the farm when the time came. And then Timothy as well. Having children about the place was a joy to him, and to Molly. He had put up a swing for them in the garden, and built them a tree house. He was very proud of the tree house, and the children had loved it. But, as they had grown up, the boys had changed. Despite having everything they wanted, and a good education (which hadn't come cheap), they had turned out to be totally unreliable, in all sorts of ways. And now they were no longer children, they ought to be pulling their weight on the farm. It annoyed him to have to pay workers when there were two grown men in the house doing nothing. Or they should be getting a job and bringing in some money – but they didn't seem to be very successful at that either. They'd each of them had jobs from time to time, but none of them had lasted long. Late for work, incompetence, lack of discipline – Will had punched the foreman on one occasion – they were usually sacked after a few weeks. Now they'd got such a bad reputation that no-one would take them on. They did help out on the farm occasionally, but always under protest. There was always something else that they just had to do that day. And when they did help, they kept doing things wrong, or breaking the machinery. He wouldn't let them near a tractor if he could help it, not after that day when Will had gone round a corner too fast and overturned the trailer. It had taken hours to sort out the mess. Sometimes he thought they were worse than useless. And always getting into trouble with the police – drinking too much and getting into fights. "How many times have I had to bail them out?" Will was the worst. By himself, Tim wasn't so bad, but he was weak and just followed what his brother did.

Miriam, though, that was a different matter. She had grown up to be a very pretty girl. And so helpful to her mother around the house. She was good on the farm too, but you couldn't expect a girl to do the same sort of work as a man. "I do hope she finds herself a good young man," he thought. "Perhaps she might find someone who could take over the farm?" So it was with mixed feelings that he climbed onto his tractor and drove down the track to the farmhouse.

When he got there, Molly called out "Tea's nearly ready."

"OK, just give me a few minutes to get my boots off and get cleaned up."

When he came downstairs again, Molly and Miriam were just putting the food on the table. Only three places set, he noticed. "Will and Tim not joining us again, then?"

Molly answered. "They went down the town. Said they didn't need any supper, they'd get something out."

"Beer and a curry, I expect. Not much of a diet."

Later on that evening, he got the phone call that he had been half expecting.

"Mr Croker? Sergeant Travers here. We've got your lads in a cell, again."

He sighed. "What's it this time? "

"Only drunk and disorderly, this time around. There was a bit a fight, but we decided not to charge them with anything else."

It could have been worse, he thought. "I can't come down now. It won't do them any harm to spend the night in a police cell. Leave them there to cool off, and I'll come and pick them up in the morning."

"OK. But I should warn you that the magistrate will probably be quite hard on them this time. He warned them last time."

"I know. I gave them a talking to as well, but it doesn't seem to have made any difference. I don't know what else I can do."

Worse was to come. A month or so later, there was a brawl in the town between two groups of lads – it would be an exaggeration to refer to them as 'gangs'. Young George Barnes was punched in the face and fell to the ground where he was kicked and stamped on. They all melted away as the police and ambulance arrived, leaving George unconscious where he had fallen, covered in blood. He was badly hurt, and if the ambulance hadn't arrived so quickly, he would probably have died. The talk in the town put the blame on Will, and the police thought so too, but there were no witnesses apart from those involved in the melee, and none of them were talking. So the police were unable to bring a case against him.

Jack and Molly were sitting alone, during the evening.

"Do you think it was Will did that to George?" asked Molly.

"I'm sure of it. I put it to him, and he tried to deny it, but the way he looked – left me with no doubt."

"What are we going to do with them?" Molly was on the verge of tears.

"I really don't know. I've tried talking to them, over and over, but it goes in one ear and out the other. They seem to have got away with it this time, but if they go on like this, they're going to get into real trouble – end up killing someone, more than likely. And there's just nothing we can do. Thank God Miriam's not like them. I hope she finds a nice lad soon."

Molly smiled at that. "I'll let you into a secret. She doesn't know that I know, but she's been seen out with Barry Turner."

"From Hanger Farm? Now he's a decent lad. Good farmers, the Turners. If they got married, we could leave the farm to them."

"Don't start building castles just yet – and whatever you do, don't let on to Miriam that we know. Until she tells us. But at least it's a ray of hope."

Jack looked at the clock. "Let's go to bed, or I'll not be able to get up in the morning."

But they neither of them found it easy to get to sleep that night, torn between dreams for Miriam and fears for their sons.

A few weeks later, Will went to Tim's room and found him sitting on the bed, with his head in his hands.

"Will, we can't go on like this. It's going to end up with us going to prison if we carry on in this way."

"Never mind that now," said Will. "There's something else we must talk about. There was some talk in the pub last night about Miriam."

"I didn't hear anything like that."

"I think you'd gone to the Gents or something. Anyway, it seems that she's been going around with Barry Turner."

"I know him. From Hanger Farm, over the other side of town. Well, she could do worse. Seems a decent enough sort of guy."

"Can't stand him – prissy stuck-up character. And running around after his parents the whole time. But that's not the point. Don't you see what's going to happen?"

"No, I don't."

Will groaned. "You're so stupid. You couldn't see a dead branch till it fell and killed you. He's a farmer; he loves all that sort of stuff. Working all day on the farm, meat and drink to him. If he marries Miriam, Dad will leave the farm to them. Not to us."

"But we don't want the farm. I don't anyway. I hate farming. The last thing I want is to inherit a farm."

"Oh, you are so thick! Of course I don't want to become a farmer. But just think how much this farm is worth. If we inherit it, we can sell it for a small fortune. We'd be rolling in the stuff. We'd never have to work again."

"We don't work now. Well, not much anyway." He thought for a moment. "Do Mum and Dad know what's going on?"

"I don't think so, not yet. But I did overhear them talking the other day, and he was saying that he hopes Miriam would marry someone who would be able to help with the farm. If that happened, then the result is obvious."

"So", said Tim. "What do you think we should do about it? Should we talk to Miriam, find out if it's serious?"

"What good do you think that would do? She's not going to take any notice of us. And we don't want just to find out if it's serious – we need to do something about it. We have to stop it."

"Well, we could try talking to Barry instead, He might listen to us."

"Oh shit. You're always on about talking to people. Talking's no good, we have to *do* something. Frighten him off."

"Frighten him off?" Tim echoed. "What do you mean by that?"

"Just wait and see, and do exactly what I tell you. If I tell you my plans, you'd only go and blurt it out somewhere and spoil everything."

Tim looked worried. "I hope it's not going to get us into trouble."

"We're only going to frighten him. No trouble in doing that."

Tim agreed, reluctantly, and with a sense of foreboding. Will's plans always seemed to land both of them in trouble, but he was never able to stop him.

Things came to a head a few days later. All five of them were sitting down to supper, unusually, when Miriam suddenly said to her mother "I think it's time that I told you that I've been seeing Barry Turner. Can we invite him over to tea on Saturday?"

Her mother pretended to be surprised. "Of course, dear. Barry's a good lad. I'm so pleased that you've found someone nice."

"They're good farmers too," said Mr Croker. "Hanger Farm's a good place, well run. And Barry works hard on the farm. You could marry someone a lot worse than him."

Miriam blushed. "It's not got to that stage yet, Dad."

But Will looked at Tim, significantly. Inviting a young man to tea was a major step; an engagement was sure to follow soon after. They had to do something quickly, and preferably before Saturday. The further things went, the harder it would be.

The opportunity came on Thursday evening. They had just come out of the pub and had walked around the corner to the side street where they had parked the car when they met Barry.

"Well," said Will. "Look who it isn't – our future brother-in-law."

Barry grinned, nervously. He knew that Will didn't like him, although he wasn't so sure about Tim. "That's jumping the gun a bit. I haven't even thought about asking her yet."

"Before you do," said Will. "There are some things that we need to talk about. Get into the car."

"But I'm on my way home. I'm late already, and Mother will be anxious about me."

"Never mind about her, a few more minutes won't kill her. Get into the car." Will opened the back door of the car and took hold of Barry's arm.

Barry didn't like the sound of this at all. Should he break away and try to make a run for it? But it was too late. Will had already half pushed him into the car. "That's more like it. Now be sensible and nothing will happen. Tim, get in – no, not in the front, get in beside him and make sure he doesn't do anything stupid."

Will drove, silently, out of the town, and turned down a narrow lane, leading to a wood. They came to where a large dead tree, broken off half way up, had left a patch of bare ground by the roadside. He pulled the car off the road and stopped. "Now, get out of the car and follow me."

Barry looked anxiously at him. "What's this all about? What's going on?"

"Just do as you're told," said Will roughly, and dragged him out of the car. He led him deeper into the wood, pushing through the thick undergrowth. Tim followed slowly behind, wondering what Will was going to do.

"This will do," said Will. He turned to face Barry. "Now let's have our little chat."

"What about?" asked Barry.

"This, for a start" said Will, and punched him hard in the face. Barry crumpled to the ground. Tim looked on, horrified. This wasn't what he had in mind at all. Will started kicking the almost inert form, in the stomach, the chest, and then the head.

"Stop!" cried Tim. "You're going to kill him!"

Will ignored him, and carried on kicking Barry's body, with a grim expression on his face, until Tim grabbed him by the arm and somehow managed to drag him away. They looked down at Barry, apparently lifeless, his face invisible through a sea of blood. He didn't seem to be breathing.

"Is he dead?" whispered Tim. "I can't touch him – you look."

Will bent over and tried to find a pulse. "I think he is," he said. "We'll need to get rid of the body. Help me to shift it into that ditch."

"You do it. I don't want to have anything to do with it."

"It's too late to back out now. Haven't you heard of 'joint enterprise'? You're in it, up to the neck, whether you like it or not."

Tim still hesitated. "I can't touch him."

"Just do it," said Will, "or you'll end up the same way."

The next day dawned, bright and clear. A few flowery clouds were scuttling across the sky.

Miriam said to her mother "Is there anything you want from the town? I'm going in to meet Barry for coffee, and I could pop into the shops if there's anything."

"No, dear, thanks. I got everything I need yesterday. You have a nice time."

"OK. I'll be back for lunch."

She came back about an hour later, looking puzzled, and a bit worried.

"Is there anything the matter, dear? You're back sooner than I expected."

"I don't know what's happened. He didn't show up. I rang his mobile, but there was no answer."

"Have you tried ringing Mrs Turner?"

"Not yet. I know she was going out this morning, but perhaps she'll be back by now. I'll try and see."

A few minutes later she came back, now looking really worried.

"Something's wrong, mother. Barry didn't come home at all last night. Mrs Turner sounded awfully worried. She was just about to call the police."

At that moment, Will came downstairs, yawning. "Is there any breakfast left? I could do with a big strong mug of coffee."

"The kettle's on the stove," Mrs Croker said. "You can make yourself some coffee."

Miriam looked at Will, but he didn't meet her eyes. He took down a mug, put in a large spoonful of instant coffee, and took it across to the stove.

Miriam said to him "Do you know where Barry is? I was supposed to meet him this morning but he didn't turn up, and Mrs Turner says he didn't come home last night."

"How should I know? Why are you asking me? He probably spent the night with some bird or other."

Miriam was livid. "How can you say such a thing? Barry's not like that. He would never do that to me. The reason I'm asking you is that I can tell that you and Tim are up to something, and someone told me he'd seen you talking to him in the street last night."

"Oh, shit," thought Will. "I was sure no-one had seen us."

"Oh, yes, that." he said. "We did bump into him when we were coming out of the pub. But I don't know where he went after that. I've not seen him since."

Miriam sat by the phone all day, waiting for Mrs Turner to ring. When she did, late that evening, Miriam could hardly bring herself to pick up the phone. But the only news was that the police hadn't found him, and he hadn't called or anything. The police were sympathetic, but they said people did sometimes just disappear, and as Barry was an adult, and there was no reason to suspect foul play, they couldn't justify mounting a full-scale search.

Miriam couldn't get to sleep that night. She just lay there, wondering where Barry had got to. Could he have had to go somewhere suddenly? But what could have called him away like that, without telling her, or his parents? And he would surely have answered his mobile. Something must have happened to him. Maybe he's lost his memory and is wandering around out there, not knowing who he is. But wouldn't he answer his phone? Perhaps he's had an accident, and is lying unconscious in a hospital bed somewhere. Should I try ringing the nearest hospitals? No, Mrs Turner will have done that. Or maybe he's crashed the car and is trapped inside it, and no-one has found it. At the thought of Barry, lying helpless in a wrecked car, in the dark, she started to cry. "Oh Barry, where are you?" At last, worn out by thinking and weeping, she fell into a fitful sleep.

The light was just starting to come into the sky when she woke with a start. "Why is my pillow so wet?" she thought, still half-asleep. Then she remembered, and started crying again. "I must go and look for him," she said to herself. Was she dreaming that she could hear Barry's voice, telling her to go to Sparrow's Wood?

Quivering with fear, she hurriedly dressed and went downstairs. She took her car keys from the shelf by the door, opened the door quietly and went out. She went over to her car in the yard, and drove off. "This is crazy," she thought. "I've had a mad dream, and now I'm off on a wild goose chase." But she kept going, through the still silent town, and up into Sparrow's Wood. Something told her to stop by the dead tree, exactly where Will had done the night before. The beaten down undergrowth leading away from the road was clearly visible. No difficulty in following the tracks. Suddenly she stopped, with her heart pounding. There, in front of her, was a place where the undergrowth had been trampled down. Next to it, a ditch with a loose pile of leaves in it. She fell to her knees and started scrabbling at the leaves with her bare hands. Underneath the leaves was loose earth, freshly dug. She didn't notice her broken fingernails, nor the blood that started to drip from her fingers, as she scratched at the earth. Suddenly she stopped, as her hands hit something that wasn't earth. She brushed the earth away. It was a hand, and on the wrist, she saw a watch. "Oh God," she cried. "That's Barry's watch." Tears as well as blood were dripping as she frantically cleared away more earth, showing first his arm, and then his shoulder. She hesitated before going further, afraid of what she would see. I must go on, she thought. I have to see his face. Gently now, she worked up from the shoulder to the neck. She could hardly bear to look as she uncovered his face, disfigured and virtually concealed by blood. She didn't need any prompting to know who had done this. "The murdering bastards," she swore, weeping bitterly. She lifted up his shoulders and slid her arm underneath as she lay down in the ditch beside him.

She was barely aware of the sun rising, and filtering through the leaves above her, nor of the birds singing around her. She lay there, clutching Barry's body. She didn't notice, as the day drew on, the light fading again, and the sun being replaced by a full moon. An owl hooted in the wood, and then brushed past her. She could almost have touched it as it swooped on an unsuspecting wood mouse nearby, but she didn't see it. Later that night, the moon disappeared as clouds gathered. It started to rain, gently at first, softly sprinkling the leaves above her but hardly penetrating. As the intensity of the rain increased, it started dripping from the trees onto the grass and brambles, and onto the two forms lying motionless in the shallow ditch, and mixing with the tears still flowing onto Barry's face. She still didn't notice.

As the light started to come back, the rain stopped. All was quiet and still in the wood. She raised her head and looked at Barry's face. She scooped some water up from the puddle they were lying in, and started to try to wash away the blood from his face. It was congealed, hard and black, but eventually she managed to clean away enough of the blood to be able to see the horrific injuries underneath. She swore again. "How could they do this to him? He had never done them any harm." She lay down again and drew his head onto her shoulder, ignoring the birds that were now starting to sing again as the sun rose, and not hearing the rustle of tiny animals in the undergrowth. Nearby, a blackbird was scratching through the leaves looking for insects and worms. She lay, still and silent, clutching Barry's body to her.

Night fell again, and as the temperature dropped, she at last became aware that she was cold and wet. And hungry too. She resented these reminders that she was still alive. And that Barry wasn't. When daylight returned, she slowly dragged herself up from the hollow, still holding Barry's hand. "Goodbye, my love," she whispered. "I have to go, but I'll not forget." Reluctantly she let go of his hand and backed away, looking at him the whole time. Brambles tore at her sodden dress, and at her legs. Eventually she turned and ran back to the car, sobbing.

She drove blindly and recklessly, tyres screaming as she wrenched the car around the bends in the lane. When she got to the town, she drove straight through a red light. Fortunately there wasn't much traffic, but several cars had to brake suddenly to avoid her. Horns blared, children and dogs ran out of the way. She drove into the farmyard, and sat in the car, weeping and shaking, and wondering what to do next. Her mother heard the car arrive, and ran out of the house.

"Miriam!" she cried. "Where have you been? Are you all right? We've been so worried about you. We've had the police out, and search parties looking for you." She opened the car door and helped Miriam out. "Look at the state of you!" Her hair was wild, her clothes were torn, sodden and muddy, her hands, face and legs were covered in blood. Worst of all, her eyes – wild, staring and strange. She didn't respond, indeed she barely saw her mother at all. Mrs Croker put her arms around her and held her close. She could feel the despair emanating from Miriam's body. "Oh, darling," she whispered. "You're home now and safe. In a minute I'll run you a bath and make you a cup of tea. And we'll get out some clean clothes. You look as though you need some food. How about some scrambled eggs, would you like that? I can do some while you're having a bath." And Miriam, stumbling and clutching her mother's arm, allowed herself to be led into the house.

Miriam had been lying in the bath for a long time, staring blankly at the wall in front of her, when her mother came upstairs and knocked softly at the door. "How are you getting on? I've got out some clean clothes for you."

There was no reply. Molly pushed the door open a crack and put her head round. Miriam didn't seem to have moved since she helped her into the bath. Her hair, still lank and matted, lay dangling in the water. "Shall I come in and help you wash your hair?" Still no reply, so Molly went in and got down the shampoo. "It's a long time since I've done this," she said, kneeling by the side of the bath as she massaged the shampoo into Miriam's scalp. "Do you remember that old earthenware jug, and how I used to pour the water over your head?" She thought Miriam's eyes flickered a bit. "No need for that now," she said, getting down the shower attachment and rinsing off the shampoo. Then she took the sponge and gently started removing the mud and blood from Miriam's face, hands and legs. "There, that looks better. Shall I help you out?" She wrapped the big bath towel around her, and dried her all over. Then she helped her to get dressed and took her hand to lead her downstairs. "It is really like dealing with a child," she thought. "No it's worse. A child responds, talks, squirms. Oh, blast. I forgot the scrambled eggs." They were thoroughly dried out, and starting to burn. She plunged the pan under the tap and started to make some more.

Miriam ate the scrambled eggs slowly and mechanically, watched anxiously by her mother. "She is at least starting to do something for herself," she thought.

She was only half-way through when Will came in. He stopped when he saw Miriam. "Hi, Sis," he said, carelessly. "So you're back then. I thought I saw the car outside. What have you been up to? You do look terrible."

Miriam finished her mouthful, and put down the knife and fork. Her eyes, up to then so dull and blank, suddenly erupted with fire. "You murdering bastard! How dare you ask that? You deserve to hang for this!"

Epilogue

The police had little difficulty in determining who was responsible. Of course they both denied it at first, but Tim soon cracked. The inconsistencies between their stories was bad enough, but when faced with the evidence of one of Barry's hairs in Will's car, and Barry's blood on Will's boots – although he had cleaned them as thoroughly as he could – he quickly gave in and admitted it. Will wasn't hanged of course. Great Britain stopped killing murderers in 1965. But he was sent to prison for a very long time. So was Tim, although his sentence was much less. Molly Croker was heartbroken at the loss of her two sons, and even more when she remembered what they had done – she never visited them in prison. Miriam threw herself into helping her father with the farm. He gradually came to rely on her completely, and had to revise his earlier opinion – she was actually just as capable of farm work as a man. By the time he died, ten years later, she was running the farm. She never married, although she had several offers. Barry's memory was too strong. She planted flowers by his grave, and every month she visited it to weed around them, and replace any that were no longer flourishing. Once a year she drove, slowly, up Gooseberry Lane, parked by the dead, broken tree (or, in later years, where it had once stood), and walked, through the re-grown undergrowth, to the well-known spot. There, she sat on the ground, hunched up in a ball, with her head on her knees, and cried until the tears would no longer come.

The river

The Haig farm was on a bluff overlooking the River Clyde. Not the majestic, if at times polluted, river that launched a thousand ships as it flows through Glasgow on its way to the sea. This was the upper reaches, in the hills, where it was little more than a gentle stream under normal conditions. But when the rains came, it turned into a violent torrent. Dangerous to try to cross it at those times.

In the farmyard, a young man stood, polishing his car. He was thinking all the time about visiting Maggie. He could just about see the top of the house where she lived, just across the river. But he would first have to confront his mother. Mrs Haig didn't like Maggie. There was a long-standing feud between them and the Stewarts. As far as he could make out, it had started with a disagreement over boundaries. For both farms, the low-lying land beside the river was important. During the summer, the sheep could graze on the rough pasture in the surrounding hills, while the fields by the river were used for making hay. During the winter the sheep had to be moved down to the lower fields beside the river, and the hay was needed to supplement the grass. The river was the effective boundary between the two farms, and that was the cause of the problem. The river tended to change course from time to time, which meant that one farm would lose some of this important land. Willie didn't know, and didn't care, whether this was legally true or not, or whether the boundary was actually defined on a map irrespective of the course of the river, but clearly a small bit of land the wrong side of the river was no practical use. So, when the river shifted its course, one farm gained a bit of land, and the other lost some. At a time in the distant past, his grandfather, or possibly even further back than that, had accused the Stewarts of deliberately altering the course of the river so that they would gain some land. The Stewarts of course denied it, and said it was just the way of nature that the river changed course sometimes. It always had, and always would; some would lose and some gain but it would even out in the end. But the upshot was that for more years than anyone could remember, they had never spoken to the Stewarts, nor vice versa. If his mother encountered Mrs Stewart in town, she would cross the road to avoid her.

It was at a ceilidh that he had first met Maggie. He didn't know who she was, but the moment he saw her, across the room, with long black hair and eyes that danced with the music, he knew she was the one for him. He'd always been scornful of romantic notions of love at first sight, but now he was confronted with the reality. He asked her to dance. And again and again. He could see his friends whispering, but he thought they were just jealous of him dancing so often with such a beautiful girl. Eventually, one of his friends took him aside.

"Do you know who that is that you've been dancing with all evening?"

He had to admit that he had been so full of himself, and enjoying dancing with her so much, that he had never asked her name.

"Well, I ought to tell you that it's Maggie Stewart. Your mother will be furious if she finds out. Her mother won't be best pleased either."

This was a bombshell. To find out that he had, he thought, fallen in love with the one girl that it would be impossible to form a relationship with, let alone marry. But he couldn't go back now, could he? Why should a stupid ancient feud, that meant nothing to him, stand in the way of his happiness? But he loved and respected his parents, and he hated the thought that this would come between them.

The next dance was starting. Before asking Maggie to dance, he said "My friends tell me that you're Maggie Stewart."

"And you're Willie Haig. Strange that we've never met before, being neighbours."

"Yes, it is that. It's all because of this stupid feud between our families. But I don't see why that should affect us. I don't care about this feud."

"I'm glad you said that. I was afraid that when you found out who I was you wouldn't want to have anything to do with me."

"Why on earth would you think that?"

"Well, your mother says such horrid things about our family. My friends hear it from their parents, so it all gets back to me. I thought you would feel the same."

"Doesn't your mother say all sorts of things about us?" Willie asked.

"Yes, she does. But I don't take any notice of that. Still less, now that we've met."

"So you wouldn't object to seeing me again some time? I've had such a nice time this evening, I'd really like to see you again."

"I'd like that, very much."

Willie was encouraged by this. This girl that he thought he was in love with would actually like to see him again, that was fantastic. But he still hesitated. "Our parents are going to be a problem though. I just can't tell my mother, she'd go ballistic."

"So would mine," Maggie agreed.

"So, we won't tell them. I don't like deceiving them, but it's the only way. We can communicate with our mobiles."

"Yes, don't ring the house. Mother would answer and want to know who you were."

"Good. Let's meet in the Swan, next Friday. Say about 8? We could go on to a club or something from there. These ceilidhs are all very well, but it would be nice to have some livelier music, and atmosphere."

One date led to another. Pubs, clubs, cinema. If the weather was good, they would go for a walk over the hills, or along paths through the secluded woods by the side of the river. Willie just told his mother he was going out with his friends. He still didn't like deceiving her. Many times he was on the point of telling her, thinking that she would come round when she realised what a lovely girl Maggie was. But he was afraid of the confrontation. She might find a way of stopping him from seeing Maggie. Eventually, the decision was taken out of his hands.

He had come back late from an evening out, with Maggie of course. He found his parents sitting up, waiting for him.

"Where have you been?" demanded Mrs Haig.

"I told you, mother, I went out with some of my friends."

"Don't lie to me! I know you've been seeing that Maggie Stewart."

"Oh, shit," he thought. "Someone must have seen us together and told her. Perhaps we should have been more careful."

"So what if I have?" he said.

Mrs Haig was furious. "Of all the girls in the neighbourhood, you had to pick one from that family. Don't you care about my feelings, or your father's? You know what we think of that family. They're all cheats, hypocrites and liars. You can't trust them an inch. She will let you down, just like the rest of them."

"Oh, mother, be fair to her. If you would only just meet her, you would see what she's like. She's not like that at all. She's clever and kind and honest; she works hard on the farm as well as in her job. And I love her. Couldn't we ask her round for tea so you can see what a nice girl she is?"

"Ask her round for tea? The very idea! I'm not having anyone from that family setting foot in my house!"

Mr Haig, who had been sitting nervously twisting his hands together, interjected "Well, dear, perhaps…"

"Perhaps nothing! If you haven't got anything useful to say, then keep quiet. That girl does not enter my house, and that's an end of it."

Maggie didn't have an easy time of it either. Mrs Stewart was just as adamant that she would have nothing to do with Willie. She also said that she wouldn't let him in the house, and if he tried calling for her she would send him away with a flea in his ear.

Mr Haig was not at all comfortable about the situation. He didn't like arguments and confrontations. As far as he was concerned, the original cause of the feud was long forgotten. Occasionally, he would see Mr Stewart at market, and they would usually go to a bar and have a drink together, quite amicably. One day, as they were sitting over a glass of whisky, he said "You know our Willie's been seeing your Maggie?"

Donald Stewart sighed. "I do indeed, and Mary's been giving me a lot of stick about it as well. She had a terrible row with Maggie. Told her to promise not to see him again, but Maggie wouldn't do anything of the sort. But Mary won't think of letting him in the house."

"Cath's the same. I don't know where it's going to end, or when. We can't stop them seeing each other. After all, they're both adults, with minds of their own. In the old days, I suppose we would threaten to cut them off without a penny – and I think Cath would like us to do that, but then who would I leave the farm to? I've always dreamed of Willie taking it over when I'm past it. And that seems to be getting nearer every day. I depend more and more on his help round the farm."

"It's like that with us too. Without the money Maggie brings in, we'd be in a poor way. And she's always ready to lend a hand round the place too. But I daren't say anything or I'd really be in the doghouse."

They both shrugged their shoulders and looked gloomily at their whisky. "Once these women get an idea in their heads, there's no shifting them."

As Mr Haig had predicted, there wasn't anything they could do to stop Willie and Maggie seeing each other. And they did, frequently. But now they were more circumspect about it. Even the secluded paths by the river were not totally safe from the prying eyes of the local gossips. So they went further afield. That of course needed transport. Maggie knew that if she took her car, her mother would be suspicious. And Willie couldn't just drive up to her house and pick her up. So he had to resort to waiting in his car at the end of the lane and ringing Maggie's mobile to let her know that he was there. He knew that, sooner or later, Mrs Stewart would get wise to this and would confiscate Maggie's mobile. He didn't know what he would do then.

This went on for several months. Their excursions were wonderful, especially lying in the heather listening to the skylarks overhead. It was on one such occasion that Willie said "I'm so looking forward to the day when we get married."

Maggie ignored the fact that he hadn't actually asked her yet. "Mm," she said, dreamily. "That would be marvellous."

Then she sat up, clasped her hands round her knees, and looked serious. "But it's not possible. Our parents would never agree. At least our mothers wouldn't, and that's the same thing."

"To hell with them. Let's do it anyway. We're old enough, we don't need their permission."

"Be serious, Willie. Where would we live? If we could only get their permission, I could move in with you. There's plenty of room. But it's not going to happen."

Willie reluctantly agreed, and they sat there, sadly dreaming of what might be, if only...

This conversation was repeated many times during those months, and always with the same conclusion. Eventually, Willie realised that they weren't getting anywhere, and the only possible course of action involved another confrontation with his mother.

So, on this evening, Willie stood polishing his car and thinking about Maggie. At that moment, his mother came out into the yard. "Willie! Are you coming in for your supper? It's nearly ready."

It was now or never, he decided. "I'm sorry, mother," he said. "I won't be coming in for supper. I'm off to see Maggie."

"What? After all we've said? I thought I'd made it quite clear, I forbid you to see that girl."

"It's no use, mother. You can't stop me. I'm in love with Maggie and I want to marry her. And I'm going to see her tonight, to ask her to be my wife."

Mrs Haig tried a different approach. "Oh, don't go" she pleaded. "I've made a lovely supper for you. That brown hen we killed this afternoon, roasted, with onions, just how you like it."

"No," he said firmly. "If you'd killed and roasted the whole flock, I still wouldn't stay. I must go to see Maggie. It looks like the weather is changing, and if I don't go now, I won't get across the ford."

He expected her to get angry and start shouting at him. But she didn't. Instead, she just said, simply and coldly "If you go, I hope the weather does change and you get drowned in the river." With that, she turned and went back into the house, slamming the door behind her.

Willie watched her go, paused for a moment, and then got into his car. He drove slowly down the lane that led to the ford, with his mother's bitter words echoing in his ears. He loved and respected his mother, and he was well aware of all the sacrifices his parents had made when bringing him up. The farm was not a large one, so they had never had much money, but they always seemed to find enough to give him anything he wanted, within reason. Even this car, he thought, had been a present for his eighteenth birthday. He remembered the look on their faces when they took him to the window that February morning, and there it was, parked in the yard, shining and new. Well, it wasn't actually new, of course, but his father must have put in a lot of effort cleaning and polishing it. Time that he couldn't really spare from running the farm single-handed. And it went like a dream. Not very fast on motorways, of course, but nearly all his driving was in the twisting lanes around the farm, and into the town where he worked. "I don't suppose they imagined I would use it mostly for going to see Maggie" he thought. He switched on the wipers as the rain started to fall. Looking up towards the hills he could see that it must already have been raining for some time up there. The river will be rising, he thought. I hope I'm in time to get across.

As he turned the last bend before the hill down to the ford, he could hear the river. When the water started to rise, the sound changed from its usual gentle rippling, first to a sort of gurgle, and then ultimately to a throaty roar. As he approached the ford, the sound seemed to be getting louder by the second. "I don't care what happens on the way back," he said to himself. "But please let me cross safely now." He put the car into low gear, and started to cross, slowly. He could feel the force of the water pushing the car sideways, and he struggled to control it. Then he felt the ground starting to rise, and he was clear. He breathed a sigh of relief. "Nothing now between me and Maggie."

Night was falling fast as he approached the Stewart farm. Most of the house was already in darkness, but he could see that there was still a light in Maggie's room. He stopped the car at the bottom of the lane, as usual, and rang Maggie's mobile. Without success. "That's odd" he thought. "It must be switched off, but she never does that. Especially as she knew I would be coming tonight. Maybe it's as I feared, and her mother has taken it off her." He thought for a while. Eventually he realised that there was only one thing to do, which was to walk up to the farm and try to tap on her window.

The lane was rough and muddy, and it was now dark. It was raining hard still, and the wind had got up. He swore softly as he stepped into another large puddle, and wished he had brought a torch. By the time he got to the farm, his shoes were covered in mud, as were his trousers up to the knees, and he was thoroughly wet. He felt his way around the house to Maggie's room, as quietly as possible. "One benefit of this storm" he thought "Nobody is likely to hear me, or to look out and see me." He tapped gently on the windowpane, and said in a low voice "Maggie, it's me. Are you awake still?"

He could hear some sounds within the room, so he knew she was there, although he couldn't make out what the sounds were.

"Maggie, let me in. I'm getting soaked out here."

Then came a reply. "I can't let you in. The house is full of people."

"Then come out and meet me in the barn."

"I can't. The barns are full of hay and cows. And my mother would kill me if she found out."

He was shocked and bitterly disappointed by her refusal to see him. "I've risked my life to come here, and I've got my mother's curse into the bargain. I never thought you would say no." And he turned away to go back to his car. He no longer noticed the puddles as he stumbled down the lane. The rain was beating down on his head, and running down his back inside his shirt, but all he could think about was Maggie's refusal to see him. "I really thought she loved me. How could she not let me in? How could she say she wouldn't even see me? She didn't even open the curtains to look out." He reached the car and climbed in. For a while he sat there, angry and bewildered. "What can I say to my mother when I get home? She will be triumphant. She will say it confirms all her worst prejudices against the Stewart family." Reluctantly, he started the engine for the drive home.

When he got to the ford, the river was roaring louder than before, and he could see that the level of the water over the ford was too high to cross safely. But he was despondent by Maggie's refusal. "If Maggie won't see me, and my mother wants me dead, what have I got to lose?" And he drove recklessly into the torrent. When he was halfway across the river, the car stalled, as the water got into the engine compartment. The car was rocking with the force of the river. With difficulty, he managed to open the door and climb out. He tried to stand up and take a few steps, but he couldn't keep his footing. He tried desperately to hold onto the car, but the force of the river tore his grip from the door handle, and he was swept off downstream, as the water closed over his head.

At the Stewart farm, Maggie woke up trembling. She ran to her mother and said "Mother, I've had the most dreadful dream. I dreamed that Willie had come to see me and you wouldn't let him in."

"Yes, dear, he was here. I had just come in to say that I was going to bed, but you were already asleep. I told him that you couldn't see him. He's long gone by now. Go back to sleep. You'll be all right now, the dream's over."

"And he took that from you? Didn't he ask to see me, or even to talk to me through the window?"

"Well, dear, the curtains were closed, so he couldn't see me. And my voice does sound rather like yours. So I suppose he thought that it *was* you speaking."

"Oh, God! So he thinks that I refused to see him! And now he's gone away, on such a night!"

Maggie dressed hastily. She was shaking so much, with a mixture of fear and anger, that she had difficulty doing up her buttons and shoelaces.

"What are you doing?" cried her mother. "You can't go after him. He'll be home by now, and it's pouring with rain."

"I must go. I can't let him think that I wouldn't let him in. I might be able to catch him by the ford. I don't suppose he'll be able to cross. The river must be too high by now."

"You couldn't have let him in. I've already told you that I didn't want you to see him, and that he was not welcome in this house."

"But mother, I love him, and I want to marry him. You've no right to try and stop us."

"Right? I've every right. I'm your mother aren't I? If all the sacrifices we've made for you mean anything at all, you ought to take some notice of what I say. If I say he's not a suitable boy for you, that should be the end of it."

"Oh, mother, you know I love and respect you both, but I love Willie as well. So I must go after him and tell him that it wasn't me who sent him away, and that I do love him."

"If you go now, that's the end for me. Don't come back again. It's either him or me. If you go after him, you're no longer my daughter."

Maggie ran down the lane, in the pouring rain, towards the ford, heedless of the puddles. When she reached the ford, although it was quite dark by now, she could just make out the shape of Willie's car in the middle of the river, being slowly swept away from the ford. "Oh God! He's stuck in the river. Is he still in the car? I must try to rescue him." After a couple of steps, the water was already above her knees and it was all she could do to stay on her feet. "I must go on," she said, and managed to take two more steps. The water was up to her waist now, and she had still not reached the car. "Willie!" she called. "Hold on, I'm coming." But Willie wasn't there. She tried to take another step, but the power of the river overcame her.

The next day, the rain had stopped and the sun came out. The river went down again, as quickly as it had come up. On the bank of the river, about a mile downstream from the ford, Mr Haig was walking with his dog, looking to see what damage had been done by the storm. The dog ran on ahead and stopped by the bank of the river, barking. When Mr Haig came up to find out what the matter was, he saw, by the river's edge, two bodies locked together in a last embrace.

The songs

These are the songs which formed the basis for each of the stories. Traditional songs come in a multitude of versions, and I make no claim that these are in any sense the 'best' version. Some have been edited to shorten them, by removing detail that is not needed for the story, and irrelevant choruses have been omitted. I have given the name of the story concerned as well as the name by which the song is usually known.

Cold Blows the Wind (The Unquiet Grave)

Cold blows the wind o'er my true love
And a few small drops of rain
I never had but one true love
In greenwood he lies slain.

I'll do as much for my true love
As any young girl may
I'll sit and weep all on his grave
For a twelve month and a day

But twelve long months were past and gone
The young man he did speak
"What makes you weep down by my grave?
And will not let me sleep."

"What is it that you want of me?
Of me, what do you crave?"
"One kiss, one kiss of your lily-white lips
Then I'll go from off your grave."

"Do you remember love the day
When you and I did walk?
The finest flower that ever was seen
Is withered to a stalk."

"My lips they are as cold as clay,
My breath is heavy and strong.
If thou wast to kiss my lily-white lips
Thy days would not be long."

"My time be long, my time be short
Tomorrow or today,
Sweet Christ in heaven will have my soul
And take my life away."

"Don't grieve, don't grieve for me, dear love
No mourning do I crave.
I must leave you and all the world,
And sink down in my grave."

Gwen (Fair Phoebe and the dark-eyed sailor)

Gwen is based, non-specifically, on a class of songs known as 'broken-token ballads'. This is just an example of this type of song.

Tis of a lady, young and fair
A-walking out for to take the air
She met a sailor upon her way
So I paid attention to hear what they did say

Said William 'Lady, why walk alone?
The night is coming and the day near gone'
She said while tears from her eyes did roll
'It's a dark-eyed sailor hath proved my downfall

It's seven long years since he left this land
I took a gold ring from off my hand
I broke the token, one half you see
And the other's rolling at the bottom of the sea.'

Said William 'Drive him all from your mind
Some other sailor as good you'll find'
'He's an honest man, not a rogue like you
To incite a maiden to slight the jacket blue'

Said William 'Lady, do not disdain
Some other sailor to treat the same
Love will come and love will go
Like a winter's morning when the land is covered with snow.'

These words did Phoebe's fond heart enflame
She said 'On me you will play no game'
She drew a dagger and then did cry
'For my dark-eyed sailor a maid I'll live and die'

Then half the ring did young William show
She seemed distracted with joy and woe
She joined together that ring of gold
'It's my dark-eyed sailor so manly true and bold'.

Then in a village down by the sea
They soon were married and will agree
Maids be true when your lover's away
For a cloudy morning brings forth a sunshine day

Hugh Bateman (Lord Bateman)

Now the turnkey had but one only daughter
The finest young girl that ever was seen
She stole the keys of her father's prison
And swore Lord Bateman she would go and see.

Now I've got houses and I've got land
And half of Northumberland belongs to me
I'll give it all to you fair young lady
Then if out of prison you will let me free

Now it's seven long years I will wait for you
And two more years to make up nine
Then if you don't wed with no other woman
Then I won't wed with no other man.

Now the seven long years were gone and past
And the two more years to make up nine
She took a ship sailed across the ocean
Until she got to Northumberland.

Now is this now Lord Bateman's castle
O is his lordship now within?
O yes, o yes, cries this proud young porter
I've just now taken his new bride in.

Go and ask him for a slice of bread
And a bottle of his very best wine
Tell him not to forget that fair young lady
That out of prison did let him free.

Then away away goes this proud young porter
And away away and away goes he
And when he came to Lord Bateman's chamber
Down on his bended knees fell he.

What news what news my proud young porter?
What news have you brought to me?
O there is the fairest of all young creatures
That ever my two eyes have seen.

Now she has got rings on every finger
On some of them she has got three
And as much gay gold hanging round her middle
That would buy half of Northumberland.

Now she's asked you for a slice of bread
And a bottle of your very best wine
And you're not to forget that fair young lady
That out of prison did let you free.

Now Lord Bateman flew all in a passion
He though he broke in three pieces three
I'll seek no more for no other fortune
Since Sophia now has crossed the sea.

Lady Geraldine (The raggle taggle gypsies)

There were three gypsies come to my door
And downstairs ran this lady, O!
One sang high and another sang low
And the other sang bonny, bonny, Biscay, O!

Then she pulled off her silk finished gown
And put on hose of leather, O!
The ragged, ragged, rags about our door
She's gone with the raggle taggle gypsies, O!

It was late last night, when my lord came home
Enquiring for his lady, O!
The servants said, on every hand
She's gone with the raggle taggle gypsies, O!

O saddle to me my milk-white steed
Go and fetch me my pony, O!
That I may ride and seek my bride
Who is gone with the raggle taggle gypsies, O!

O he rode high and he rode low
He rode through woods and copses too
Until he came to an open field
And there he espied his lady, O!

What makes you leave your house and land?
What makes you leave your money, O?
What makes you leave your new wedded lord?
To go with the raggle taggle gypsies, O!

What care I for my house and my land?
What care I for my money, O?
What care I for my new wedded lord?
I'm off with the raggle taggle gypsies, O!

Last night you slept on a goose-feather bed
With the sheet turned down so bravely, O!
And to-night you'll sleep in a cold open field
Along with the raggle taggle gypsies, O!

What care I for a goose-feather bed?
With the sheet turned down so bravely, O!
For to-night I shall sleep in a cold open field
Along with the raggle taggle gypsies, O!

Soap starch and candles

Verses 3 and 5 are my additions

It was on one Easter Monday on a trip to Ilfracombe
'Twas there I met a pretty girl with cheeks like a rose in bloom
It was on the steamer when we met, she made my heart go 'hop'
When she told me about the contents of her father's corner shop, which sold:

Soap, starch, candles, liquorice and turpentine,
Pepper, glue and mustard, and cod liver oil and scent,
And dried eggs, clothes pegs, creosote and fishing line,
Linseed oil and treacle, and paint brushes lent.

When they played at kissing-in-the-ring well I joined her in that scene.
She often threw her glove at me, and I chased her round the green
And when I caught her, oh what bliss, to span that tender waist
And when I kissed her, then I said "O heaven those lips do taste of:

Well, many happy days we spent, it was just her and me
And then one day her Mum and Dad invited me to tea
With bread and jam and buttered scones the table it was graced
And chocolate cake and sandwiches, but all that I could taste, was:

Now a year went by, and her and me – we decided to get wed
And in the back room of the shop we had a grand old spread
And then her father came to me and he made me heart go 'hop'
For he said to me that we could carry on the corner shop, with:

More years went by, and then one day her father passed away
I remember well, the truth to tell, it was on his funeral day
I said to my wife, the time has come, things have to change
So we threw out all the old stuff and stocked a different range
Now we sell...
Dried fruit, ginseng, olive oil and herbal teas,
Fenugreek and bath oil, peppercorns and mead,
And beeswax, arrowroot, incense sticks and goats cheese,
For the modern customer, we have all you need

The Stranger (The Outlandish Knight)

An outlandish knight from the north land came
And he came a-wooing of me;
And he told me he'd take me to that northern land
And there he would marry me.

Well, go and get me some of your father's gold
And some of your mother's fee
And two of the very best stable steeds
Where there stand thirty and three.

She mounted on her lily white horse
And he upon the grey,
And away they did ride to the fair river side
Three hours before it was day.

"Pull off, pull off, your silken gown
And deliver it unto me
For I think it's too fine and much too gay
To rot in the salt water sea."

She said "Go get a sickle to crop the thistle
That grows beside the brim
That it may not mingle with my curly locks
Nor harm my lilywhite skin"

So he got a sickle to crop the thistle
That grew beside the brim
She catched him around the middle so small
And tumbled him into the stream.

"Lie there, lie there, you false-hearted man
Lie there instead of me
Six pretty maidens thou hast drowned here before
And the seventh hath drowned thee."

Then she mounted on her lilywhite horse
And she did ride away
And she arrived at her father's stable door
Three hours before it was day

Now the parrot being in the window so high
A-hearing the lady did say
"I'm afraid that some ruffian has led you astray
That you've tarried so long away."

"Don't prattle, don't prattle, my pretty Polly
Nor tell no tales of me
And your cage shall be made of the glittering gold
And your perch of the best ivory."

Sylvie (Sovay or The Female Highwayman)

Sovay, Sovay all on a day
She dressed herself in man's array
With a sword and a pistol all by her side
To meet her true love away did ride.

And as she was a-riding over the plain
She met her true love and bid him stand
Your gold and silver kind sir she said
Or else this moment your life I'll have.
And when she'd robbed him of his store
She says kind sir there is one thing more
A golden ring which I know you have
Deliver it your sweet life to save.

Oh that golden ring a token is
My life I'll lose, the ring I'll save.
Being tender-hearted just like a dove
She rode away from her true love.

Next morning in the garden green
Just like true lovers they were seen
He spied his watch hanging by her clothes
And it made him blush like any rose.

What makes you blush at so silly a thing
I thought to have had your golden ring
It was I that robbed you all on the plain
So here's your watch and your gold again.

I did intend and it was to know
If that you were my true love or no
For if you'd have given me that ring she said
I'd have pulled the trigger and shot you dead.

The Beggar Girl (The Beggar Wench)

Have you heard of the merchant's son?
From the battle he has run
He has mounted on his milk-white steed
And away for pleasure he did ride

A beggar wench then he chanced to meet
A beggar wench of low degree
He took pity on her distress
And he said my lassie you've a bonny face

Now they both inclined to take a drink
Into a public house they went
They drank whisky gin and brandy punch
Till the both of them were rolling drunk

Now they both inclined to go to bed
And under cover soon were laid
Strong drink and brandy went to their heads
And they both were lying as they were dead

Now a little while later this girl she rose
And she put on the young merchant's clothes
With his hat so high and a saucy gleam
And away she went with the merchant's gear

Now a little while later this merchant rose
And looked around for to find his clothes
There was nothing left unto that room
But a ragged petticoat and a wincey gown

Now a stranger the merchant was to the town
But he put on the lassie's gown
And down the street he soundly swore
That he never would lie with a beggar no more.

The Birthmark (Y Blotyn Du or The Black Spot)

This is my adaptation of the literal translation, from the original Welsh, accompanying the record. "Stable-loft Songs (Caneuon Lloft Stabal)" Now available on CD (without the translation): SAIN SCD2389. The song is believed to refer to a murder that occurred in Penryn, Cornwall, in 1618,

A story I'll unfold
About a sailor bold
A cruel tale I have to tell
of murder and of gold.

There was a poor farmer
with a farm down by the water
His only son away had gone,
the wide world for to wander.

For seven long years he wandered
to where the cannons thundered
A pirate wild on the ocean wide
and many a ship he plundered.

By storm and water riven
by seas and weather driven
Their sails all rent, their rigging wrecked,
at last they found a haven.

To his sister's house he went,
to test her was his intent
He said to her "Is your brother here?
With a message I am sent."

She answered with alarm
"I fear he's come to harm
But I'll know him sure if he comes here.
He's a black spot on his arm."

He bared his arm straight way,
"I'm your brother" he did say
She welcomed him with open arms
and bade him there to stay.

When he showed her all his plunder
Her eyes were wide with wonder
"You're just in time to save the farm,
you must go and tell your father."

He went next day at dawn
to the house where he was born
A stranger then he was to them
with his hair and beard unshorn

Said the father to the mother
"Here's a chance like no other
We'll kill him when he sleeps and then
We can steal all his plunder."

When the night it was quite dark
They took a knife so sharp
The mother brought the lantern bright
The father pierced his heart

His sister came there early
Bearing gifts so fairly
I'm looking for that man so fair
Who came last night quite newly

Her father answered straight
"No man came here last night."
"O yes, I swear it was my brother fair
You surely can't deny it."

"I saw he had a black spot,
and gifts that he had brought
That he had seized upon the seas
from the battles he had fought."

The old man began to swear
"There's no way we can repair
What we have done, killed our own son
His fate we now must share."

The mother began to moan,
"I bore him in my womb
I share the guilt, I held the light,
the gallows must be our doom."

The Blind Husband (Marrow bones)

'Twas of a jealous old woman
as I've heard them tell
She loved her husband dearly,
but another man twice as well.

She went unto the doctor
to see what she could find
To know what was the very best thing
to make her husband blind.

You boil him up some good rum punch –
I'm sure that's very good
And stew him up some marrow bones
to circulate his blood.

But this old man being a crafty blade
and knowing the scheme before
He drank it up and said
"My dear, I can't see you at all."

"I'll go down to the river
and there myself will drown."
Says she "I'll come along with you
in case you should fall down."

Oh they went along both hand in hand
till they came to the river's brim
The old man tripped his foot to one side
and the old woman went rolling in.

Good Lord! How she did holloa
and loud for mercy call
But the old man said
"I'm so very blind I can't see you at all."

The Farmer's Sons (Bruton Town or The Bramble Briar)

In Bruton town there lived a farmer,
Who had two sons and one daughter dear.
By day and night they were contriving
To fill their parents' hearts with fear.

He told his secrets to no other,
But unto his brother this he said:
"I think our servant courts our sister,
I think they have a great mind to wed.
I'll put an end to all their courtship.
I'll send him silent to his grave."

They asked him to go a-hunting,
Without any fear or strife,
And there these two bold and wicked villains,
They took away this young man's life.

And in the ditch there was no water,
Where only bush and briars grew.
They could not hide the blood of slaughter,
So in the ditch his body they threw.

When they returned home from hunting,
She asked for her servant-man.
"I ask because I see you whisper,
So brothers tell me if you can."

"O sister, you do offend me,
Because you so examine me.
We've lost him where we've been a-hunting.
No more of him we could not see."

As she lay dreaming on her pillow,
She thought she saw her heart's delight;
By her bed side as she lay weeping,
He was dressed all in his bloody coat.

"Don't weep for me, my dearest jewel,
Don't weep for me nor care nor pine,
For your two brothers killed me so cruel.
In such a place you may me find."

As she rose early the very next morning,
With heavy sigh and bitter groan,
The only love that she admired,
She found in the ditch where he was thrown.

And the blood upon his lips was drying
Her tears were soft as any rain
She sometimes kissed him, sometimes crying
"Here lies the dearest friend of mine"

Three days and nights she did sit by him,
And her poor heart was filled with woe,
Till cruel hunger crept upon her,
And home she was obliged to go.

When she returned to her brothers:
"Sister, what makes you look so thin?"
"Brother, don't you ask the reason,
And for his sake, you shall be hung."

The River (Clyde's waters)

Young Willie stood at his stable door,
Leaning o'er his steed
And looking through his white fingers,
His nose began to bleed

Bring some corn to my horse
and give my young man mead
And I'll away to Maggie's bower,
I'll be there before she sleeps

Stay at home my Willie dear,
O stay at home with me
And the best fed lamb in all my flock
will be well-dressed for thee

All your lambs and all your flocks
I value not a pin
And I'll away to Maggie's bower
I'll be there e'er she lies down

If you go to Maggie's bower
it's sair against my will
The deepest part of Clyde's waters
my malison you'll feel

He's rode up yon high high hill
and down yon dowy den
And the rush that rose in Clyde's water
Would have feared a thousand men

Clyde, O Clyde, ye roaring Clyde,
your waves are wondrous strong
Make me a wreck when I come back
but spare me as I gang

Maggie, Maggie, Maggie dear
Rise up and let me in
For my boots are full of Clyde's waters
and I'm shivering to the skin

My stables are full of fine horses
and my barns are full of hay
And my beds are full of gentlemen
Who will not leave till day

He turned his horse right round about
with a salt tear in his eye
I never thought to come here
this night and be denied by thee

He's rode up yon high high hill
and down yon dreary den
And the rush that rose in Clyde's waters
took Willie's cane from him

Leaning out of his saddle bows
to catch his cane by force
The rush that rose in Clyde's water
took Willie from his horse

Up arose his Maggie dear
Out of a fearful dream
I dreamed my love was here this night
and ye would not let him in

Go to bed my daughter dear
Lie down and take a rest
Since your love William was here this night
It's but three quarters past

She's away to her chamber
and clothes she quickly put on
And she's away to Clyde waters
as fast as she could run.

When she came to the waters side
So quickly she stepped in
And loudly cried her true love's name
but louder blew the wind

The next step that she stepped in
It took her to the chin
And the deepest part of Clyde's waters
She found her Willie in

You've got a cruel mother Willie,
And I have got another
And here we'll sleep in Clyde's waters
Like a sister and a brother.